The Mountains at the
Bottom of the World

The Mountains at the Bottom of the World

A NOVEL OF ADVENTURE BY

Ian Cameron

William Morrow & Company, Inc.
NEW YORK   1972

Payne, Donald Gordon, 1924-
    The mountains at the bottom of the world.

    I. Title.
PZ4.P344Mo [PR6066.A9]   823   70-170248
ISBN 0-688-00002-9

Contents

The Mountains at the
Bottom of the World

OUR ROUTE TO THE VULCAN VIEDMA

Prologue
The Coast of Tierra del Fuego

A clear night. A hunter's moon. Swell rolling in from the Pacific. And the wind a typical Cape Horner: steady Force 6.

The bay faced west, and great waves were surging up the beach and streaming like avalanches of milk over the rocks. It was so cold that the sea water, where it lay in little pools, was turning to ice. The cold, however, didn't seem to worry the bay's six or seven hundred occupants. Oblivious to wind and spray, the elephant seals slept.

They slept according to the grades of their hierarchy. At the water's edge the harems of cows, each with its bewhiskered bull; inland the pups, from two to four weeks old; and huddled disconsolate in random groups along the shore the bachelors, ever hopeful of prizing a cow from her harem but fearing the gash of the old bull's teeth. Another couple of weeks and they would have left their breeding ground for the safety of the Weddell Sea. But less than half of them were to survive the night. For a little after 3 A.M. a sloop, her lights doused, came nosing into the bay.

She was black as a witches' Sabbath: black sails, black hull and a deck stained black with blood; her figurehead was of Diana the Huntress, and this was apt because she had been seal poaching so long, it was whispered in Punta Arenas, that she could smell out the breeding grounds as surely as an excise officer rum. As she dropped anchor, her crew gathered beside the rail, their eyes on the shore, their hands resting lightly on pistol, gutting knife or club. They didn't need orders; they had learned their trade on a dozen bloodstained beaches round the bottom of the world.

The elephant seals stared at the sloop with neither interest nor fear, their infinitesimal brains unable to cope with this unexpected development. Even when the crew of the *Huntress* lowered dories and came rowing purposefully toward them, they gave no more than a blink of surprise.

The seal poachers * wasted no time. Within five minutes of landing they had lit kerosene flares and were clubbing their victims to death.

It was bloody work. The less experienced members of the crew broke the seals up, driving the sleekest (and richest in oil) to the water's edge. Here the more experienced did the killing. A rip across the throat or a pistol shot between the eyes, and another body was added to the growing pile at the water's edge. It was David Miles' initiation to one of the cruellest callings in the world.

To start with, the boy was keyed up with excitement. He used his club with vigour and dodged the rushes of the infuriated bulls with skill. It was, for a fourteen-year-old, all part and parcel of the Big Adventure of Running Away to Sea. After a while, however, the noise and the stench and the weird yellow light began to make his head ache; and the cruelty sickened him. He didn't care so much what happened to the parents—elephant seals are singularly unattractive creatures—but the sight of the pups being crushed to death in the panic-stricken stampede made his stomach churn.

"Look lively, young varmint!"

The voice of the boatswain galvanized him for a few mo-

---

* In the early nineteenth century elephant seals were hunted with such efficiency that they became virtually extinct. In 1874, however, they were classified as "protected," and since that date no one without a government license has been permitted to kill them. This law is enforced by Protection Boats, based in Leith Harbour and Punta Arenas.

[2]

ments to renewed activity. But it was no good. His heart was no longer in killing. He bided his time; and when the boatswain was busy with one of the bulls, he slipped out of the circle of flarelight and into a gully between the rocks.

The gully was jagged, dark and lacquered in rime; and for several minutes David Miles lay shivering with cold and wondering what on earth had possessed him to run away from his comfortable home in the Ayrshire hills. Then, taking care not to be seen, he began to worm his way out of the rookery. He had too much sense to go far. So long, he told himself, as he kept the sealers in sight, there was no risk of getting lost. He climbed an outcrop of rock which lay between the rookery and the beach next door, and here he rested, looking down on a scene which might have been lifted straight from Dante's *Inferno*.

Killing was giving way to skinning now, and the poachers were ankle-deep in blubber and blood. They worked fast, anxious to be back at sea before a Protection Boat discovered them. With short knives—which they honed after every cut—they removed a seal's entire pelt in four long strips. These were then attached to toggles on a wire strap and drawn out by steam winch to the waiting sloop. Knives flashed, winches hummed, dories plied to and fro between ship and shore, and skuas, stinkers and sheathbills darted in and out of the carnage like a macabre *corps de ballet* of the air.

David knew that he ought to be helping. But perversely he stayed in the hollow: I'll not go back, he told himself, till the butchery is over. He huddled into a crevice in the rock, trying not very successfully to keep warm. The stars faded. A pearl-grey light seeped into the sky in the east.

He was watching the birds when, out of the corner of his eye, he noticed a movement at the water's edge. It looked as though something was being washed ashore on the beach next door to the rookery. He decided to see what it was.

It would be an hour till dawn, he thought, as he wandered, hands in pockets, across the deserted beach. The light was deceptive: with the sky pale, the ground dark as if in shadow, and the flares spluttering away in the distance so that every now and then little ripples of light fanned out across the water. He had no forebodings as he picked his way that morning over the coarse grey sand: no premonition that what he was about to see would haunt him for the rest of his life. But as he neared the sea, he became aware of a peculiar smell: pervasive, foetid, nauseous. It was a smell he was to experience years later, in the mud of Passchendaele and Ypres.

It was a sea-fed pool that his nose led him to. Waves flowed into it in rhythmic succession: the larger with élan, the smaller gently, so that the body was hardly disturbed.

His eyes widened.

He thought at first that it must be one of the sealers. He took a step forward. Then, as a bigger-than-usual wave swirled the body almost to his feet, he screamed.

For perhaps ten seconds he stared at the thing that lay in the water, rigid with terror. His first impression was of the nightmare creature which was to haunt his dreams for the next seventy years: a monstrous great ape, its jaw protruding, its skin bloated, its body matted with rust-red hair. It can't, he told himself, be true. And indeed, as another wave drifted the body away, it seemed in the half-light to become transformed to a mass of sea kelp: no creature, but a figment of the mind.

How many times David Miles was to curse himself, in years to come, for not having had the courage to look at whatever it was more closely. But he was an imaginative boy, alone, and keyed up already by the butchery of the seals. His mind, quite suddenly, went blank. He turned and ran.

He could hear nothing except the crunch of his boots in the sand and a series of ear-splitting screams. It distressed him that crunches and screams didn't coincide; it was only when he tried to synchronize them that he realized the screaming was his. As he rushed headlong back to the rookery, the nearest sealers came running to meet him. He tried to push past them, desperate to get as far as possible from whatever it was he had seen. But the boatswain grabbed him, shook him, and clapped a hand to his mouth. For a moment David fought him, blind with panic; then he collapsed limp as a rag doll to the sand. The boatswain bent over him. His voice was not unkindly. "What scairt yeh, lad?"

He drew a shuddering breath, trembling like a man in the grip of fever.

The boatswain unscrewed his flask. He forced it between David's teeth, tipped back his head and poured. Most of the rum went over his chin or inside his shirt, but a trickle found its way down his throat. He sat up, retching and coughing.

"Now, young 'un. What yeh seen?"

"A body."

"A sealer's body?"

He moistened his lips. "I dunno."

Another five minutes and there would have been no mystery: none of the doubts and heart-searchings which were to plague David Miles for the rest of his life. But the reconnaissance party, organized by the boatswain with orders to bring back whatever it was, was still picking its way across the rocks when a searchlight cut a sudden swathe of brightness out of the night. It swept the shore. It came to rest on the dories, the piled-up bodies of the seals, and the crew of the *Huntress* frozen into a tableau of guilt. A gun barked warning of no-nonsense as the Protection Boat dropped anchor in the lee of the bay.

The seal poachers were caught with their pants down. They could neither fight nor run.

Most of them came quietly—there wasn't anything else they could do. A couple tried to hide in a cleft in the rocks, but they were soon winkled out, handcuffed and flung none too gently into a dory; and only the boatswain showed fight. "No bastard puts handcuffs on me!" His bellow rang out defiantly above the roar of the wind, and the first man to lay hands on him was sent reeling back, blood trickling from his mouth. The crew of the Protection Boat were in no mood to be trifled with; and more than one saw the justice of it as their clubs thudded into him, until, like a great bull seal, he fell senseless to the sand.

David tried to attract the attention of one of the officers. "Sir!"

"Quit whining, lad."

"I'm not. But just before you came, I found a body."

"A body! Where?"

"Back o' yon rocks."

The officer looked at him doubtfully. "Whose body, lad? A sealer? An Indian?"

"Dunno." A pause; then with a shudder, "He was all red an' hairy!"

They were joined by a seaman from the patrol. "Sounds like a patch o' kelp, sir."

"Or a pack of lies!"

They were questioning him further when the voice of the skipper came over the loud-hailer. "Landing party, look lively!"

It was no time, the officer decided, to start a hare: they had more important things to see to than the tall story of a half-hysterical boy. "If he's dead, lad, there's naught we can do for him!" He picked David up and dumped him into the stern of a dory.

The boy rocked to and fro, hugging his knees. They don't believe me, he thought. Nor could he blame them. For truth to tell he could hardly believe himself that the thing which he had seen at the water's edge was real.

He was sentenced to three months in Port Stanley jail (there was no "binding over" in the early 1900s). The judge was not impressed with his story of the body—"a lot of moonshine," he called it. But the recorder took the boy's statement down; and it can be seen today, archaic spelling, flecks of quill powder and all, in the rare documents department of the British Museum.

The crew served their sentences—eighteen months in the

case of captain, boatswain and mate; the *Huntress* ended her days in an aura of unlikely respectability on the nitrate run from Tocopilla to San Francisco; and no one gave more than a passing thought to what it could have been that was washed ashore that night on one of the loneliest beaches of the world. No one, that is, except David Miles.

His nightmares were vivid enough at first for the guard to find him clawing in terror at the bars of his cell. For there was no doubt in his dreams what the waves washed up: a monstrous barrel-chested ape, its forehead sloped back in ridges, and its body matted with rust-coloured hair; and in the moment before he woke, it sprang at him out of the sea, its great teeth dripping with saliva. He tried in his waking hours to convince himself that he must have been wrong: that there were no monkeys within a thousand miles of Tierra del Fuego, let alone man-sized apes. Yet if it wasn't an ape, what was it? Certainly not a man. A patch of seaweed perhaps: a mass of kelp torn from the rocks and woven into the likeness of a body? This, on the face of it, seemed the likeliest explanation. But it had a flaw. It wasn't the smell of seaweed which had led him, that morning, to the water's edge.

The memory of what he had seen haunted him. And when, later in life, he joined the Merchant Navy, he gravitated half by accident, half by design to the South Pacific. He paid several visits to Valparaiso, Concepción and Punta Arenas, half-expecting somewhere along the Chilean coast to pick up a clue as to what it could be he had seen. He drew a complete blank.

Inevitably, with the passing of time, the incident receded into the limbo of things that it was more comfortable to forget. In his heart he never ceased to believe that the creature he had seen was real; but common sense and every shred of evidence cried out that this couldn't be so.

It was a mystery: a mystery which remained unsolved till the day he died, and was heightened rather than resolved by a strange little incident in the penultimate year of his life.

A few days after his eighty-third birthday, David Miles

was glancing idly through one of his grandchildren's books, *Early Man* by F. Clark Howell and The Editors of *Life*, when, quite out of the blue, he came across a picture which made his heart falter and the breath catch in his throat. It was a full-page colour reproduction that he stared at, a reproduction of the creature he had seen, seventy years ago, washed up on the shore of Tierra del Fuego. As he peered at the drawing he could hear again the cries of the sheathbills and skuas, and could smell once more the foetid stench which the trenches of the First World War had taught him to identify. He polished his glasses and studied the drawing more closely. Every detail was identical. The matted rust-red hair, the grey face, the receding forehead, the flattened nose, the huge jaw and the massive salivated teeth; the foot even had the same short, splayed-out toes which he could remember grounding for a moment on the coarse grey sand of Tierra del Fuego.

The drawing, a caption told him, was an accurate reconstruction of *Paranthropus*, a species of pre-man which had been extinct for over half a million years.

1

A Voice from the Past

My great-uncle David Miles died in Emsworth on midsummer eve. I remember very clearly the circumstances in which I heard of his death. It was a Sunday afternoon, the wind was fresh, the sky was blue, and my friend Ted Carson and I had just come back from sailing out of the Helford. The telegram was pinned to the door of the bungalow we were renting: "UNCLE DAVID DIED IN HIS SLEEP SATURDAY NIGHT. PLEASE COME IF YOU CAN. SARA."

I hadn't known my great-uncle well, but the cry for help from his daughter was something I couldn't ignore. I looked at the picture-postcard sky and the Fireball at the water's edge and cursed. But Ted knew, and I knew, that I had to go.

To cut a long story short, I found myself twenty-four hours later in Emsworth, just in time for the funeral. And after the funeral, Sara and I, as executors, went back to Great-uncle's house to make an inventory of his effects.

It was a small, rather drab little house, of the sort that had mushroomed between the wars. But it was situated by the water's edge, and the view across Chichester harbour was delightful: all browns and greens and shifting light and wheeling birds.

Sara had the key to the front door. She was very business-like. "I'll do upstairs. You do down."

"O.K.," I said. "But what do I list?" Being twenty-two and a student of zoology at the University of St. Andrews, I felt I wasn't going to be much use as an executor.

"Anything," she said practically, "that's worth selling is worth listing."

So we set to work.

My great-uncle had spent several years in the Merchant Navy, and his house was full of the accumulated bric-a-brac of travelling—Maori paddles, Satsuma bowls, conch shells from the Great Australian Bight—most of it more interesting, it seemed to me, than valuable. Since the death of his wife, three or four years before, he had lived by himself, but everything was neat and orderly—shipshape I expect he would have called it—and in next to no time I had filled half a dozen pages in the exercise book which the efficient Sara had provided.

To start with, as I worked my way from room to room, I could hear my aunt rummaging about upstairs: the slam of a cupboard door, the pulling open of a drawer and the occasional creak of floorboards. But after a while I became aware of a vaguely disconcerting silence. I went to the foot of the stairs. "All right, are you?"

There was no reply. If I had given the matter a bit more thought I would have called again, more loudly. As it was, I simply went upstairs and pushed open the nearest door. She was sitting on the bed in her father's room, crying her eyes out. She wasn't a good age for crying: her makeup had run, her muscles had sagged and she looked a right old mess. But I suddenly liked her better. "Sara," I said, "snap out of it."

The moment she saw me she jumped up and started dabbing at her face. "Sorry. Can't think what came over me."

"Don't apologize," I said. "I'd think it odd if you *didn't* cry."

She blew her nose with vigour. "I'm O.K. now. I'll make a cup of tea."

Ten minutes later she reappeared, mascara and composure

restored; she had even remembered the tea cozy. But I couldn't help noticing that her hands were shaking and that there were lines of strain round her mouth and eyes; she looked washed out. "Aunt Sara," I said, "why don't you push off home? I'll finish the inventory."

She didn't give in without a fight. But it had been an exhausting week for her; and she admitted in the end that she'd be glad of an early night. So a little after seven o'clock I persuaded her into her battered old Mini, and off she went.

It was nice and peaceful by myself in the old man's house. The light was fading, the tide was flooding and looking out of the window I could see a family of swans in line astern, gliding down the path of the sun. Sara hadn't liked the idea of my spending a night in the house alone. But ghoulies and ghosties had no terrors for me, and the sooner the inventory was finished, the sooner I would be back on the Helford. So I worked my way first round the kitchen, then round the sitting room and eventually, round about ten o'clock, I came to my last port of call, Uncle David's desk.

I had asked Sara if she would prefer me to leave the desk, but she had said, "Go through it for me. Please. You'll find no skeletons in Father's drawers." So I set to work.

You can tell a lot about a man from the way he deals with his correspondence and bills. Uncle David's were in apple-pie order: bills paid up-to-date, and correspondence kept to a minimum and neatly filed. Sara, I reflected, was right: I would find no letters here from a mistress of the past, no disclosures to ruffle the wake of a conventional, well-ordered life.

Soon only the bottom drawer remained to be looked through. This, to my surprise, turned out to be in complete contrast to those I had opened before. It was in chaos: bundles of old letters, diaries, newspaper cuttings, sheaves of paper covered with notes and a copy of the Time-Life edition of *Early Man* with pages torn out and a number of passages underlined. It looked as though Uncle David, in the last years of his life, had begun to take an interest in anthropology. This struck me as a little surprising, but my curiosity wasn't really roused until I started to read the draft of a letter he had written to F. Clark Howell, professor of anthropology at the University of Chicago. My great-uncle had obviously had the greatest difficulty composing this letter (indeed I learned afterward it was never posted). Nor, when I saw the content, was I surprised. In fact I burst out laughing. For my great-uncle, whom I had regarded up to now as a model of probity, seemed seriously to think that he had seen, washed up on the shore of Tierra del Fuego, the body of a male *Paranthropus,* a species of pre-man which had been extinct for the better part of a million years.

It was strange, I thought, how a man could be ninety-nine percent normal and one percent complete and utter crank.

The harbour was white with moonlight by this time, and I suddenly realized I had had nothing to eat and only a cup of tea to drink since the funeral. I couldn't be bothered to cook, but I collected corned beef, pickles and water biscuits from the larder, and in between mouthfuls began to sort through my great-uncle's papers, determined to find the cause of this most unlikely bee in his bonnet.

The obvious cause, I told myself, was anno Domini, but as I worked my way through the complex, and often quite technical letters and notes, I could find no trace in my uncle's correspondence of senility; no trace either of the arrogance that one usually associates with a crank.

It would be hard to pinpoint the moment when I stopped being amused and became intrigued, but it could have been when I discovered the diary. This was an old leather notebook, about 9″ x 7″, filled with sloping handwriting which though faded, was mercifully easy to read. My uncle, I learned later, had kept the diary in his sea chest and had written it up each night. It contained several references to the thing he had seen washed up beside the breeding ground of the seals, including this passage written during his first night in Port Stanley jail:

[12]

"*I want to get down right away,*" the entry ran, "*what it was I saw. He was like a muckle great ape. Tall: he could have been almost seven feet, I reckon, and covered all over with coarse hair, a sort of half-brown, half-red like the spikes of old heather on summer braes. His face was enough to scairt the devil. The skin a sort of grey-white, the forehead sloping back in ridges like a ploughed field, and the jaw enormous and full o' the most awfu' great teeth. One of his feet I remember especially clear. The toes were all stiff and spread out like a fan, the big toe being small and separately jointed, like a thumb.*"

Now this was intriguing. Being a zoologist, I was familiar with the basic principles of anatomy; and I knew that the feet of primates such as *Solo* and *Paranthropus* were pretty well unique in having a small and separately jointed big toe. But I knew too that this fact about them had only been discovered recently. I didn't see how my great-uncle, writing in 1902, could possibly have known it. . . . It made me think. . . . Was it just possible, I asked myself, that he had indeed seen something "rare and strange," something in the same category perhaps as a coelacanth?

Now I can't begin to explain what happened next. I suppose it must have been the late hour, the stillness and the fact that I was alone in the house where the old man had died, but I suddenly had the feeling that my great-uncle was beside me in the room. I don't mean that I saw his ghost or heard his voice or anything as fanciful as that. But I felt his presence: felt as though all the bewilderment which had plagued him for seventy years was being sloughed off onto me. What on earth, I wondered, could the creature have been?

The noise of a plane taking off across the water from Thorney Island brought me back to reality. Uncle David, I told myself, had never known what it was that came drifting in on the Pacific tide. I would never know either. Not all the inspirational guesses in the world would bring the truth to light. So I might as well go to bed.

It was midnight by the time I had tidied away the last of the papers. Then, thankfully, I climbed into pyjamas and bed, and within five minutes I was asleep.

It would not have surprised me if I had dreamed that night of a "muckle great ape" rising like some nightmare creature out of the sea. But in fact I slept soundly, and didn't wake till 8 A.M. when I heard the crunch of the postman's feet on the path next door.

In the sober light of day, my speculations of the night before seemed farfetched, even farcical. My great-uncle, I told myself over breakfast, had let his imagination run riot, and for the rest of his life he had made a mountain out of a mole-hill. I must admit, however, that at the back of my mind there remained a residue of doubt. And to placate this, I typed out a couple of passages from the diary and made a précis of his correspondence. These I posted to Fergus Mc-Bride, our senior lecturer of anthropology at St. Andrews. McBride, I knew, had taken part in expeditions to South America, he had a penchant for lost causes and unconventional beliefs, and the affair of the great ape would be right up his street.

Having thus salved my conscience, I locked up the house and invited Aunt Sara to lunch at the Crown. She was almost effusively grateful for the little I had done, and raised no objection when I told her I wanted to be on my way to the Helford.

"You're very keen to get back," she remarked archly over her lager and lime. "I hope she's nice."

"A Fireball's a fast boat, Auntie," I told her. "Not a fast girl."

She pouted. "A pity!"

Well, that was a matter of opinion. I was happy with *Petrel*. Boats you can understand.

Summer ended in a riot of high winds and heavy seas: not easy weather for sailing, but *Petrel* had a robustness which her racing lines belied. Ted and I sailed from sunrise to sunset, from The Manacles to Pendennis Point, and enjoyed every minute of it, capsizings and all. Then, too soon, it was autumn and I was in a northbound train for St. Andrews.

On the Helford, I had hardly given a thought to my uncle's monstrous ape. But the moment I set foot in my digs, I was reminded of it in no uncertain fashion.

One of the letters waiting for me was addressed in green ink and a violent sprawling hand. Its contents were brief and to the point:

> *The Harbour Wall*
> *St. Andrews*
>
> Sir,
>
> *Be good enough to call on me at your earliest convenience.*
>
> *Fergus Alexander McBride*

2
"The Big Red Men from the Hills."

I knew our senior lecturer only by reputation. He was, to those outside his faculty, a flamboyant figure, whose forays into the limelight seemed always to end in uproar and recrimination. It occurred to me that before I called at The Harbour Wall, I ought to know more about him, so I arranged to meet John Hawksworth in the bar of The Links.

John was a second-year student of anthropology with whom I sometimes went climbing—we were both members of the Universities' Mountaineering Club. "McBride," his mouth thinned in dispproval. "Brilliant but unstable."

"You mean he's a crank?"

"Let's say an eccentric. He's a first-class 'stones and bones' man, I'll give him that. On anything a million years old he's one of the leading authorities in the world. But he won't put his mind to conventional work: seems to think it beneath him. He's always dashing off on some harebrained expedition."

"What sort of expedition?"

"Searching for living primates—yeti or Neanderthal man, or whatever the latest craze is."

"I thought so. Didn't he go to South America three or four years ago?"

"He did. And came back with a right old story."

"Go on."

John sipped his beer. "As far as I can make out nobody's sure what *really* happened. But I think he gave an interview to Reuters, somewhere in Chile. Made the most fantastic claims: said he'd discovered the missing link! When he was asked for evidence, not surprisingly, he couldn't produce any! Came up with some cock-and-bull story about his photos being damaged and his specimens lost. In the end, I'm pretty sure he retracted, and the whole affair was hushed up. One or two people were inclined to take him seriously, but he soon choked them off."

"How?"

"By being damned rude. He seemed to think that anyone who didn't swallow his story hook, line and sinker was a moron."

"Charming!"

The light was fading now, and through the windows of the bar we could see the last of the golfers coming in from the Old Course. John looked at me curiously. "It's not Chile you want to see him about?"

I nodded.

"Well, watch it! He slung a couple of journalists who tried to interview him out of his house. I'm not sure there wasn't a case for assault."

I smiled. I am six foot two, weigh thirteen stone and play rugger for Eastern Scotland. "I'd like to see him try! Let's have your glass. . . ."

An hour later I was phoning The Harbour Wall. It was a girl who answered. And when I told her my name, she said very politely, "Oh yes, Daddy would be happy to see you at three-thirty tomorrow."

It sounded O.K. to me. But John had his doubts. "Mc-Bride's a tricky customer," he said. "I bet he either has you for a sucker or slings you out!"

The Harbour Wall turned out to be at the top of the Scores, overlooking St. Andrews Bay. It was built of local stones (pinched, I imagine, from the old harbour), an austere, forbidding residence about as up-to-date as a dodo. The door was opened by the girl who had answered the phone. "Peter Miles?"

I nodded. "Your father's expecting me."

She showed me into a dimly lit, Victorian-style front parlour, and shut the door purposefully behind us. She was about seventeen and decidedly attractive, with long corn-coloured hair, a too wide mouth and chameleon eyes (I couldn't make out if they were blue or green); I looked at her with some apprehension.

"Have you met my father before?"

"No."

"Then I warn you in advance. He's got the devil's temper. I hope you won't argue with him."

"My knees," I said, "are trembling."

She tossed her head; and her eyes, which up to now had been friendly, went cold. "Suit yourself, Tarzan. But he's thrown bigger boys than you into the street. . . . I hope it's not Chile you want to see him about?"

"As a matter of fact it is."

"Well, be tactful. If"—she looked at me doubtfully—"you can. And if he turns violent, ring the bell. He's got old-fashioned scruples about brawling in front of a woman."

"Alison!" The roar echoed down the stone-flagged passage. "Show my visitor in."

She held open the door. "Come on then, Daniel. Don't keep the lion waiting."

With these encouraging words, she led me to a massive oak door. A tap, a bellow of "Come," and I was face to face with the professor.

I don't know which was more imposing, the room or the man. It was a big, high-ceilinged room, its panels festooned with paintings of misty braes and lugubrious cattle. Dominating it was a huge inglenook fireplace and a huge flat-topped desk, the latter littered with books, maps and specimen

[18]

frames. And dominating the desk was Professor Fergus Alexander McBride.

Having only seen him before from a distance, I was unprepared for so commanding a personality. His size quite took my breath away. His head was huge, with a massive high-domed forehead; his nose was hooked, with wide flared-back nostrils; a luxuriant rust-red beard rippled almost to his chest; and his eyes were a brilliant sapphire blue, very clear and very masterful. Wide shoulders, a barrel chest, great hairy hands and a rumbling booming voice completed my first impression of the notorious professor.

"Now, young man." He eyed me as might a vivisectionist a not very promising specimen. "Are you the author of these documents?" He waved the extracts I had copied from my great-uncle's diary.

"I didn't write them," I said. "I simply passed them on to you."

"Why?"

I shrugged. "I thought you might be interested."

He leaned forward, his great hands splayed out on the desk like spiders about to jump. "Gibberish. That's what they are. Complete and utter gibberish. Do you expect a man of my intelligence to be taken in by a schoolboy prank?"

I was considerably put out. "If that's your opinion, sir, we needn't waste one another's time." I turned for the door.

"Wait. You deny these are fakes?"

"I hoped I'd made it plain in my letter," I said. "They're extracts from a perfectly genuine diary, written in 1902. If you doubt it, I can show you the original."

"A likely tale!"

His daughter's warning was forgotten in a rising tide of anger. I hadn't come to this man's house to be insulted. "Are you calling me a liar?"

He leaned forward, stroking his great red beard. "I warn you, young man, if you *are* lying, I've promised myself the pleasure of showing you out of the house—on the toe of my boot."

"You and who else?"

He sprang to his feet, catching the edge of the desk as he did so, and knocking a pile of specimen frames with an almighty crash to the floor. We glared at one another, like cocks in a pit, and even in the heat of the moment my first reaction was surprise. He was a good head shorter than I was: a mini-Hercules, all run to breadth and brain. I believe we would have had things out there and then if his daughter hadn't burst into the room. She had heard the crash, and half-expected, I think, to find us locked in mortal combat. As it was, she took one look at our angry faces and the pile of broken frames, and planted herself in front of her father like an outraged chicken confronting a bulldog. "You ought to be ashamed of yourself. Aye brawling. Aye trying to prove you're stronger than others. Where's your dignity?"

"Dirty linen," he grumbled.

"Indeed it's no secret. You'll be the laughing stock of the university."

"It was my fault," I said. "I provoked him."

They both stared at me. Some of the anger ebbed out of Alison's eyes; indeed at the back of them I thought I discerned a glimmer of amusement, though she tried not to let it show. "Then you're as bad as he is!"

"Now, miss," the professor started to pick the frames off the floor, "with your permission Mr. Miles and I will continue our discussion. So perhaps you'll bring us tea."

"I'm not sure—" I began.

He glared at me. "Sit down! I've not finished with you yet!"

I was in two minds to walk out of the house. In fact, I believe to this day that it was only a chance question of Alison's that induced me to stay. "You'll be wanting pikelets?" she asked me.

I am amazed at the incredible chain of events which stemmed from my weakness for homemade scones.

The professor and I tidied up the floor and the desk; Alison brought in tea with commendable promptness; and the pikelets were all I had hoped for, crisp and newly cooked and thinly buttered. We ate in silence, eyeing one another over the rims of our tea cups. For perhaps ten minutes the only sounds were the tick of a clock and the appreciative mastication of the professor. Then he pushed the tea tray aside and leaned back in his chair like a complacent bullfrog. "I invited you to remain, young man," he announced pontifically, "for two reasons. First, your reaction to my very justifiable accusation that you were the perpetrator of a schoolboy prank. This was violent enough to convince me you truly believe your uncle's documents to be genuine. Second, I was favourably impressed by your admission to my daughter that the blame for our little contretemps lay with yourself. This stamped you as a person of some mental detachment and maturity of view; you swam, as it were, into my notice; I perceived that you might be a useful ally. I have therefore decided to take you into my confidence. If you wish to smoke, kindly deposit ash in the bowl beside the Polish Atlas Swiata."

All this he boomed forth, like a lecturer addressing a crowded hall. He was ferreting about in the desk now, eventually coming up with an official-looking document—I could see, embossed on the notepaper, the blue flag and four stars which, I learned later, were the insignia of the commander-in-chief of the Chilean Navy.

"I take it," he went on, "you sent me these extracts because you couldn't believe your uncle's story yourself but you felt there might be something to it?"

I nodded. "It's an impossible story. But he was such a well-balanced chap. It's hard to believe he made the whole thing up."

The professor leaned forward. "I can promise you, young man, that the creature your uncle saw was flesh and blood. As real as you and I." He laid a hand on my shoulder, smiling —a sudden emanation of *bonhomie* which was almost as overwhelming as his violence. "I too, Mr. Miles, have seen strange sights on beaches at the bottom of the world!"

I was skeptical. But I had nothing to lose by listening.

"You have to understand," he began, "that southern Chile is one of the least-known parts of the world. Most countries nowadays are crisscrossed by air routes, and have lost their aura of mystery. Not Chile. It's out on a limb, you see, a narrow ribbon of land, hemmed in to the east by the Andes, and to the west by the Pacific. Look at a map of the world's population density, and you won't find many blanks on it. But there's a blank in austral Chile: ten thousand square miles of forest, glacier and ice cap: one of the last great open spaces in the world to be marked not only 'uninhabited' but also 'unexplored.' In recent years the Chilean government has tried to encourage settlement along this southern coast. It's been an uphill struggle, for the terrain is formidable, and the climate about the worst in the world. A handful of families, however, have at last taken root: a couple of houses here, another couple there, at the foot of glacier or fjord. Their survival depends on the Chilean Navy, whose vessels call three or four times a year with supplies. And it was an officer of the Chilean Navy whose report triggered the affair off."

He leaned back in his chair, eyes half-closed, hands clasped to his stomach. "Three years ago I was in Punta Arenas. I had been making a study of the Yagan and the Alacaluf, a couple of Fuegian tribes, who, by the by, are among the most primitive people on earth. We had finished field work and were waiting for the boat home when I was called unexpectedly to naval headquarters. The Chilean Navy, you have to understand, had been keeping a fatherly eye on us; they were interested in our work; and they now showed me a report from one of their officers." He paused. "To the author of this report I am always happy to lift my hat. Indeed when the credit for this fantastic business comes to be shared out, his name will stand in the roll of honour not far below my own. . . . Now the gist of the officer's report was this.

"The *Laubaro,* a six-hundred-ton patrol boat, had called to drop off supplies at a settlement on the Golfo de Peñas. The crew, it seems, realized the moment they anchored that something was wrong, because they couldn't attract the settlers' attention; and when the landing party were put ashore they soon found why. The two homesteads had been demolished, and the occupants not a sight for the squeamish—men, women and children were lying dead with their heads screwed completely off. Their first thought was that the settlers had exterminated one another in a family feud, but this they soon ruled out. Their second thought was the Alacaluf. A group of them were camped on an island a couple of miles offshore, and late that afternoon an officer and a party of seamen paid them a visit. Now the Alacaluf are unbelievably primitive—as an indication of their mental capacity, their speech contains no number higher than five. They were suspicious, frightened and unable to speak the same language as the landing party. But the officer, a Lieutenant Juan Sarmiento, managed by signs to establish three facts: one, the Alacaluf knew what had happened to the settlers; two, they denied that any of their tribe were responsible for the massacre; three, they said the settlers had been killed by 'big red men from the hills.' Now the hills at the back of the Golfo de Peñas are known to be uninhabited, and ninety-nine people out of a hundred would have dismissed the story as moonshine. Sarmiento, however, was a man of discernment. He had a feeling that improbable as it sounded, the Alacaluf might be speaking the truth. And eventually he winkled out of them the fact that they had an important piece of evidence. They could show him the body of one of the big red men.

"Light was fading as they led him to a cave at the foot of the cliffs where, according to Alacaluf custom, the body had been buried. The cave was dark, wet and stank to high heaven. But Sarmiento had guts and a torch; and leaving a couple of seamen to guard the entrance, he squeezed in. I now propose to tell you, in his own words, what he saw."

As the professor picked up what was obviously a transcript of Sarmiento's report, my interest quickened.

"I quote: 'The beam of my torch spotlit first, on the floor of the cave, a miniature oval hut about eighteen inches high made of twigs and fern. At the side of it lay a heap of ash and a handful of mussel shells.* The beam of my torch moved on. It came to rest on the body, and I felt the hair prick up on my head. He was like nothing I had seen or heard of. Enormous: in appearance half-man, half-ape. The body had started to decompose, but I made what measurements I could. Height six foot eight inches. Chest fifty-eight inches, arms very long, not less than forty-two inches. Head with a pushed-back appearance, the brow receding in ridges like the foothills of a mountain range. Jaw huge, brain small, teeth very large. Skin of face, feet and hands a curious grey-white. He appeared to have died from gunshot wounds in the chest, sustained, I assume, during the attack on the settlers' farm. I could not stay long because the battery of my torch was fading. On leaving, I instructed my men to roll boulders across the entrance, and to mark our route with arrows, to facilitate the cave being found again.' . . . Now, young man, what do you make of that?"

I was intrigued. For this was something very different from the cock-and-bull story John Hawksworth had led me to expect. "I suppose," I said, "Sarmiento's report was verified?"

"By no less a person than myself. . . . It was three weeks from the time Sarmiento found the body to the time the *Laubaro* dropped anchor off Punta Arenas, and another three weeks before I had read the captain's report and found myself a ship that was bound for the gulf. Eventually, however, I managed to talk my way aboard a small nitrate freighter which was heading, via the inshore channels, for Puerto Aisén. Her skipper promised me a landing party, and five or six

---

* I have since learned that it is common practice among the Alacaluf to provide the spirit of those who die with shelter, food and warmth: to keep it going, I suppose, till it finds another body to move into.

hours to crate up the body. This should have been time and to spare. But from the moment we stepped ashore everything went wrong. We found the cave all right. But when we rolled away the stones, the fear that had been nagging at me for weeks was realized. It wasn't a body we stood staring down at, it was a skeleton. Time, sea water and the beaks of skua and albatross had transformed Sarmiento's magnificent specimen to little more than a pile of bones. Well, it was no use crying over spilt milk. We crated the skeleton up and carried it to the water's edge. The weather, however, had worsened while we were in the cave; fair-sized waves were now rolling down through the Narrows, and the wind was rising. The freighter signalled us that we were in for a storm. We had better, she said, look lively or wait for it to blow over. I still think we made the right decision. We decided to wait. We weren't to know that the bad weather was to continue, without letup, for more than seventy-two hours. Picture the scene, young man. Outside, sleet driving in from the sea in great horizontal swathes; inside, myself, three Chilean seamen and the skeleton, huddled together in a dark, wet, stinking cave. Within a couple of hours we were white with rime and spray, and shivering with cold. If it hadn't been for the fuel and food packs—which are standard equipment in a ship's boat— we might well have died of exposure. As it was, we spent three most miserable days in the cave, our vitality being sapped and our judgment, I can see now, being progressively impaired. On the fourth day, the wind and sleet eased off; we decided to make a dash for it; and the freighter moved as close inshore as she dared, leaving us no more than a couple of hundred yards to row. After three days and nights in the cave, it is obvious in retrospect that we weren't as much on the *qui vive* as we ought to have been. We none of us saw the williwaw until, midway between ship and shore, it hit us: a great current of air sweeping down through the Narrows, against the prevailing wind. One moment it was blowing a zephyr from the south, the next a cyclone from the north. The sea and sky disappeared in a great wall of rain. And our boat heeled over, broached to and started to sink."

McBride levered himself to his feet, walked to the fire and tossed on a log. "If we hadn't jettisoned the crate," he said, "we would have drowned."

"So," my voice was thoughtful, "you lost your evidence?"

"In ten fathom of fast-flowing water. Beyond hope of recovery."

Well, it was a strange, inconclusive story. But it contained a number of facts which, it seemed to me, could easily have been checked. "Surely," I said, "you had only to tell this to the right people, and the whole affair would have been looked into?"

"So, in my simplicity, thought I. But not a bit of it. I was met at every turn by incredulity and derision—the result partly of jealousy, partly of ignorance. It is not in my nature, sir, to suffer fools gladly. When my word was doubted and my reputation blackened, the whole affair became distasteful to me. I resolved to go, as it were, into hibernation until such time as my discovery could be verified."

"Surely it could have been verified right away? By Sarmiento?"

He spread his hands in a gesture of resignation. "Sarmiento," he said, "was sent on special leave, to report his findings to the University of Chile. On his way north, he stopped for the night at the little port of Puerto Aisén to visit his family. He was there for less than twenty-four hours. But during the night he spent there, there was an earth tremor, quite a small one by Chilean standards: two dozen houses demolished, half a dozen people killed—including Sarmiento and his wife."

I stared at him. "So you lost first your evidence, then your witness?"

He nodded. "Like the prophet who cries in the wilderness, I have nothing to offer but truth."

It was silly, I know, but I felt quite suddenly the way I had felt that night in my great-uncle's house in Emsworth:

as though I was being caught up in events beyond my control, dragged along like a cork in the wake of the old man's life. "What on earth," I said slowly, "do you suppose the creature was? A sort of missing link?"

A snort of exasperation. "As you know very well, young man, the term 'missing link' is a catchphrase abhorrent to the serious anthropologist. Without doubt the creature will prove to be an aberrant species of early man: *Oreopithecus, Solo* or—most likely of all—*Paranthropus.*"

His assurance irked me. "If you're so sure," I said tartly, "I wonder you don't take an expedition to Chile and bring one back."

"I will leave tomorrow if you provide the necessary twenty-five thousand pounds."

It was a complication I hadn't thought of. He had unfolded a map of the Southern Andes now, and was staring at it, stroking his beard, apparently lost in thought. I walked round the desk and stood beside him, peering down at the mosaic of glacier, ice cap and lake. "I suppose," I said, "it would be a difficult area to search."

"The conventional type of search would not be necessary. Since I know where the creatures are."

I stared at him in amazement. "You must be joking!"

"Study the map, young man. There is only one place they *could* be. Not on the coast, for dense as the forest is, they would have been seen from passing ships. Not beside the lakes of the Argentine border, for this is *estancia* country, dotted with sheep farms. Which leaves us with what?"

"The ice cap?"

"Exactly. The Hielo Continental of the Andes, one of the bleakest terrains on earth: an ice plateau, in almost perpetual cloud, swept by some of the strongest winds on earth, and cold as the wastes of Antarctica. How do you suppose they survive there?"

"I can't think!"

He shook his head, more in sorrow than anger, and pointed to the northern extremity of the Hielo Continental, where the symbol of a volcano was suffixed by the words "Vulcan Viedma (position unverified)."

"You think they live near the volcano?"

"It seems an eminently reasonable supposition. The whole plateau is volcanic in origin. The Viedma is known to be active—though it is so inaccessible that no one has ever set foot on it: even its position, I gather, is in dispute between the Argentine and Chile. I would expect to find the creatures existing in caves, close to the volcanic fumarole."

"Why on earth in caves?"

"Both your uncle and Sarmiento remarked on the grey-white colour of their skin: the hallmark of a troglodyte."

He certainly had it all worked out. But the arrogance of his assertions made my hackles rise. "If you're so sure you're right," I said, "I wonder you haven't found yourself a sponsor to explore the Viedma. Anyone who climbs a twopenny-half-penny mountain can get a subsidy nowadays."

He stared at me, breathing heavily, mouth hanging open like an asthmatic bulldog. I thought for a moment he was speechless with rage. Then, to my amazement, the most beatific smile spread slowly over his face. His cheeks dimpled, his eyes took on a mischievous glint and a great fist smacked into the palm of his hand. "Eureka!" With an *entrechat* which would have done credit to Nureyev, he leapt to the far end of the desk and snatched up a university calendar. What he saw in it seemed to confirm his good humour. "Who would have believed it! Out of the mouth of babes and suck-lings! . . ."

"You have an idea?"

"Indeed, young man, it is your idea more than mine. You will observe from your calendar that the raisin-day lecture will be given this year by Eric Westerman, a dry little stick of a fellow, but a mountaineer of repute, who knows South America. Pray attend this lecture, sir. It will surely be an historic occasion." He looked pointedly at his watch.

"You hope," I said, "to persuade Westerman to lead an expedition? To climb the Viedma?"

"Just so." He pressed a bell. "And now I must not detain you further. . . . Alison, Mr. Miles is leaving now. I look forward to seeing you, young man, at the lecture."

My last impression of the professor, as the door closed, was of his great hairy hands moving purposefully over the map of the Cordillera. He was already, I guessed, planning a route to the Viedma.

I felt that I ought to say something to Alison as we walked through the hall. But all I could think of was "your pikelets were jolly good." This struck me as trivial, so I said nothing, except "thanks" as she opened the door and "good-bye" as she was about to close it. Her eyes, I decided, were green: like a deep sea pool it would be rather fun to dive into.

"Bye, Tarzan," she said.

I walked up the Scores, past the harbour and over the Kinkell Braes. It was a lovely evening: pale yellow sky, big waves and a blustering wind. I was glad of the wind: it helped to clear my head. But even after a couple of hours' walking, I still wasn't sure if McBride was charlatan or prophet.

John Hawksworth had no such doubts. I found him waiting for me when I got back to my room. "How," he asked, "did you get on with Professor Munchausen?"

"I'm not so sure he *is* a fraud."

John laughed. "Missing links: alive in our day and age! I'd as soon believe the Arabian Nights!"

"He's got a case."

"But no evidence?"

"Nothing concrete, I admit. But a good deal of what you might call circumstantial evidence."

"These things are easy to cook up if you've got the know-how. Remember Piltdown Man."

I shook my head. "I don't see why a man of his standing should *want* to cook things up."

He shrugged. "I don't see why some people *want* to be Napoleon. But they do. Delusions of grandeur, I suppose."

I began to feel uneasy. Perhaps, after all, I had been unduly credulous. "Maybe you're right," I said. "But in all fairness we ought to give the old boy a hearing. He's planning some sort of coup at the raisin-day lecture. Let's go."

John was none too keen to start with, but in the end he agreed. "If nothing else," he said, "it'll be good for a giggle."

3

An Expedition Is Formed

Raisin-day is rag day at St. Andrews: a day of little work and much festivity, the latter reaching its climax in the evening lecture at the Younger Halls. This, by tradition, is popular rather than academic and is open to the public.

By the time Hawksworth and I arrived at the Halls, they were already three-quarters full. Both town and gown, it seemed, had turned out in force to listen to Eric Westerman, who was giving a lecture with ciné-film on the Southern Andes. There was an atmosphere of expectancy among the audience, and I wondered if rumour of McBride's intended intervention had leaked out. He was there in the front row, together with his green-eyed daughter and a number of dignitaries from the university.

"I wonder," I whispered to John, "what he's dreamed up?"

"I shudder to think. He can't open his mouth without putting his foot in it!"

Westerman was introduced by the vice-chancellor. He was a slightly built man with an unassuming, almost diffident, manner, but he knew and loved the lonely places of the world, and he had the knack of communicating this love to his audience. He began with a brief account of exploration in the Southern Andes—"one of the least-known ranges in the world." Few expeditions, he told us, had managed to penetrate more than a few miles into the great Andean ice plateau, the Hielo Continental, which lay between the forty-eighth and fifty-first parallels. None, prior to 1968, had succeeded in crossing it. But that summer he and a couple of companions had set out from Lago San Martín on the Argentine border. . . . He had a nice sense of humour, and the trials and tribulations of his party among the foothills made good entertainment. It was not, however, until he came to the meat of his lecture, the actual crossing of the ice cap, that he had us wholly under his spell. Then we might have been with him: cowering under the eighty-mile-an-hour lash of the Patagonian wind, and staring in wonder at the bizarre beauty of the great cornices of ice. The latter featured in his slides: arrases of fluted white, clinging against all the laws of gravity to rock faces that were near-perpendicular. "They are formed," he explained, "by the moisture-laden wind blowing in from the Pacific and striking the summit ridge. This ridge is precipitous in the Hielo Continental, being volcanic in origin, though it contains no active volcano."

"Question!" boomed a voice from the stalls.

For a moment Westerman was nonplussed; then his eyes came to rest on McBride, who was leaning back in his chair, his eyes closed and his lips composed into a beatific smile. "I see," Westerman said with a shrug, "it is our friend the senior lecturer in anthropology."

The audience laughed. But the affair was far from over. For on several more occasions, while describing the Hielo Continental, Westerman remarked on the fact that it contained no active volcano, and on each occasion he was interrupted by the same bull's bellow from McBride. The audience was in just the mood for it. And soon, each time the word volcano was mentioned, before the professor's beard had a chance to open, a great shot of "Question!" erupted from every part of the hall. Eventually the vice-chancellor rose to his feet. "Professor McBride. If you please, sir. Questions at the *end* of the lecture."

The professor, quite unabashed, bowed, smiled, puffed out his cheeks and subsided into his chair.

"I told you," John hissed, "he'd make a fool of himself."

Westerman wasn't easily ruffled. He continued his lecture, apparently unmoved by the buzz of expectation. But I learned afterward that he showed only two reels of film instead of three. For he could sense the mood of his audience.

When it came to question time an anticipatory hush descended on the hall. There was a moment of anticlimax when an earnest young man in horn-rimmed glasses asked a highly technical question about the protein content of the expedition's diet. Then McBride rose ponderously to his feet.

As luck would have it, the *Eastern Gazette* published a full account of the events that followed, and I quote from this verbatim:

"The professor addressed the hall in a paternal manner. Mr. Westerman, he said, was to be congratulated on crossing the ice cap. One crossing, however, didn't constitute a survey. Hundreds of square miles of the Hielo Continental remained unmapped and unexplored; and just because Mr. Westerman and his party had seen no active volcano, it certainly didn't follow that none existed. He pointed out that the whole mountain complex south of the forty-ninth parallel was virgin ground. And it was here, he claimed, among the peaks of the Mariano Moreno, that there existed an active volcano, the Vulcan Viedma.

"Mr. Westerman replied that in his opinion the Vulcan Viedma was like the Loch Ness monster: several people claimed to have seen it, but no one could produce definite evidence of it. Both Chile and Argentina, for example, claimed that the Viedma was in their territory, yet neither had been able to locate it, let alone triangulate it and place it on the map. Its existence, therefore, must be regarded as unproved.

"In reply the professor embarked on a lengthy and detailed analysis of the evidence that a volcano existed among the peaks of the Moreno. This was not to the audience's liking. They became restless and bored. Cries of 'Sit down,' 'Prove it' and 'Question!' were heard from various parts of the hall. The professor became first disjointed in his argument, then angry. His anger was directed initially at the students who interrupted him, but after a while he rounded on Mr. Westerman, who had, during the furore, been preserving a discreet silence. 'I claim,' he shouted, 'a volcano exists. You doubt my word. Then let us put the matter to the test. If I provide evidence of the Viedma's latitude and longitude, will you lead an expedition to survey and climb it? Here is a challenge for you, sir: to put one of the last unconquered peaks of the world fairly and squarely on the map.'

"Westerman was inclined at first to prevaricate. The audience, however, clearly regarded the challenge as a fair one, and cries of 'Call his bluff,' 'Chicken!' and 'Have a go!' greeted the lecturer's efforts to break free from the web that he found himself suddenly ensnared in. Eventually he was goaded into a reluctant undertaking. If—and he took pains to stress the word—*if* McBride's evidence turned out to be conclusive, he would do his best, he said, to get an expedition together. This was the signal for much cheering and applause. . . ."

Up to now I had been a mere observer, watching with some amusement as McBride netted his quarry with the cunning of a poacher his salmon. Suddenly, however, and before I quite realized how it happened, I was netted too!

Westerman said that he would need a couple of competent mountaineers to make up his team. There would, McBride intimated, be no problem here. The well-known Chilean climber Eduardo Corbella was likely, he said, to be available. "And perhaps," he added, almost as an afterthought, "we could find another volunteer from the hall?"

Everyone's life, I suppose, has its moment of crisis. Suddenly and without premeditation I found myself on my feet and heard myself saying, as if in a dream over which I had no control, "I volunteer." Beside me John was tugging at

my sleeve. "Sit down, man! Don't make a fool of yourself."
But I stayed on my feet. "I'd like to volunteer," I repeated.

"Your name, sir?" Westerman eyed me appraisingly.

"My name is David Hamilton Miles. I am a graduate of
zoology. And a member of the Universities' Mountaineering
Club."

The professor favoured me with a paternal smile. "Mr.
Miles," he said, "appears to have the essential qualifications.
A zoologist would be welcome. I propose he is invited to
join us."

And so, amid a mounting hubbub of speculation, good-
humoured ribaldry and cynical dissent, our expedition was
conceived.

Soon after this the meeting broke up, and I allowed myself to be borne away in the great human current that was
spilling out through the doors. Outside the hall I was conscious of a great concourse of people and an excited babble
of talk; then the crowd thinned out, and I found myself
walking alone, through quiet streets, in the direction of my
digs.

Yet not completely alone. I was suddenly aware of footsteps behind me, and as I turned, a hand touched my elbow.
"Mr. Miles?"

I nodded. I didn't recognize Westerman at first. In the
half-light he looked frailer and older than on the platform of
the Younger Halls. "I'd be grateful," he said, "if you could
spare me a few minutes? There are one or two questions I'd
very much like to ask you."

4

"I warn you. It's the most God-forsaken corner of the earth."

We didn't say much as we walked down Union Street toward Westerman's hotel. He did, however, ask me where I'd done my climbing, and whether I knew a couple of young mountaineers who were friends of his. I got the impression that he wasn't sure what to make of me, and that he thought the whole affair might turn out a rag-day hoax. As we neared the hotel, he felt in his pocket, pulled up short and cursed, "Damn it! I've left the key in my room."

"I should think," I said, "there'll be someone to let us in."

He shook his head. "The night porter turns in at eleven-thirty. We're locked out of the hotel."

It seemed to me that if we banged on the door and rang the bell, we would soon wake somebody up. But Westerman said that he had left his bedroom window open, and it would be a simple matter to climb in. I dare say if my head hadn't been full of more important matters, the idea would have struck me as preposterous. As it was, I merely shrugged and contented myself with observing that I hoped the police didn't spot us.

His hotel was at the bottom of The Scores, a comparatively new building, faced with blocks of local stone, with the cement-rendering in between affording about enough toe-hold for a small monkey with prehensile feet! Westerman pointed to an open window on the second floor, and asked me what I reckoned was the best way up. Well, the light was bad and the façade intimidating, and I didn't fancy the look of it. It occurred to me, however, that perhaps I was being put to some sort of test; and although I am certainly no braver than the next man, I have an almost pathological horror of being thought a coward. So I pointed to a boxed-in gutterpipe which ran from ground to roof, and suggested to Westerman that he give me a leg up. When he made some comment about the danger of falling onto the patio beneath, my irritation spilled over. "There's no point," I said, "in putting it off. If we wait till sunup the danger won't be less."

He muttered something I didn't catch, and pulled out his wallet. "What an ass I am! I remember now, I put the key in here."

I was not amused. "You knew it was there," I said, "all the time."

He had the grace to look sheepish. "I hope you don't mind, Mr. Miles. But if we *are* to go climbing together, I want to know something about you. At least I'm sure now you've plenty of nerve. . . . But come in. I really do want to talk to you."

I followed him, by no means mollified, into the hotel. There was a light still on in the room behind the reception desk; and after asking me what I'd like, Westerman ordered "as big a pot of coffee as you can manage." We then retired to a corner of the lounge, which at this hour of the night was deserted.

He came to the point right away. "This Fergus McBride. He seems a cantankerous old bird. What do you know about him?"

I told him of my great-uncle's diary, and my visit to The Harbour Wall. He listened closely, asking the occasional question. At the end, I could sense that he still wasn't sure what to make of it—which was not surprising really. He asked me to help myself to coffee while he got some papers from his room. After about five minutes he reappeared, and spread out on the table a large-scale map of the Hielo Continental. "Have you ever been to South America?"

I shook my head.

"I've spent ten years," he said, "in and around the Andes. They're mountains I love. But they're not everyone's cup of tea. And before you even think of joining an expedition, you ought to realize quite clearly what you'd be letting yourself in for. Here is where we'd be going"—he smoothed out the map and pointed to the area of the great lakes on the Chile-Argentine border. "This," he went on, "is one of the least-known corners of the earth. The land is so rugged, you see, and the weather so bad, that it sometimes takes as much as a week to cover a couple of miles. Just look at the terrain. Here's the main range of the Andes, running roughly north and south; and here are the foothills. The foothills are covered in forests of evergreen beech. These beech are so stunted and flattened by the wind that they form a low matted tangle of branches that is literally impenetrable. So the only way to approach the mountains is via the lakes—Lago Argentino, Lago Viedma and Lago San Martín. These lakes are swept by high winds, their currents are tricky, and crossing them isn't easy. Their western arms, which fan out like fjords into the mountains, are ringed with some of the most spectacular glaciers in the world. But the glaciers are fast-moving; they are so broken up and crevassed that they're difficult to climb; and there are none of the nice easy traverses of moraine that you find, for example, in the Himalaya. And finally, at the head of the glaciers, we come to the Hielo Continental itself. This is guarded by almost perpendicular walls of ice, and it's about the bleakest spot on earth. It doesn't compare in size, of course, with the ice caps of Antarctica or Greenland, but for sheer windswept desolation it hasn't an equal." He paused. "As for the weather, it beats even an English summer! It rains or snows on seven days out of eight. Fine spells are rare and seldom last more than a few hours. And the wind is a steady twenty to thirty knots, often gusting well over a hundred knots in storms that go on for weeks. I want to make it abundantly clear, Mr. Miles, an expedition to the Hielo Continental would be no picnic."

I looked at him curiously. "And you say you love the Andes."

He smiled. "Let's say they're a challenge." There was a faraway look in his eyes; and it came to me that this unassuming little man, now sipping his coffee with almost genteel fastidiousness in the hotel lounge, was cast in the same mould as the very greatest of the world's explorers: men like Nansen, Thesiger and Saint Exupéry, who have sought out the lonely reaches of land, sea and sky, and wrung from them not only adventure, but the best and hardest-won fruits of it—philosophy.

"How," I asked him, "would you rate our chances of success?"

"If you mean our chances of finding the Vulcan Viedma, I'd say this was quite on the cards. I can only give a tentative opinion, of course, without seeing McBride's evidence. But he's right in saying the whole range of the Moreno is virgin ground. For years there have been reports of volcanic activity there—the sighting of smoke plumes, falls of pumice and ash—and an active volcano somewhere along this part of the border is perfectly possible." He helped himself to coffee. "If, on the other hand, you mean what are our chances of finding a tribe of prehistoric apes, well, that's a different kettle of fish. I've heard some pretty tall travellers' tales in the Andes—lost cities, Nazi hideouts, veins of gold—but never anything on a level with this! Common sense surely rules it out."

"I suppose," I said not very happily, "you're right. So what's the next move?"

"I'm meeting McBride tomorrow. He'll hand over his evidence—I gather he's got photos and survey reports, though heaven knows where from! If it adds up to anything, I'll have a word with the Royal Geographical Society."

"And they'll finance us?"

"If I ask them to. But the evidence will need to be pretty convincing. I'll not be conned into a wild-goose chase."

Silence, while I drank the last of my coffee, and Westerman rolled up his map. "What do you know," I said eventually, "about this Chilean chap who's coming with us?"

"Corbella? I met him once, but I've never climbed with him. He's an officer—a pretty high-ranking one, I think—in the Chilean Navy, and he doesn't get much time for climbing. But I'm told he's a more than competent mountaineer, and he seemed pleasant enough."

"So there'd be just the four of us: you, McBride, Corbella and me?"

"If you're sure you want to come. I warn you. It's the most God-forsaken corner of the earth."

"It'll be a challenge," I said.

And I knew from the way he smiled that if we did eventually fetch up in the wilds of Patagonia, the two of us would be *en rapport*, which in a small expedition is a matter of some importance.

Westerman warned me that night—or rather I should say early that morning—as I left to walk back to my digs, not to count too much on our going. Most expeditions, he pointed out, were like aeroplanes: sometimes they never got off the ground, and this one in particular looked to have more than its share of imponderables.

A week later, however, much to my delight, I received a telegram: "EXPEDITION APPROVED BY R.G.S. LETTER FOLLOWS. WESTERMAN."

"We're off!" I exclaimed exultantly that night to John Hawksworth in the bar of The Links.

"Off your head!" he grunted.

I won't bore you by describing the events that led up to our departure. They were hectic: especially for Westerman, who got landed with the assembling of our equipment and supplies. For me, the hardest part was getting leave of absence from the university. They were not keen on letting me go at first, but were won over in the end when I promised to write a thesis on "The Fauna of the Patagonian Andes"—though just how momentous a document this would turn out to be, no one had an inkling at the time. Anyhow, to cut a long story short, December 2 found us in the departure lounge of London Airport. Westerman and McBride were coping with reporters, who still hoped for a last-minute release of our expedition's destination and plans, while I was talking to Alison. After a while one of the reporters came up to us. "I believe you're a member of Westerman's team?"

I nodded.

"Have you had much experience of the sort of climbing you'll be doing?"

"Sorry," I said, "no comment."

"How dull! . . . Is this," he smiled knowingly at Alison, "your girl friend?"

Alison, to my surprise, blushed, which I thought rather charming. "This," I said, "is Professor McBride's daughter."

He favoured her with a knowing leer that I didn't care for. "I bet *you* know where the expedition's going?"

Her eyes were wide and innocent. "Of course," she said. "To Loch Ness."

His pad snapped open.

"My father has this thing about the monster," her voice was deadpan. "He's leading a team of mountaineers in aqualungs down to the bottom of the lake."

I could see that he wasn't sure how to take this. "Are you going too?"

"Yes, isn't it exciting?" She gave a little shiver of anticipation. "I'm the bait!"

As he ripped the page angrily out of his pad, I heard them call our flight to Buenos Aires. "When we get back," I said to Alison on our way to the barrier, "remind me to give you an Oscar."

Unexpectedly she reached for my hand. "Daddy's getting a bit long in the tooth for this sort of thing," she said. "Look after him for me, Tarzan. Please."

"I'll try."

"And yourself," she added.

5

"You are guests of the Chilean Navy."

It was cold and windy as our Boeing climbed out of London Airport through flurries of rain. It was colder and even more windy when we landed three days later on the opposite side of the world in Punta Arenas. The Cape Horner which had built up unchecked across nine thousand miles of sea made us feel that we had come indeed to the uttermost part of the earth.

Punta Arenas is a schizophrenic town. In good weather it has an almost ethereal beauty, with its buildings hung fairy-tale-like midway between mountains and sea. But when the weather is bad—and it is bad on seven days out of eight —it has a look of drear impermanence, like a Klondike stage set long after the Forty-Niners have come and gone. What doesn't change is the good humour and hospitality of its inhabitants.

We were met at the airport by a lieutenant of the Chilean Navy, a voluble, ungrammatic little man who said that he had been a friend of Sarmiento. He wouldn't hear of our booking into a hotel. "I have cancel your reservations," he announced cheerfully. "You are guests of the Chilean Navy."

It was our first intimation of a relationship which was to prove in the weeks ahead delightful but vaguely mysterious. Why, I found myself asking more than once, were the

Chilean authorities going out of their way to be so kind to us?

I was naïve enough to imagine at the time that it must be because of Corbella. We met him soon after our arrival, in the operations department of naval headquarters: a long, low-ceilinged room, with a scale model of austral Chile running the length of one wall. The three of us were a bit apprehensive, I think, as we clustered round the model, studying the approaches to the Hielo Continental. For Corbella was an unknown quantity; and in an expedition like ours, compatibility among members is a prerequisite of success. Suddenly we were startled by a great gust of Rabelaisian laughter, quickly suppressed as footsteps came to a halt outside the operations room; the door was flung open, and Corbella came toward us, hand outstretched. He was a tall, sallow man, sparely but strongly built; his hair was thick and dark, flecked at the temples with grey; and his manner, on being introduced to us, was (like his English) formal and impeccably correct. His eyes, however, were humorous; and I got the impression that once he knew us better he would unbend.

There were two things we wanted to discuss at this first meeting: a timetable and a route.

January to March is the best time for exploring the Southern Andes, for temperatures in these months are maximum and rainfall minimum. We had arrived, in other words, at the right time; and provided there were no delays in assembling equipment and supplies, we reckoned we should be approaching the Hielo Continental by mid-January. This would give us a good two months to locate and survey the elusive volcano.

Our route depended principally on just where we thought the volcano was. Since both Chile and the Argentine laid claim to it, we assumed it must be close to the border, i.e., on the eastern side of the ice cap. This precluded an approach via the Pacific, and left us with the prospect of an approach via one of the great Argentinian lakes: either

Lago San Martín or Lago Viedma. We decided in the end to approach via the latter: a route which necessitated our expedition being lifted first by boat to Río Gallegos on the "toe" of Argentina, and then by truck to the shore of the lake.

It was during these discussions that I saw for the first time McBride's "conclusive evidence" that the Viedma did indeed exist.

Most of South America, Corbella explained, had been mapped in detail in the 1960s by high-flying planes of the U.S. Strategic Air Force. These planes, however, had been hampered in the Southern Andes by almost perpetual cloud and the scarcity of airfields. Their photographs of the Hielo Continental were particularly poor; and to supplement them, the Chilean government had agreed to attempt a survey by helicopter. This was a formidable undertaking, for the helicopters were operating at the very limit of their range and in the worst weather in the world. They had, however, after a number of extremely hazardous sorties, managed to bring back a more or less complete coverage of photographs, the originals of which Corbella now produced from the Chilean Navy's top secret files. The ones we were specially interested in were of the Mariano Moreno. These showed three interesting phenomena: (1) A number of dark bands radiating from a glacier near the top of the east face of the Moreno; these bands were identified by experts as deposits of volcanic ash. (2) Smoke plumes issuing out of a vent beside a rocky plateau close to the head of the same glacier. And (3) a small ice-free lake, situated in the center of the above plateau. I gathered the professor had somehow got hold of copies of these prints, and had used them to convince Westerman. And convincing they certainly were. "It looks," I said, "as if this plateau is the key."

"Our young friend," McBride boomed, "has moments of lucidity."

"The plateau must be volcanic," I persisted. "And active. Or the lake wouldn't be free of ice."

"Without doubt," the professor said condescendingly, "the plateau contains both an active volcano and a number of hot springs—similar to those of the Reykjavik area of Iceland. It is in caves beside these springs," he added, "that we shall find the *Paranthropus.*"

Corbella and Westerman exchanged glances.

"I suggest," the latter said mildly, "we proceed one step at a time. Your Vulcan Viedma, I admit, may exist: we have some sort of evidence of it. Your *Paranthropus,* to say the least, are unproven."

"The pace at which you proceed, sir," McBride replied, "must naturally be governed by your intelligence. Truth, however, is truth, no matter how long it takes you to perceive it."

It was Corbella who came to the rescue. "I have for you gentlemen a surprise," he said quickly. "Our expedition may shortly be joined by a fifth member."

Westerman frowned. "A mountaineer, I hope?"

"His name is Chris de Garcia. We have not met, but have been in correspondence. He is a student of geology, I understand, at the University in Santiago. What is more to the point, his family owns an *estancia* on the shore of Lago Viedma."

"We go through his land?"

He nodded. "And he has offered us peons and horses, to lift our supplies. And his services as a guide."

Westerman and McBride had reservations. I, on the other hand, rather welcomed the prospect of a companion more my own age; and as Corbella pointed out, a geologist might be useful. In the end we agreed to send Chris de Garcia a message by radio, accepting his offer of help.

The meeting was about to break up when there occurred an incident which seemed trivial at the time, but which, I can see now, should have given us food for thought. I was collecting together the prints of the helicopter survey when I noticed on the back of them a series of figures—"6%, 7%, 64%, 67%, 70%," the percentages building up sharply over the plateau of the Viedma, then tailing away to nothing in the lower slopes of the Moreno. "What are the figures?" I asked.

Corbella fairly snatched the prints from me, muttering in Spanish. "They are," he said after a moment's hesitation, "reference numbers, for our files."

I felt sure he was lying. But there didn't seem any point in making an issue out of it.

We left Punta Arenas on December 17 and made the voyage to Río Gallegos in style, in a frigate of the Chilean Navy. This, we knew, was likely to be our last taste of comfort for several months, and we made the most of it: hot showers, clean sheets, morning tea, and aperitifs in the wardroom before a four-course evening meal. "Does your navy," I asked Corbella, "always entertain so lavishly?"

He winked. "Our captain is—how do you say it?—on the make for promotion. He tries very hard to impress."

Late the next afternoon we arrived in Río Gallegos. It took us a couple of hours to unload our supplies, and another couple to get them through the customs. Then we said good-bye to our friends, the Chilean Navy. They had been good to us. And as the frigate, on her way back to the Strait of Magellan, disappeared into a rain squall, we felt very much on our own.

Next morning we set off for Lago Viedma.

It was, for me at any rate, the start of the expedition proper, and the scene was one I shall never forget. Our Land-Rovers, crammed to bursting point with supplies; the main street, deserted in the cold, grey dawn; and ahead of us the pampas, mile after hundred mile of barren grassland, its silver-white flowers streaming away in the wind like the spearheads of a medieval host. And beyond the pampas, out of sight but by no means out of mind, the foothills of the Andes, bastions of the unknown. Who knew, I asked myself, what strange adventure might befall us among these mountains at the bottom of the world?

I append a list of our equipment and stores. I make no

apology for giving this in full, since good and well-chosen supplies are essential to any expedition, and in our case a wrong choice would very likely have cost us our lives.

*1. Two Land-Rovers. These were kindly lent by Shell Argentine Ltd: robust, reliable vehicles which would take us first by road and then by dirt track to the shore of the lake.

*2. One inflatable "Zodiac" boat of the type used by Dr. Bombard in his voyage across the Atlantic. We had given a great deal of thought to crossing the Lago Viedma. A launch would have been the ideal answer, but the cost of buying and transporting one would have been prohibitive. We therefore settled for the largest and strongest inflatable rubber-cum-wood dinghy we could find: the Zodiac. It turned out to be a splendid vessel. When deflated, it folded into a neat pack 4' x 2' x 2'; when inflated it measured 15', could carry up to a ton and was able to withstand a surprising amount of battering from rocks and ice.

3. Two Pyramid double-skin tents. There are basically two types of expedition tent: the Pyramid (used in the Antarctic) and the Mead (used in the Himalaya). The latter is the more popular nowadays, being lighter, easier to pack and easier to assemble. Westerman, however, insisted—and thank heavens he did!—that a Pyramid would stand up better to the snow and wind of the Hielo Continental. He therefore ordered two standard models from Camtors of the Falkland Islands. Their outer skin was made of Ventile 19, and their inner skin of nylon and cotton. Each weighed a little under sixty pounds and could accommodate three people.

4. Two detachable groundsheets.

5. Five sets of Alpine climbing equipment (boots, ice axes, crampons, pitons, goggles and rope).

---

* The Land-Rovers we planned to leave at de Garcia's *estancia*. The rest of the equipment marked with an asterisk we planned to leave on the far shore of Lago Viedma, so that on the actual climb we could travel light.

6. Five sets of snowshoes.

7. Five Jaegar sleeping bags. These were made of wool-fleece and eiderdown and were wonderfully warm and light.

8. One set of aluminum cooking utensils.

9. Two large Primus cooking stoves, plus twelve gallons of paraffin. It is always difficult for an expedition to estimate its consumption of paraffin. So much depends on whether it is snow or water which has to be brought to the boil, how much draft there is in the tent and how often the stove is used for drying clothes, etc. Westerman thought a gallon a week would be sufficient, and this in fact turned out to be almost exactly right. The fuel was stored in army-type plastic containers, of the so-called unbreakable type used in parachute drops.

10. One medicine chest, containing everything from Elastoplast to morphia.

11. One set of surveying equipment. This was Corbella's responsibility. And to judge from the number of theodolites, sextants, plane tables and tachymeters that he insisted on bringing, he intended to triangulate the elusive Viedma to the exact inch!

12. Ten pounds of spare clothing apiece. We all took slightly different items. Following Westerman's advice, my choice was as follows: one pair trousers, two pullovers, two shirts, two pairs pyjama bottoms, one string vest, six pairs socks, one pair gloves, one balaclava.

13. Approximately 300 pounds of food. Expedition food is always a matter of controversy. In the Arctic and Antarctic, explorers' diet has, by long tradition, tended to be Spartan. Mountaineers on the other hand, especially among the higher peaks, have always insisted on their food being both plentiful and varied. In our case we had no choice. We *had* to travel light. For we had none of the porters and pack mules used to carry supplies halfway to the top of Everest. We worked out that we could each carry a 60 pound load, i.e., five of us could shift 300 pounds in a single journey. Practi-

cally the whole of this 300 pounds, however, was accounted for by the weight of our tents, clothes and equipment, which meant that to ensure a reasonable supply of food we would have to shift everything in two relays. On Westerman's advice we budgeted on the following scale of rations per man per day:

Sugar	7 ounces
Rolled oats	4 ounces
Meat	4 ounces
Biscuit	3 ounces
Milk powder	3 ounces
Butter	2 ounces
Cheese	2 ounces
Bacon	1 ounce
Soup powder	1 ounce
Drinking chocolate	1 ounce
Rum fudge	1 ounce
Extras (mainly potato, lemon and curry powder, raisins, onion flakes and barley sugar)	4 ounces
Daily total:	33 ounces
	4,600 cals.

The food was packed by the Raslin method: that is to say a day's ration for five men was weighed out, put into a Raslin bag and then subjected to vacuum-sealing. The effect of this was to compress the food into a hard flat slab (very handy for travelling), though when the bag was opened and the vacuum released, the food expanded to its normal consistency and size.

14. One fiber-glass sledge: very light, very strong, very smart in orange paint, and collapsible into sections so that it was easy to carry. We hoped to use this sledge on the ice

cap to shift our equipment and food, thus avoiding the arduous business of double-tracking.

*15. Two fishing rods.

16. Two cameras and a plentiful supply of film.

*17. One Redifon SSB Manpack radio of the sort used by Wally Herbert in the Arctic.

*18. Two twelve-bore shotguns, excellent for small game or birds for the pot.

19 (and finally). Two Parker-Hale rifles excellent for shooting puma, men or, of course, *Paranthropus*. These were McBride's idea, and caused the rest of us no little amusement.

"You don't seriously imagine," Westerman teased him, "we're going to indulge in a running fight with a tribe of prehistoric apes!"

"You would be less flippant, sir, if you had read the report from Chilean Naval Intelligence on how the settlers on the Golfo de Peñas were killed."

We looked at him inquiringly.

"The head of every man, woman and child," he said, "had been screwed completely off."

It was silly, I know, but I shivered. And for the first few miles of our journey we were all of us unusually subdued.

6

El Condor

There is no need for me to describe our journey from the coast to Lago Viedma in detail. It was like any other journey across the Patagonian lowlands: dull, damp and depressing. Enough to say that it took us three days to cover the 190 miles, for the road got progressively worse, the terrain progressively more desolate and it rained to all intents and purposes nonstop. There were times when the Land-Rovers seemed to be sailplaning over a sea of mud.

In spite of this somewhat dismal prelude, the four of us quickly settled into a *modus vivendi.* And here, on the threshold of our adventures, I would like to describe my companions more fully.

McBride, at fifty-one, was the oldest. Back in England Alison (from whom I had had a couple of letters in Punta Arenas) had asked me to look after him, but now that we had started to rough it, it was obvious he was well able to look after himself. He was, I think, the strongest man I have ever known. I remember Westerman and myself struggling to load a 180-pound pack into the Land-Rover, and McBride picking it up quite casually and tossing it into place. The life of the camp was nothing new to him, for he had been with Shipton in the Karakoram and with Harrison in Borneo. In temperament he was mercurial in the extreme; but if it was impossible to be at ease with him because of his formidable temper, it was equally impossible to be bored. In appearance he was excessively untidy, letting his hair and beard grow wild, until at the end of a couple of weeks he rather resembled one of his *Paranthropus*—whose existence, by the by, he continued to regard as established fact rather than dubious supposition.

Westerman was forty-three. In many ways he was the antithesis of the professor: being small, neat in build and habit, and equable in temperament. Like many slightly built men, he appeared to have limitless energy, though after observing him closely I formed the opinion that his energy was not so much inexhaustible as shrewdly conserved; that is to say he had the true mountaineer's knack of never making a foolish or unnecessary move. In conversation he had a dry, laconic wit—frequently directed, though without malice, at McBride. The two men indeed could easily have rubbed each other the wrong way. Fortunately for the rest of us, however, they regarded one another with good-natured, if somewhat patronizing, amusement. They disagreed about everything—though only on the subject of the *Paranthropus* did their disagreement threaten to rock the boat. For Westerman made no attempt to conceal his belief that although the Viedma might exist, our quest for the ape-men was a wild-goose chase so patently absurd that it could bring us nothing but ridicule. He had one other trait which was not immediately apparent, but which was later to stand us in good stead: he was, in a crisis, quite the coolest customer I have met.

Corbella was in his late thirties. A captain in the Chilean Navy, he had seemed in uniform a somewhat daunting figure: formal, dignified and reserved. In camp, however, he soon thawed out and became the most entertaining of companions. He had a lively wit, and, of all the improbable tastes, a liking for limericks. We must have taught him hundreds—some of which I only hope he didn't repeat in mixed company! On the more serious level, he was a man of many parts: intensely patriotic, a devout Roman Catholic and, we discovered by accident, a fully qualified metallurgist. This latter accomplishment came to light in a rather unexpected way. On our second day out from Río Gallegos the pack containing his surveying instruments burst, and out tumbled not only theodolites and plane tables, but also a metallurgical microscope and a dilatometer.

"What on earth," I asked, "are you bringing those for?"

His embarrassment was obvious. After a good deal of humming and hawing, he tried to make us believe that the instruments were for Chris de Garcia. He was a poor liar. But if he chose to make a mystery out of his penchant for metallurgy, this was his affair, not ours.

Late on the third afternoon we squelched down to the shore of Lago Viedma. It was difficult, in the driving rain, to get much idea of the surrounding country, but late that evening the weather cleared a little, and we had a brief glimpse of well-wooded hills, and away in the distance, seen dimly through drifting banks of cloud, a range of snow-capped peaks. We pitched camp on a spit of gravel, taking care, on Westerman's advice, to keep well above the high-water mark. And it was as well we did. For in the small hours of the morning we were catapulted out of our sleep by the most appalling roar—a sort of continuous twenty-second sonic boom. It was, Westerman explained, a glacier "calving" several million tons of ice into the lake. A few moments later a succession of waves, like those from the wake of a ship, came swirling up the bank of the spit. And the water level rose three feet in as many minutes.

Next morning I woke early. For a moment I couldn't think what was different. Then I got it: for the first time since leaving Río Gallegos there was neither roar of wind nor lash of rain. I went outside. And the beauty of the morning made me catch my breath.

It was very still. The sun was rising like an oriflamme out of the pampas. And the limpid waters of Lago Viedma mirrored with exact precision the beech-covered hills and the great snow-clad peaks of the Moreno. The peaks were magnificent, rising sheer ten thousand feet from the head of the lake. Though they were forty miles away, the air was so clear that their every detail was sharply delineated: the glaciers, the snowfields, the overhanging cornices of ice. And in all this scene of grandeur there was no hint of man: no homestead, no noise of tractor, no coil of smoke nor trail of vapour in the sky.

Not wanting to wake the others, I walked a little way down the shore and sat on a grassy knoll, looking out across the lake like Adam surveying his Eden. For some time the only sounds were the chatter of parrots, the twitter of wrens, and the occasional "plop" as a trout jumped close inshore. Then I became aware of the drum of a horse's hooves, distant at first but coming steadily nearer.

She came out of the beech woods less than twenty yards from where I was sitting. A girl on a bay Colorado. She didn't seem in the least surprised to see me. "Hi, there!"

I got to my feet and gaped at her. The scene might have come straight from a glossy magazine: thoroughbred horse, beautiful girl, a setting to take one's breath away; I half-expected her to offer me a menthol cigarette or a can of Harp!

My astonishment seemed to amuse her. She swung off the horse and came toward me. "You *are* one of Westerman's party?"

"Yes."

She held out her hand. "I'm Christina de Garcia," she said.

We arrived at her parents' *estancia*, El Condor, late that afternoon. We would have been happy to camp outside, but Christina's father insisted we stayed in the house. And a very fine house it was too, built of *nothofagus* beech and equipped with running water and electricity—the latter generated by windmill. Its setting, looking out across the lake to the Moreno, was out of this world.

After supper, I gave Christina a hand with getting ready for the Christmas *sortija* (a sort of Argentine gymkhana), which was due to take place the next day. It was hard work, setting up the jumps and erecting apparatus for the various games; and when we had finished, we stood leaning over the fence of the corral, watching the sun disappear behind the rim of the hills.

Christina was an exceedingly pretty girl: aged twenty, height around 5′ 7″. She had dark hair, brown eyes and a figure that went in and out—but not too much so—in all the right places. "And to think," I said, "we reckoned you were a boy!"

She moved her hand closer to mine, a gesture which rather pleased me, until I realized she was drawing my attention to her engagement ring.

"Who's the lucky chap?" I asked her.

"His name is Cedomir. He's at the university too, reading law." Her English was every bit as good as Corbella's, and I learned later that she had spent a couple of years at Boston University.

"What are *you* reading?"

"Metallurgy," she said.

I looked at her in surprise. "So Corbella *was* bringing the instruments for you!"

"What instruments?"

"The microscope. And the dilatometer."

"I don't know," she said sharply, "what you are talking about."

She knew very well. She looked thoroughly put out: as though she had dropped her bag and out had leapt a large and very disreputable cat. I was about to ask her what all the secrecy was about when Corbella came out of the *estancia* and joined us, and the two of them embarked on a highly technical discussion about tomorrow's *sortija*.

It took some time for the penny to drop, but after several minutes of somewhat desultory conversation, it dawned on me that they wanted to be on their own. It was I who was put out now. Something odd, I told myself, was going on. But as there was obviously no point in my staying where I wasn't wanted, I wished them a somewhat grumpy good-night.

Christina smiled very prettily at me. "Night, Pete," she said. "And thanks for helping."

I watched them from behind the lace curtains of my bedroom window. What I expected, I'm not sure: some dramatic denouement perhaps, or that they would go wandering hand in hand into the woods. My expectations were not fulfilled. For the better part of an hour they stayed beside the corral, talking earnestly. A couple of times Corbella pointed to the Moreno, now etched in indigo against a backdrop of stars; once Christina gestured impatiently and stamped her foot. Then they came back to the *estancia,* to their respective beds.

Well, we had enough on our plates, it seemed to me, without bothering our heads over a mysterious naval officer and his metallurgical girl friend. Christina obviously wouldn't be coming with us—the Hielo Continental was no place for a woman—so I might as well, I told myself, forget her and go to sleep, which I promptly did.

The guests for the *sortija* began to arrive at dawn. And very picturesque they looked: the men with black broad-brimmed hats, coloured scarves and curiously wide trousers: the girls in their traditional buttons and bows. Most of them had been travelling overnight from neighbouring farms, and they were soon tucking into the *asado* which had been prepared for them—beef roasted with the hide on, and whole lambs and suckling pigs suspended on spits over a bed of red-hot ash, the meat being washed down with liberal quantities of wine or beer. Our hosts went out of their way to make us at home, introducing us to their friends, and explaining the games such as *Taba* and *Las Tres Marias,* which the peons were soon playing wherever there was a convenient patch of shade. It was a colourful scene: an exciting scene too, when, in the afternoon, the horse racing got under way. But we had other things to think of.

Christina was the problem. And while she was taking part in the *sortija*—and winning, as far as I could see, just about every race she went in for—the rest of us held a council of war.

Neither Westerman, nor McBride nor I thought it desirable for her to come with us. She, however, when she got our radio message, had blithely assumed that she was part of the expedition; and in this she had the support of Corbella. "She has lived in El Condor most of her life," the Chilean pointed out. "She knows the approaches to the Moreno. She'd be a useful guide."

"She'd be a damned nuisance," McBride grunted.

"In more ways," I added, "than one."

Corbella shrugged. "She is a competent climber. A member of the Santiago Mountaineering Club. The same sort of qualification," he smiled at me, "as you have."

"I'd have thought," Westerman said mildly, "there were certain practical objections to four men and a girl climbing in the Hielo Continental. When the weather is bad, for example, it will be impossible for any of us to leave the tent for days on end."

"Quite out of the question," boomed the professor. "I suggest you inform the young lady of our decision."

Thus adjured, Westerman set out to find her.

We were all, I think, half-expecting a scene. And sure enough, after about half an hour they returned to the living room, Westerman looking considerably put out and Christina as though butter wouldn't melt in her mouth.

"I am told," the former said curtly, "that if we don't take Christina with us, her parents are unlikely to loan us peons or horses to shift our supplies."

I didn't care for blackmail. "We can shift the supplies ourselves," I said. "By boat."

"Possibly, if we have to. But I think we ought to talk the whole thing over, quietly and rationally."

We tried to, for the better part of an hour. But we got nowhere. And in the end our tempers became more than a little frayed. What we none of us could understand was why Christina was so determined to accompany us when she obviously wasn't wanted, and why Corbella supported her.

"There's something fishy going on." McBride thrust out his beard. "What the devil are you two up to?"

Corbella gave him the sort of look that would have withered a junior officer-of-the watch, then turned to Westerman. "May I have a word with you, sir, in private?"

Westerman didn't like it. Neither did the rest of us. But in the end we went trooping out of the room, and left the pair of them to it.

It was an hour before we were called back, and I could see at once from Westerman's face that something had happened he didn't care for. His voice was curt. "As leader of the expedition," he said briefly, "I have decided Christina comes with us. This is my decision and my responsibility. The matter is now closed."

McBride started to argue, but Westerman cut him short. "I said the matter is closed. . . . Now I suggest we all get a good night's rest. Tomorrow we set out for the Viedma."

I have one other memory of El Condor.

The festivities ended with a dance, which was held in the largest of the shearing sheds—a great barnlike building that had been especially cleaned, decorated and made gay with lanterns and flowers. In spite of Westerman's advice about early to bed, I decided to go. On my way to the shed, however, I happened to notice a young peon, trying not very successfully to tune his guitar. It was a Martin folk guitar, and had cost him, I found out later, the better part of a year's wages, but there was no one in El Condor who could teach him to play it. He would have had no problem in most parts of the world. But the de Garcias' *estancia* was almost unbelievably remote, and I doubt if anyone within 250 miles had ever played a modern guitar. Except myself. I spent a couple of hours with the peon, explaining its intricacies, and he was almost embarrassingly grateful. When he had grasped the rudiments, I started to teach him some Dylan and Simon and Garfunkel songs. Soon we had attracted quite a crowd—almost as many in fact as were dancing in the shed. It was a scene I shall never forget. The Moreno spearing the stars, the tang of resin from the larch woods, the aroma of wine and *carne con cuero,* and the circle of dark faces, rapt in concentration as I sang "Blowin' in the Wind," "Mr. Tambourine Man" and "The Times They Are A-Changin'." I have a vague recollection of Westerman's arm on my shoulder. "Don't be too late, Peter. We're making an early start." Then someone refilled my glass and I was singing "The Sounds of Silence" and "Sad-Eyed Lady of the Lowlands." Hackneyed stuff, perhaps, to those with sophisticated palates, but to peons in the shadow of the Andes, a wine both heady and evocative.

The de Garcias' wine was heady too. And insidious. To start with, it buoyed me up, like the applause and the shouts of encore and bravo which greeted the end of every song; then it slurred my voice; and finally, after many hours and many songs and many refillings of my glass, it caused the peaks of the Moreno to gyrate in slow procession across the sky. It was 2 A.M. before guests and peons started to drift away, and by this time I could hardly keep my eyes open or my legs from folding beneath me. I have a vague recollection of a seemingly endless procession of people patting me on the back and shaking my hand. Then, quite suddenly, the three of us were alone under the stars: the peon with his guitar, Christina and myself.

And the peon was trying to tell me something.

"You go to the mountains, Señor Miles?"

I nodded.

"To the foothills of the Moreno?"

"And beyond," I said portentously, feeling like the hero of a Boy Scout adventure.

He laid a hand on my arm, and his hand, to my surprise, was trembling. "Do not go, señor. It is bad country."

"Bad? Why is it bad?"

"No one goes there. The wind is terrible. And the sheep disappear."

"We're not sheep," I said, with drunken wit. "So why should we worry?"

Christina said something to him in Spanish, and he broke into a torrent of supplication, rolling his eyes and waving his arms, like a footballer trying to convince the referee he's been fouled.

I looked at him in surprise. "What's he on about?"

"It isn't important," she said. "And it's high time you were in bed."

"*He* seems to think it's important." I turned to the peon. "Why do the sheep disappear?"

He crossed himself. "They are taken by the devil."

At 2 A.M. after half a dozen glasses of vino the idea seemed really rather hilarious. "You mean the devil lives in the Moreno? And he comes down from the mountains to pinch the sheep?"

He nodded.

"Heaven help us," I said to Christina. "We'll have to look out for little black men with pitchforks!"

The peon backed away from me. My levity, I suddenly realized, both frightened and appalled him. For the sake of the good turn I had done him, he had tried to warn me of the danger that lay in the Moreno; if I wouldn't listen, on my own head be it. He walked away, with dignity. His voice came faintly, like that of a disembodied spirit, out of the night. "The señor shouldn't mock the devil. The señor knows very well that he isn't little and black but big, red and hairy."

I was about to run after him, but Christina stopped me. "He is offended," she said. "You'll get no more out of him tonight."

I started to question her, but she said—quite rightly—that it was too late and I was too pie-eyed. She would tell me about the peons and the big, red devil of the Moreno, she said, in the morning.

7

Threshold of the Unknown

Our first day out of El Condor was one I would prefer to forget. We left the *estancia* at 9 A.M., on horseback, together with a retinue of peons and pack mules. It was pouring with rain, my head ached and I'm no great shakes at the best of times on a horse. The fact that the others were in excellent spirits did nothing to alleviate my hangover.

Christina was solicitous. It had been put to her, I gathered, that she would have to pull her weight or be left behind. And certainly that first day she did all that could have been expected of her, exhorting the peons with fluency and picking a route through none too easy terrain, with aplomb. She even found time to commiserate with me. "How's the head, Pete?"

"O.K."

She looked at the pack that I had strapped not very expertly onto the saddle. "My horse is fresher than yours," she offered. "Let me take the pack."

"Don't be silly," I said.

About an hour later we came to a small but steep-sided ravine. The others prudently dismounted. I, however, decided to stay in the saddle; my horse, I told myself, must surely be used to picking his way down the sort of grass-cum-scree that dipped away in front of us. It was tempting providence. Halfway down the girth slipped, and I catapulted ignominiously over the horse's neck, and rolled head over heels down the slope. The others were clustering round me almost before I came to rest.

I got to my feet, covered in mud but more angry with myself than hurt. "I'm all right," I muttered. "Don't fuss." When the others realized I hadn't broken any bones, they were quick to see the funny side of it. Christina and Corbella were in hysterics. The latter intoned:

> *"El que comitó, tomó y montó,*
> *No preguntes de que murió."*

"What was that crack?" I grunted.

Christina was doubled up with laughter:

> "He who has eaten, drunk and mounted," she gasped,
> "Do not ask what he died of."

Westerman eyed me with disapproval. "And I've a quotation for you too, from Tibet. 'If your horse can't carry you uphill, he is no horse. If you can't lead him downhill, you are no man.'"

My back was aching now as well as my head; I felt thoroughly put in my place; and I've seldom been so thankful as when we came to a halt, a couple of hours later, at a spot where a fast-flowing river entered the lake.

It was still raining—hard, stinging little drops on the verge of hardening to hail—and though we soon had the tents up and a fire lit, I can't say the scene was exactly cozy. After supper I reminded Christina of her promise to tell us about the peons' big, red devil of the Moreno.

Now this sort of travellers' tale is, I know, traditionally told round the camp fire, with woodsmoke coiling up to a canopy of stars. Our setting was less romantic: the five of us huddled round a smelly old paraffin stove in an overcrowded tent. But the story Christina told us had all the classic ingredients of mystery, terror and the truth that is stranger than fiction.

Some years ago, she said, a friend of her parents had tried to establish an *estancia* at the head of the lake, about twenty miles west of El Condor. It was difficult country: scenically beautiful and rich in flora and fauna, but too intransigent to be easily tamed. The cattle went roaming into the hills and became half-wild, the sheep disappeared with depressing regularity and the peons evinced a stubborn reluctance to work there; the land round the head of Lago Viedma, they said, was "devil country." It was the peons indeed who were responsible in the end for the *estancia* folding up. They had Indian blood in them; many of them were only a couple of generations removed from the primitive; according to their lore the devil lived in the mountains at the head of the lake, and as ill luck would have it a series of unfortunate incidents seemed to prove their point.

"What sort of incidents?" I asked.

Christina shrugged. "At first," she said, "it was only the sheep that disappeared: literally hundreds of them, and their bodies were never found. Then peons started disappearing as well. It was hard to keep track of them," she explained—"for they were often away for weeks at a time, rounding up cattle or sheep—and it was thought at first that they had simply wandered back to their villages or gone to work somewhere else. But this wasn't the case, and in the end inquiries proved that a fair number of men too had disappeared: nine or ten of them, vanished off the face of the earth. And to cap it all, early one morning the headman and his son were found only a few hundred yards from the *estancia,* murdered."

McBride's voice was deceptively casual. "How were they murdered?"

"Their heads," she said, "had been screwed off."

The tent rocked to a sudden buffet of wind. And I shivered.

It must have been fifteen years ago, Christina went on to tell us, that the *estancia* packed up. But from that day to this, no peon had dared to set foot in the "devil country"—indeed our present recruits had only agreed to come with us on condition we paid them off this side of the lake: not for all the gold in El Dorado, she said, would they cross to the farther shore, where, they were convinced, the devil stalked the foothills of the Moreno, carrying off or killing anyone unlucky enough to cross his path.

Well, it was an inconclusive sort of story. It didn't make me lose any sleep. But I did notice, rather to my surprise, that later that night when Westerman thought the rest of us were asleep, he made an inventory of our rifles and ammunition.

In spite of wind and rain we slept well, and the following morning set off along the shore; our objective, the tip of a small peninsula from which we hoped to launch the Zodiac on our voyage across the lake.

The going was hard. For dense woods of *nothofagus* extended to the water's edge, while the shore itself was choked with icebergs, which had calved from glaciers at the top of the lake and been blown onto the beach. It was an odd sight to see the great glistening blocks of ice, many of them the size of a house, mixed up with the tropical-looking trees. Needless to say it rained nonstop all day and it took us five hours to cover a couple of miles.

Late that afternoon, wet and bedraggled, we struggled through to the tip of the peninsula where we were lucky enough to find a cove that was sheltered from the worst of the wind. Here we pitched camp. As soon as the tents were up, we climbed an outcrop of rock and stood looking out across the lake. We could just make out the farther shore: a lowering massif seen dimly through driving squalls of sleet. Though it was only six or seven miles away, there was obviously no hope of our getting across till the weather cleared. We therefore spent the rest of the day inflating the Zodiac, testing its outboard motor and giving it a run in the comparative shelter of the bay.

We had resigned ourselves to spending Christmas in the cove. However, during the night of December 23, the weather took a turn for the better, and the next day dawned cloudless and still. It was the start of one of those rare fine spells, which, in the Southern Andes, are beautiful as some exotic butterfly—and usually as short-lived.

By 8 A.M. we had the Zodiac loaded with about four hundred pounds of food and equipment, and Westerman, Christina and I were ready to embark. (The boat could, at a pinch, have taken all five of us together with our supplies, but this would have meant loading it to the very limit of its capacity, and it seemed wiser to attempt two easy voyages rather than one hazardous one.)

"Cast off!" Westerman shouted. The outboard warmed to a steady roar, and we were under way.

The morning was very still, and instead of the long, cold haul against wind and spray that we had anticipated, we found ourselves gliding over smooth waters under a sun that was almost tropic in its intensity. Every now and then we had to alter course to avoid the icebergs which were drifting hither and thither in random currents, like futuristic ships in a silver sea. To start with, our view was restricted by the hills of the peninsula. But as we moved clear of the shore, a magnificent panorama of snow-clad mountains opened up to our left, peak after spectacular peak, the Moreno, rising sheer 10,000 feet from the head of the lake, and a little to the north of them the symmetrical pyramid of Mount Fitz-Roy (11,066 feet) reaching for the sky in solitary grandeur. There wasn't a sound, except for the occasional roar as one of the glaciers calved huge pieces of ice, many of them the size of a city block, into the lake. Whenever this happened, waves fanned out across the water, like ripples from a stone tossed into a pond.

The Zodiac had a fair turn of speed—at least six knots, Westerman reckoned—and we made such good progress that when we were halfway across we decided not to head for the shore immediately opposite but to make for the head of the lake where the glaciers terminated in a spectacular cirque of ice walls. Landing was a bit of a problem, but eventually we spotted a spit of moraine-cum-gravel running parallel to the shore, and here a little before midday, we ran the Zodiac aground.

As we stepped ashore, I was conscious of a quickening of excitement. For this was "devil country": the threshold of the unknown.

It took us a couple of hours to unload the supplies, for Westerman insisted that everything be carried well clear of the lake to a spot where the moraine gave way to a grassy knoll surrounded by *nothofagus*. It was a bizarre spot: the great gnarled trees, in front of them the sparkling waters of the lake, and behind them the glacier, a huge expanse of ice riven into a fantastic battleground of serac and crevasse, while overhead flew flocks of bright green parrots uttering cries as raucous as were ever heard in an Indian jungle.

Here Westerman left us, with instructions to set up camp and not to go out of sight of it. It was silly, I know, but as the Zodiac headed back to pick up the others, Christina and I felt very much alone.

"We'd better," she said, "see to the tents."

"First things first." I took the rifles out of their waterproof cases, made sure they were loaded and stacked them against a crate in the center of the clearing.

Christina was half-amused, half-reassured; and for some time we were too busy with guy ropes and groundsheets to give our environs a great deal of thought.

When the tents were up, we rested for a while on the edge of the moraine, looking out across the lake.

For a while we sat in silence, she studying the hills, I studying her. "Peter," she said suddenly. "Don't make things difficult. Please."

I was rather put out to know that my thoughts had been so transparent. "Don't worry," I said. "I was only window-shopping."

Though her English was good, the phrase was unfamiliar to her; and when I tried to explain it, she didn't seem very pleased. "If you choose to regard me," she said, "as merchandise in a shop window, then please remember I have a little notice on me, 'not for sale.'"

"There's no need," I said, "to get on your high horse."

"Please?"

When I had explained this too, she looked at me with annoyance. "You think I'm a spoiled child? Coming to the Moreno just—how do you say it—for kicks?"

"I don't," I said truthfully, "know what to think."

"It isn't true."

"Why *are* you coming then?"

For a long time she was silent, and when she did speak I thought at first that she was trying to change the subject. "You have to understand," she said, "that this eastern part of the Andes has been settled by people from Chile, not by people from the Argentine."

"So?"

"About a hundred years ago a treaty was signed between our countries. This said that the boundary line between us should, I quote the exact words, 'follow the highest peaks of the Andes, which form the watershed between Atlantic and Pacific.'"

"So?"

"In places," she said, "the line of the highest peaks and the line of the watershed do not coincide. In these places the boundary always has been and always will be in dispute."

I looked at her in some surprise. "Are you trying to tell me that you and Corbella are some sort of unofficial boundary commission?"

"Not exactly."

"What then?"

She frowned. "Please, Peter. I have already told you more than I should."

"It seems to me," I said slowly, "that we're all looking for something different in the Moreno. McBride for his missing links. Westerman for his volcano. And you and Corbella for a new international boundary!"

"Let's hope," she said, "we all reach our rainbow's end."

The rest of the afternoon was uneventful. The sun sank slowly toward the peaks of the Moreno. The shadows of the *nothofagus* lengthened. There was no sign of the Zodiac.

Christina looked at her watch. "They'll be cold and hungry," she said, "by the time they get across. If you do the fire, I'll do the supper."

So we set to work: I collecting firewood, she fishing.

I ought perhaps to have explained before this that ever since leaving El Condor we had made a point of living off the land, for our food packs would be needed on the Hielo Continental, and were too precious to be broken into. There was a fair variety of game round Lago Viedma—small deer (huemul), guanacos and rhea—and an abundance of waterfowl and fish—in particular trout, the lakes of the Chile-Argentine border providing some of the finest fishing in the world. Christina used a spinner, and in less than an hour she had landed eight rainbow trout, all over two pounds. We cooked them wrapped in newspaper in the hot ashes of the fire.

Now I didn't say anything to Christina, but all the time I had been collecting firewood I had felt ill at ease. It must, I suppose, have been the silence and the solitude and the fact that the pair of us had been left by ourselves on a shore about as remote from civilization as the face of the moon. Anyhow, whatever the cause, I found myself continually looking over my shoulder and jumping like a scared old woman at the snap of every twig. For I had the feeling that I was being watched. I remembered the peons' devil and McBride's *Paranthropus*, and this of course made matters worse. I was thankful when a good stack of firewood had been collected, and I could return with a clear conscience to the camp. After a while, however, I noticed that Christina too kept glancing into the shadow of the trees.

"What's up?"

"I know it's silly," she said. "But I think we're being watched."

The sun dipped under the Moreno and the camp turned suddenly dark. I shivered. "The others," I said, "will be back soon." I brought the rifles to where we were sitting. And instinctively we moved closer to the fire and to each other. "It must be imagination," I said. "All those ghost stories you told us the other night!"

She was trying not very successfully to smile when her eyes went wide with fear. "Listen!"

I heard it at the same moment: faint but unmistakable, the rustle of leaves and the snap of twigs. Something was moving toward us through the trees.

We reached for the rifles.

The sun had vanished now behind the hills. The *nothofagus* were close packed, and their shade was too dense for our eyes to penetrate. But a stir in the undergrowth gave us a point to focus on. And Christina's rifle steadied on a tunnel-like opening between the trees. "There it is," she whispered.

In the shadow of the beeches I could make out a deeper shadow still: black, squat and menacing. Faintly through the silence came the slow pant of breath and the pad of feet as the creature, whatever it was, edged purposefully toward us. A pair of amber eyes glowed for a moment like oriflammes in the dark; and I could feel the sweat, cold and damp, break out in sudden beads on my forehead. "If it comes any closer," I muttered, "aim for its eyes."

A rasping cough, and he stalked into the clearing, sniffing the air: an enormous jet black bull. He was an ugly-looking customer, but after the nightmare creatures my imagination had conjured up, I could have leapt for joy at the sight of him. He came to a halt about twenty yards from where we were standing, lowered his head and started to paw the grass. I felt sure he was about to charge, and my sights steadied on the center of his massive forehead. Then quite suddenly he wheeled away, bellowing, into the undergrowth. And that was the last we saw of him.

Christina sat down, hurriedly, and it made me less ashamed of myself to see that she, too, was trembling. "When the *estancia* folded up," she said, "I suppose their cattle went wild."

We were both of us more than a little shaken. Indeed we didn't wholly recover our composure until, in the gathering twilight, the bow of the Zodiac grounded a second time on the moraine. With the return of the others, however, it wasn't long before our spirits revived. We slept soundly that night, and woke on Christmas Day to a chorus of wrens and a spectacular sunrise—shafts of red and gold fanning out across the lake like a Catherine wheel of the gods.

After an early breakfast we embarked in the Zodiac, and set off on a voyage of reconnaissance round the head of the lake, our object being to spot a likely looking approach route to the Hielo Continental. Christina, who probably knew the terrain as well as anyone alive, favoured an ascent via one of the glaciers. And with reservations Westerman agreed. "We want to keep clear of the broken ice," he said, "where it calves into the lake. The crevasses there are a death trap."

Corbella nodded. "To be on the safe side, I reckon we ought to avoid the last thousand feet of the glacier."

After a morning's reconnaissance we worked out what seemed a feasible plan: to tackle the Moreno's lower slopes via the beech woods, the middle slopes via the most southerly of the glaciers, and the upper slopes via a smooth unbroken snowfield which, so far as we could see, led straight from the head of our glacier onto the plateau of the Hielo Continental itself.

The next few days were like a summer idyll: cloudless skies, gentle winds and a sun that smiled benignly from dawn to dusk. The scenery was magnificent: spectacular vistas of blue water, steep-sided valleys and walls of ice. And to add to our euphoria, we found the ideal spot for a base camp, only half a mile from the glacier we intended to climb. We moved in without delay.

We were in virgin country now. No one, except perhaps the odd peon in search of his sheep, had ever penetrated more than a few hundred yards into the hills which rose, mysterious and inviting, immediately behind our tents. As Corbella said—though I didn't fully appreciate the innuendo at the time—"From now on we make our own map."

8

"It looks like the north face of the Eiger."

A good base camp, any mountaineer will tell you, is one of the prerequisites of success; so I make no apology for describing ours. It was sited about two hundred yards from the shore, where, in the shade of the forest, an overhanging cliff some hundred feet high formed a roof over an area of dry mossy ground, which was further screened from wind and rain by a belt of undergrowth. Firewood was plentiful and so was water, the latter trickling down the face of the cliff and forming a little pool less than a dozen yards from the overhang. We lost no time in moving into this delightful spot, where, free from the cramping confinement of tents, we could spread ourselves in abandon in front of a blazing fire.

The weather for the next few days was almost too good to be true: clear skies and gentle winds. Westerman and Corbella took full advantage of it. And within seventy-two hours, climbing light, they had pioneered a route up the glacier and onto the ice cap. It was a remarkable achievement, and when, on New Year's Eve, they returned to the base camp they were full of optimism; provided the weather held, they said, we should be camped on the Hielo Continental within a week. We planned to start the ascent the next morning.

After supper I strolled down to the shore of the lake. There was no wind, and the Lago Viedma lay still as glass, reflecting the whole magnificent range of the Moreno. It was very quiet, except once when the peace was shattered by a thunderous roar, as blocks of ice cascaded off the face of the glacier. The sky in the south was laced with clouds, little mare's tails of pink, which I hoped weren't an augury that the weather was about to break. I don't think I shall ever forget that evening: the beauty, the peace and the savour of anticipation. It is not, in my experience, necessarily true that anticipation is better than fulfilment, but it has a special quality—fear perhaps is part of it—which makes a more lasting impression on the mind. We were about to embark on a journey into one of the loneliest and least-known ranges in the world; and I would, I think, have been dull indeed if I hadn't been conscious of an undercurrent of excitement.

We set off next morning in the pale half-light of dawn, anxious to be on our way while the weather held. We left behind a small cache of food, together with our shotguns, fishing rods, radio and of course the Zodiac, all lashed down under a tarpaulin and protected by a barrier of thorn scrub. We took with us our tents, sledge, climbing gear and some 300 pounds of food, plus a number of small items such as personal clothing, survey equipment and (at McBride's insistence) the Parker-Hale rifles. All in all we had about 550 pounds to carry, and we divided it into ten packs of 55 pounds apiece. This meant that we had to double-track, i.e., to lift half our supplies to a convenient spot, dump them and then go back for the rest; laborious work, but, in the absence of porters, unavoidable.

To start with, our route lay through the beech woods. All morning we plodded forward in single file, through pleasant, undulating forest. Wild animals were scarce: indeed the only creature we caught sight of that first day was a solitary fox. Birds, on the other hand, were plentiful: plover, ibis, parrots, teal and a great number of birds of prey such as eagles, hawks and condors—the latter, magnificent birds which hovered over us morning and evening, stooping and soaring on unseen air currents with hardly a movement of their wings. After a while we fell into a routine that was acceptable to us all: an hour's walk, then ten minutes' rest, then back to collect the remainder of our supplies, with another rest as soon as this second load had been humped up to join the first. My pack consisted of a Pyramid tent, and once I got the frame adjusted so that its weight was properly balanced, I found it less trouble than I had anticipated.

As we gained height, the trees became gradually closer-packed and more stunted, until in the late afternoon we came to the "emerald band"—the upper reaches of the forest, which consisted of a mass of dwarf *nothofagus*, their twisted trunks so flattened by the wind that they lay almost horizontal, with their branches forming a sort of interwoven latticework about six feet high. It was appalling stuff to struggle through; and on Westerman's advice we made no attempt to push into it that evening, but camped in a little clearing close to the edge of it. By six o'clock we had the tents up, a fire lit, and half a dozen rainbow trout grilling on an improvised spit. We had, Corbella told us, covered a shade over five miles that first day, on a course of 293 degrees, and had climbed 1,040 feet.

It was the sort of exact computation that we came to expect from Corbella at the end of each day's climb. For from the moment we left El Condor he kept a running plot, on which he recorded both our route and our environs with meticulous accuracy. It was comforting to feel that whatever else might happen, we certainly wouldn't get lost!

We slept well that night. But when I woke next morning I found, much to my disgust, that my body ached all over, as though it had been beaten with rubber clubs. The others, I noticed, seemed equally stiff and sore; and we eyed our packs with a decided lack of enthusiasm. Westerman, however, didn't give us time to feel sorry for ourselves. By 8 A.M. we had struck camp, and were forcing a way through the *nothofagus*.

The *nothofagus* lay in a solid belt, a mile wide, between us and the glacier. Climbing light, Westerman and Corbella had forced a way through without too much difficulty. With packs, however, it was a different story, for we had to step heavy-laden from branch to branch, and our footholds frequently broke so that we fell into the morass below and became trapped in the network of tentacle-like branches. It took us an hour to cover a couple of hundred yards.

Soon, to add to our troubles, it started to rain.

It didn't rain very hard to start with: just the occasional shower, interspersed with bursts of sun strong enough to make the moisture-laden foliage steam like a cauldron of soup. By midday, however, the rain had settled into a steady downpour: stinging little drops driven out of the south by a cold unremitting wind. We slipped with increasing frequency off the rain-wet branches; our packs which yesterday had felt reasonably light became instruments of torture; and we had the mortification of knowing that every step we took would have to be retraced and then taken again carrying the equipment.

It was the end of our honeymoon with the Moreno.

A psychologist would, I am sure, have drawn profound conclusions from the way we reacted to our changed circumstances. Westerman was equable as ever. He had warned us before we left Punta Arenas that there was only one way to treat the Chilean weather. Ignore it. And this he proceeded to do, pushing ahead steadily hour after hour, not only without complaint but with as much enjoyment, apparently, as if he had been approaching some sunlit summit in the Alps. McBride was less phlegmatic. He cursed the rain, the *notho-fagus*, his pack and the rest of us in language that would have made the savants of St. Andrews raise their eyes to heaven. But he was always ready, I noticed, to lend a hand where wanted, using his enormous strength to cut through or prize apart the tangle of branches that blocked our way. Corbella apparently decided that we needed cheering up, for he assumed the role of expedition jester, full of funny stories and humorous asides. His *pièce de résistance* was when Christina suddenly disappeared down a microscopic slit in the carpet of branches over which we were walking. We peered down at her as she picked herself up, unhurt, some four or five feet beneath us. "How the devil did you get through there?" I exclaimed.

Corbella intoned:

"There was a young lady of Bath,
    Whose figure was slim as a lath.
She was cleaning the grate
    When, sad to relate,
She slipped through a crack in the hearth!"

We needed something to laugh at. For not only did it take us half an hour to extricate Christina, but her pack had been ripped in the fall, and a goodly proportion of the expedition's powdered milk lay effervescing in the rain.

Christina had the roughest time. For although she weighed only about half as much as McBride, she insisted on carrying a pack that was just as heavy. This, it seemed to me, was unnecessarily quixotic, and I offered several times to give her a hand. She was fiercely determined, however, not to be an encumbrance, and toted her fifty-five pounds with never a word of complaint—though I don't think any of us realized quite how much the effort cost her.

As for myself, I was young, strong and (I liked to think) fit; and if an old man of fifty and a slip of a girl could keep going, so I told myself could I. But I can't say I enjoyed it. The rain was drenching, mist and cloud obscured the view, and the *nothofagus* stretched away in front of us in seemingly endless morass. I disciplined myself not to look at my watch for at least ten minutes, and amused myself by trying to estimate how long it would take us to reach various objectives. And after what seemed like a lifetime—but was in fact almost exactly nine hours—we struggled through to the timber line, and stood staring down through eddies of mist and rain at the glacier. With its unstable pinnacles and fear-some crevasses, it was hardly an inviting prospect, but any-thing would have been welcome after the *nothofagus*.

Left to ourselves, we would have camped on the spot and crawled exhausted into our sleeping bags. Westerman, how-ever, insisted that we find a better place for the tents. It was, he said, a basic tenet of mountaineering that no matter how tired a team might be, they choose their camp site with care —for a few minutes' extra effort at the end of the day might save many sleepless hours in the night. We therefore climbed down into the moraine trench—a sort of no-man's-land of boulders and mud which lay between forest and glacier. It was a bleak place: a wilderness of muddy stream, mini-lagoon and dead ice (ice which has been left behind by the reces-sion of the parent glacier). The going was none too easy, but as luck would have it we soon found a spot on which to camp: a flattish outcrop of rock, sheltered from the wind and unlikely to be flooded. Here, gratefully, we dumped our supplies.

It was cold that evening; and after we had put up the tents we built an enormous fire, feeding it with the largest tree trunks we could roll down from the nearby forest. The branches of *nothofagus* burned cheerfully, and from the circle of their warmth we watched with smug satisfaction the curtain of sleet driving near-horizontal over glacier and beech wood. We were too payed out, however, to sit up late, and by nine o'clock we were asleep, oblivious to the forces of nature which were soon reshaping our environment.

I woke early next morning, to a strange stillness. The wind had dropped; shafts of sunlight were streaming down through rifts in the cloud; and forest and glacier lay silent under a six-inch blanket of snow.

The others were asleep, but it struck me as a shame on such a lovely morning not to be up and about, so I pulled on boots and anorak and made my way to the forest with the idea of collecting dead wood to resurrect the fire—one of the peculiarities of *nothofagus* being that it burns quickly and completely leaving little ash, so that however large a fire we made at night it was always dead by morning. I was grubbing about in the undergrowth, trying to wrench off a likely looking branch, when I heard a rustle behind me.

I froze.

For a moment my mind conjured up the most horrific possibilities: black bulls, red apes or could it be the devil himself come to see who had dared set foot in his domain? Then common sense took over, and I forced myself to look round.

They were less than ten yards from where I was crouching: a pair of huemul, gazing at me with moist brown eyes. Huemul are Patagonian deer, about the size of a small chamois; they are widely distributed throughout the forests of the Southern Andes, but are so shy they are seldom seen. I rose to my feet, fully expecting them to bolt, but not only did they hold their ground, they showed not the slightest sign of alarm. I walked toward them until I was less than six feet from where they were standing, and still there was no reaction. I believe I could actually have touched them, had I wished; but I was so enchanted by their confidence that I was loath to do anything that might destroy it. So I tossed them a piece of biscuit that I happened to have in my pocket. They ignored this friendly gesture, and, evidently becoming bored with me, started to nibble the grass. After a while one of them came across the biscuit; he sniffed at it, but left it alone. I had often read that in places undisturbed by man, wild animals were without fear; and actually to meet such creatures was a delightful experience. I left the huemul to their grazing, and made my way back to camp.

The others were awake by this time: Christina and Corbella busy with compass and theodolite, Westerman and McBride packing up the tents. A quick breakfast, and by eight o'clock we were continuing the ascent.

Westerman pointed out the route: up the moraine-trench for roughly half a mile, then across a small lake and finally onto the glacier itself. He set a cracking pace, anxious to push on while the weather was fine.

The weather, however, didn't stay fine for long. The sun, all too soon, disappeared, the wind rose, and by midday it was sleeting steadily out of a drear grey sky. It was some consolation—but not much—to know that in the trench we were at least sheltered from the sort of blizzard that, five thousand feet above us, was sweeping the ice cap.

In the early afternoon the trench petered out, and we came to our first serious obstacle: a small, ice-blue lake at the head of the moraine.

The lake barred our way: deep, about fifty yards wide, and flanked to the left by a sheer wall of rock, and to the right by a series of unstable ice towers. There was no way round it. It had to be crossed. Westerman and Corbella, on their reconnaissance, had stripped off and swum it, carrying their clothes in bundles on top of their heads; but this was a technique we could hardly emulate with 550 pounds of supplies. It was Corbella who came up with an ingenious suggestion: "Could we use the sledge?"

"As a boat?" Westerman pursed his lips. "I doubt if it's watertight."

"We could," I said, "caulk up the joints with lavatory paper."

After several other suggestions had been put forward and rejected, we decided to give Corbella's idea a try, and the sledge was duly unearthed.

It was an odd-looking contraption: coloured orange, shaped like a punt and consisting of four fiber-glass sections which could be slotted into each other like eggshells. When assembled, it was eight feet long but only nine inches deep, and on launching it we found there was a bare three inches of freeboard. There seemed, however, to be little if any seepage, and we could load it with a couple of hundred pounds before it shipped water. It looked a dubious craft, and we eyed it with some apprehension. "Who'll volunteer," Westerman said, "for the maiden voyage?"

Every expedition has its sucker. I was the youngest in ours

—apart from Christina—and as I think I have already mentioned, I have a horror of being thought a coward. "I'll have a go," I said.

So while the others plied me with encouragement and advice, I took off my boots and anorak. I then lay facedown in the bottom of the punt, Westerman pushed me off and I began very gingerly to paddle across. The lake was comparatively sheltered and without currents; even so, the crossing was a delicate operation, for the punt was highly unstable. Halfway across it began to oscillate, and I shipped a fair amount of water. However, by lying perfectly still I managed to get it steady. I was about ten yards from the far shore, and congratulating myself that I had things well under control, when I must have leaned too far to one side, for the wretched thing gave a sudden lurch and capsized.

The water was ice-cold: so cold that for a second I couldn't breathe, and my body felt as though it had been dipped in fire. Blind with panic, I struck out for the shore, and crashed straight into the sledge, which was floating upside down. The shock brought me to my senses. With dry land within spitting distance, I wasn't, I realized, in danger. So I dived for the Pyramid tent that had been my cargo, and dumped it on top of the sledge, and began to push them toward the shore. Within a minute I was scrambling onto the beach of moraine. My difficulties, however, were not yet over. I had brought with me an ice ax and a length of rope, the idea being to rig up an improvised pulley so that the sledge could be hauled to and fro across the lake. But my teeth had begun to chatter so violently and my hands were so devoid of feeling that, although I managed to drive the ice ax into the moraine, I couldn't for the life of me attach the rope. Much to the hilarity of the others, I had to strip off my sodden clothes and sprint up and down the moraine before my circulation was sufficiently restored for me to rig up the recalcitrant pulley.

"For heaven's sake," I shouted, hopping up and down like

the proverbial brass monkey, "bring me some dry clothes!"

"Coming, darling!" Christina shouted, and the four of them dissolved into fits of laughter.

It was, however, McBride—much to my relief—who was next across, bringing with him a change of clothes.

Our ferry operations took the rest of the afternoon and evening, and by the time we were safely across, it was almost dark: far too late to venture onto the ice. So we climbed a little way up the moraine and pitched our tents.

We spent a peaceful enough night on the moraine; but the weather next morning was too bad for us to venture out —high winds and driving snow—so we stayed with a clear conscience in the warmth of our sleeping bags. It was late the following afternoon before the blizzard began to ease off and Westerman and I were able to make a brief reconnaissance of the approaches to the glacier.

There seemed to be only one way to approach it: up a narrow tongue of moraine, flanked by cliffs on one side and a fast-flowing stream on the other. We were walking along quietly, heads bowed against the wind and without any sort of premonition, when we made the most alarming discovery.

It was Westerman who literally stumbled across them: the skeletons, laid out on a slab of rock.

We stared at three piles of bones in consternation.

"Looks as if we've found some of the missing peons," I said.

Westerman nodded. "But what the hell were they doing up here?"

Silence, while we felt our way, reluctantly, toward the only possible conclusion. "They can't have died here," Westerman said. "In the rainy season these rocks would be under water."

"Perhaps they were drowned?" I suggested. "Or brought down by the glacier?"

He shook his head. "It looks to me as if they were put here. Deliberately."

He was right. Now that we studied the skeletons more

closely, it was obvious they had been laid out, in a neat little row, blocking our path.

I moistened my lips. "Look at the skulls."

Each was by itself, a little to one side of the main skeleton. And McBride's warning came back to me, like a soothsayer's prediction of doom: "You would be less flippant if you knew how the settlers on the Golfo de Peñas were killed. . . . The head of every man, woman and child had been screwed completely off." I looked up at the encircling hills, and shivered. "We'd better," I said, "call the others."

Half an hour later we were listening to McBride.

He was in his element. Seated on an outcrop of granite, one of the skulls in his hand, he proceeded to address us as though delivering an inaugural lecture. "Without laboratory tests," he boomed, "it is wisest not to be dogmatic. But I estimate that poor Yorick"—he tossed up the skull—"died between fifteen and twenty years ago. From his bone structure, I deduce he was a South American Indian, probably, as our young friend surmised, a peon. The cause of his death was the twisting apart of the upper discs in his vertebral column. His head, in other words, was screwed off. As to how he and his companions in misfortune got here, there is to my mind only one explanation. Glacier and moraine are in constant movement, so we can rule out the theory that the peons died on the spot and that their bodies have remained here ever since. We can also rule out the theory that they were disgorged from the glacier, for the bones, you will observe, are neatly—indeed symmetrically—laid out. In other words, they must have been put here: deliberately and recently. As to who can have done this, here again, in my opinion, there can be only one explanation. No peon has dared to set foot this side of the Lago Viedma for years: no other expedition has ever been here; and the Moreno are known to be uninhabited by man. The bodies, therefore, can only have been put here by the Indians' 'big red devils from the hills': the *Paranthropus*. And put here," he added, "as a warning."

It was a thoughtful party who made their way back, in gathering darkness, to our camp on the moraine.

When we had eaten, Westerman did some straight talking. "We have come here," he said, "to locate and climb the Vulcan Viedma. We are *not* here," he turned to McBride, "to search for a tribe of missing links. Or," he swung round on Corbella, "to get involved in a frontier dispute. Do I make myself plain?"

Corbella had the grace to look sheepish. But McBride thrust out his beard. "In my opinion, sir, you should consider yourself fortunate. As leader of the expedition that discovers pre-man alive in the twentieth century, you will be sure of a place in history. What is climbing a paltry volcano compared to such a claim to fame!"

Westerman was not amused. "My orders from the Royal Geographical Society," he said curtly, "were to find the Viedma. For this, may I remind you, they put up a great deal of money."

"Finding the Viedma," I said, "won't do us—or the R.G.S. —much good if we end up with our heads screwed off."

"Our young friend," the professor boomed, "displays a measure of common sense. I endorse his warning. We would do well to bear in mind what happened to the settlers on the Golfo de Peñas."

I don't know that any of us—except McBride—really thought we were in danger. But we were probing into one of the least-known corners of the earth, and there was no harm in being prepared. We therefore agreed to take three precautions: never to go wandering off by ourselves, never to go anywhere without our guns, and to have a sentry keeping watch throughout the night. And I must admit that I for one slept more soundly that evening for the knowledge that McBride was on the *qui vive*.

Next morning we got to grips with the glacier. Most glaciers in the Southern Andes are fast-moving and unstable. The one we had chosen to climb was no exception. As soon as we set foot on it we found the ice broken and twisted into a chaotic mass of ridges and spires, intersected by a labyrinth of crevasses; it was impossible to choose a route for more than a few yards ahead, and often we would cut steps to the top of a ridge only to find that we couldn't descend the far side. Although it was only a week since Westerman and Corbella had pioneered a way up, the formation of the ice had altered so much in this short period that we had to blaze what was virtually a new trail.

Neither McBride nor I had done much climbing with crampons; we were therefore sandwiched in between the experts, and told to tread exactly in their footprints. A few tips from Westerman about balance and breathing, a quick test of the rope that linked us and off we set.

The glacier lay in a couloir, writhing snakelike between cliffs of rock to the right and cornices of snow to the left; the latter looked liable to avalanche, so we gave them as wide a berth as we could. To start with we made fair progress; Corbella, who was in the lead, kicking out steps in ice so soft and unstable that he had little need of his ax. On rounding a bend in the glacier, however, we were met by the full force of the wind, which whipped up the powder snow and the loose particles of ice and flung them straight into our faces. As we gained height, the wind increased and the clouds darkened and lowered; and it wasn't long before snow—like a curtain of arrows shot by celestial bowmen—was scything steadily out of a sepulchral sky. We struggled on, heads bowed, having at times to use all our strength to prevent ourselves being plucked out of our footholds and bowled head over heels across the ice. By midday we had had enough. We dumped our packs in the shelter of an ice wall, marked the spot and went back for our second load. It was six o'clock before the rest of our supplies were humped up, our tents erected and our Primuses alight; and by this time we were all of us suffering from exhaustion; in addition Christina and I had splitting headaches, caused not by altitude—for we had ascended a mere twelve hundred feet—but by the unremitting wind.

Although we all took aspirin, none of us slept very well that night. I for one couldn't get used to the glacier's cacophony of sound: the rumble of collapsing seracs, the trickle of rivers running far beneath us under the snow, and the everlasting complaint of ice squeezed this way and that by pressures too great to be endured. As the night wore on, snow began to pile up in the lee of the ice wall. And at dawn we had to dig ourselves out.

We would have been thankful for a day in our sleeping bags, but once again by 8 A.M. Westerman had us on the move. As we hacked away at the ice wall, the Hielo Continental, four thousand feet above us, looked a very long way away.

It took us five days to climb the remainder of the glacier: slow progress by Himalayan standards, but good going, Corbella told us, for the Andes. The weather, during the whole of the ascent, was abysmal: thick cloud, a steady gale-force wind and violent squalls of sleet by day and snow by night. On the fifth evening, however, as we debouched onto the more or less level snowfield, there was a momentary clearance.

We were putting up the tents when the sky in the west turned from grey to mother-of-pearl; wisps of nimbostratus went scudding overhead like the rear guard of a defeated host; and with the passing of the front, the sun appeared briefly out of a waterlogged sky.

Corbella and Christina got to work with plane table and theodolite while Westerman, McBride and I set off to climb a small peak from the top of which we hoped for a glimpse of the Hielo Continental, or even perhaps of the Viedma.

We were not disappointed.

The sun was low in the west as we struggled onto the summit ridge, and stood staring at the magnificent panorama which stretched away in front of us as far as the eye could see: the Hielo Continental—the only substantial ice cap in the world wholly outside the Arctic and Antarctica—a level plateau from which the peaks of the Moreno protruded like medieval castles festooned in battlements of ice. Most of the time the plateau is shrouded in mist or cloud. But we were lucky. And for a brief spell that evening we were able to feast our eyes on a scene of such grandeur that even Mc-Bride was awestruck. "Which do you reckon," he whispered, "is the Viedma?"

We studied the ice cap methodically, section by section. Away in the distance, half-hidden by intervening peaks, we could make out the outline of a cliff-girded plateau. We stared at it intently, shading our eyes against the glare of the dying sun. For a few moments the plateau was clearly defined: a dark mass splayed out like some crouching monster against a backdrop of snow. Then the clouds swirled over it, and it was gone.

But we had seen enough to feel sure it was the Viedma.

"If the weather holds," Westerman said, "we could be there in a couple of days."

We made our way back, in twilight and high spirits, to the tents. It was bitterly cold that night. As the sun dipped under the Moreno, the peaks, which a moment before had been touched with fire, reverted from rose-red to a cold translucent green. The snowfield took on a deathly pallor. Frost gripped the night. The stars shone down on a scene of stupendous desolation.

Next morning, much to our relief, the weather took a turn for the better: alternate flurries of snow and bursts of sun. We assembled and loaded the sledge. Sledging, we reckoned, would be a welcome change from double-tracking our packs. It was, therefore, with a sense of pleasant anticipation that we strapped on snowshoes and harness and took up our positions: the taller (Corbella and myself) in front, and the shorter (Westerman, McBride and Christina) in the rear. "One, two, three," Westerman exhorted us. "Heave!"

We took up the strain. Nothing happened. We heaved again, but again nothing happened. We might have been chained to a wall of rock.

"Come on," Westerman panted. "Heave!"

And at last, with a mighty effort, our bodies angled forward against the traces to almost 45 degrees, we managed to stagger forward about five yards. Then the front of the sledge sank deep into the snow, and we came to a halt.

We looked at one another. The implication of our pathetic failure struck me as all too obvious: the sledge was a write-off. Westerman, however, was not defeated so easily, and we spent the rest of the morning in experiment. First, we removed a pair of slats from the bottom of the sledge. These had been put there to prevent it sliding sideways in crosswind or traverse, and the loss of them made the wretched contraption highly unstable; it did, however, reduce its surface friction. Next, we applied to the bottom of the sledge a lavish coating of ski wax. And finally we discarded our snowshoes (for to use the latter one has to walk virtually upright, while to pull a sledge one has to lean well forward). Without the snowshoes we sank almost up to our knees in the sticky, wet snow; but at least we were able to maintain a more or less continuous pull on the traces. As a result of these experiments we were able, in the afternoon, to move forward, if not with élan at least with a certain dogged persistence. Progress was slow, but we managed that day to cover a couple of miles before exhaustion forced us to halt, about halfway to the plateau, which, we could now see, was roughly circular in shape and ringed by dark precipitous cliffs.

The nearer we drew to it, the more convinced we became that it was indeed the Viedma. And this was confirmed a little before sunset when, as we were hammering in the tent pegs, we spotted a thin spiral of smoke curl briefly out of its summit. I don't know who was the more excited: Westerman at the thought of an unknown volcano to conquer, Corbella at the thought of a disputed spot on the frontier to triangulate, or McBride at the thought that we were at last approaching the hideout of his *Paranthropus*.

We spent the rest of the evening, in between snow showers, taking bearings and photographs and making sketches. And by the time the sun set, the east face of the elusive Viedma had been well and truly triangulated.

We made an early start next morning, in the hope that while the snow was crisp it would prove easier to sledge over. By 6 A.M. we had breakfasted, struck camp and were on our way. A strong southwest wind was blowing into our faces, but the clouds were several hundred feet above us and visibility was at least a mile; we had, therefore, no difficulty in maintaining course with only the occasional glance at our compass. To start with we made fair progress. As we approached the plateau, however, both terrain and weather deteriorated.

We couldn't understand why the snow became steadily softer and more unstable. The air temperature, 17 degrees Fahrenheit, remained way below freezing; yet time and again, as we neared the plateau, we found ourselves sinking almost up to our waists in pockets of slush. Hauling the sledge became a labour of Hercules; indeed I doubt if we could have kept it moving at all if it hadn't been for McBride. As for the weather: no sooner had the sun risen than battalions of mist came flooding out of the west and moved round the plateau, as though mustering to its defense. Here they remained, rising and falling, a sullen army undecided as to their next move, perversely blocking our view. Not that we had much time, that morning, for admiring the view, for all our energies were taken up in picking a route through what, it suddenly dawned on us, was highly treacherous terrain.

Our first hint of danger was when we came within a hairsbreadth of falling six hundred feet into a "moulin." Moulins are huge circular shafts, plunging vertically into the ice. I had always associated them with glaciers rather than snowfields; yet there the yawning cavity was, less than a dozen yards in front of us, its walls echoing to the sinister roar of underground water. We backed away from it, hurriedly.

"I suppose," I said, as we paused to look back from what

we thought a safe distance, "that *is* spray, coming over the edge?"

We stared at the nebulous haze of white, rising and falling, like a giant's breath, round the perimeter of the moulin.

"I think," Corbella said at last, "it's steam."

McBride nodded. "I endorse your opinion, sir. Without doubt we are traversing an area of thermal activity. Hence the softness of the snow."

"Then I vote," I said, "we traverse out of it. As quick as we can."

McBride raised his eyebrows. "You should cultivate the scientific outlook, young man. To an observant mind, the terrain surrounding the Viedma is of the utmost interest. Its moulins, underground rivers and thermal springs are phenomena to be marvelled at. I trust I shall have the chance to study them more closely."

"You'll be studying them a bit too closely," Westerman observed dryly, "if you don't jump to it!"

With a bellow of alarm the professor leapt out of the depression which, he suddenly realized, had been forming while he spoke, under his very feet. And from the snow where only a few seconds before he had been standing, there coiled up a sinister spiral of smoke.

We grabbed the sledge and fled. Nor did we come to a halt until, gasping for breath and wet with sweat, we were standing half a mile away on snow that was mercifully firm. I doubt if even then we would have ended our flight if it hadn't been for Westerman.

"This," he said matter-of-factly, "looks a likely spot for lunch."

More than a little ashamed of our panic, we let the sledge lose way. The meal was therapeutic—it is hard to feel panic-stricken while eating something as mundane as biscuits and cheese. Within the hour we had regained our composure and were setting out to reconnoiter a new approach to the Viedma: an approach which took us well to the north of the area of moulins, mist and thermal springs.

Soon the plateau was less than a mile ahead of us, and although we could catch only an occasional glimpse of it through the low cloud and driving snow, we were able to form a fair idea of its shape and size. It appeared to consist of a more or less circular massif, ringed by high black cliffs. The whole formation was larger than we had anticipated and was clearly volcanic in origin. It was clearly active too, for in the late afternoon we came across deposits of pumice, scattered like fine black ash across the surface of the snow. We collected a sample for analysis.

"This," Corbella pronounced, "is from a recent explosion. Within the last couple of days. Or it would have been washed away."

We stared at the volcano, looming like some great black monster out of the mist. "I hope"—Westerman spoke for us all—"it won't turn out to be *too* active!"

"You need have no fear of that," McBride reassured him. "Or the *Paranthropus* wouldn't have made it their home."

The argument didn't strike us as especially convincing; and as we neared the plateau, I for one found myself eyeing it with apprehension.

We camped that night in the shadow of its cliffs.

It would be hard to picture a more desolate scene. Behind us the vast waste of the Hielo Continental, with a 50-knot wind whipping up great plumes of snow and streaming them near-horizontal over the ice; in front of us the cliffs, rising black, formidable and straight as a clipper's mast, into the mist. The rock face was curiously striated—a characteristic peculiar to basalt—so sheer that in places it overhung, and we could spot neither toehold nor crevice. Westerman, it was clear, didn't fancy our chances of an ascent. "It looks," he said, shaking his head, "like the north face of the Eiger."

9
Land of Ice and Fire

That night we discussed our next move. It didn't take us long to decide our best bet was to work our way round the Viedma till we found a place where the cliffs could be scaled.

"What," I said, "if they're sheer all the way round? And there's no way up?"

"Such a supposition, young man," the professor boomed, "is hardly viable."

"Why not?"

"The *Paranthropus*, it is clear, have found a way up and down. . . . I suggest, by the way, we keep an extra-sharp lookout. They can hardly fail to know we are here."

I don't think any of us took his warning all that seriously at the time. But in the small hours of the night, when it came to my turn as sentry, I must admit that I felt unaccountably nervous; for I had the sensation, once again, that we were being watched. I checked my gun, turned up the wick of the Tilley lamp and took a careful look outside. Needless to say it was snowing, hard little flakes scything out of a leaden sky; the great black cliffs, towering above us so sheer that in places they overhung, were hardly a reassuring sight; but there was no sign of life. Indeed I told myself that nothing— not even an Abominable Snowman or a Stone Age ape— could exist amid such desolation.

I felt even more certain of this next morning when we were hit by a blizzard of unbelievable ferocity. We had just finished breakfast, and I was helping Corbella to take bearings when I saw a great wall of white, like a tidal wave, surging toward us across the snowfield. Before I had time to cry warning we were knocked off our feet by a hammerblow of wind, the air was full of choking particles of ice and snow, and the plane table and Corbella's snowshoes were plucked up as though they were feathers and whirled out of sight. We couldn't get to our feet. Indeed we were hard pressed to crawl on hands and knees to the comparative safety of the tents.

It was the prelude to four days of unremitting tempest: sleet by day, snow by night and a wind that never dropped below 60 knots and rose to over 120 knots in squalls of terrifying violence. It seemed as though the wind was trying to rip up the Hielo Continental and spin it screaming off the face of the earth. I doubt if our Pyramids would have survived if they hadn't been protected by the Viedma—though their position in the lee of the cliffs had the minor disadvantage that it wasn't long before they were deep in snowdrifts. On the second night, after a particularly heavy fall, the weight of snow was so great that Christina and Corbella's tent, which we had been careless enough to erect in a small hollow, started to flood. They could do nothing to drain it; so at 2 A.M. they brought in their sodden sleeping bags and dossed down with us. Here the five of us remained, cold, damp and packed tight as the proverbial sardines, for forty-eight hours. Sleep was impossible, and time dragged—though we whiled away some entertaining hours by extending Corbella's repertoire of limericks.

During the fourth night the storm at last began to ease off; and Christina, who was nearest the entrance, looked out at frequent intervals and reported a gradual lessening of wind and lifting of cloud. We slept fitfully, longing for dawn and the chance to extricate ourselves from our sodden surroundings.

By first light, conditions were back to normal—that is to say the snow was intermittent and the wind a mere 30 knots; so we set to work to dig ourselves out. There was an incredible amount of snow. It made everything look different. Outcrops of rock which a few days before had been familiar landmarks had vanished now, and the Hielo Continental lay silent under a uniform carpet of white. Nothing seemed to be broken except a couple of guy ropes, and nothing was missing except the plane table and snowshoes. I took our binoculars, walked to the top of a small hillock and scanned the snowfield section by section in the somewhat forlorn hope of spotting the missing equipment.

It was not, however, plane table and snowshoes that showed up in the binocular's magnified circle. It was something quite different. Footprints: clear-cut and unmistakable, circling the tents.

My frightened shout brought the others tumbling into the open; and we stood in a little circle, staring at the prints in the snow. Something—or somebody—had climbed down the Viedma in the small hours of the night, made a reconnaissance of our camp and climbed back the way it had come.

"Our friends the *Paranthropus*," McBride observed, "are early risers!"

As he spoke of *Paranthropus*, I noticed that Westerman, for the first time, made no dissent; indeed his usual smile had given way to a look of reluctant credulity. The professor, unfortunately, saw it. "Of course," he boomed with ponderous sarcasm, "Mr. Westerman will understand that when I speak of a *Paranthropus* I mean an Indian: only the sort of Indian who is seven feet tall, has red hair, the skin of a troglodyte and lives in a temperature of minus twenty degrees Fahrenheit!" He smirked, blinked and bowed until Westerman turned away in disgust.

We took photographs of the footprints, and made what deductions we could: that they were recent (or they would have been filled in by snow), and that the creature which made them was large and heavy (for the indentations were widely spread and deep). McBride squatted down in the snow, his finger tracing their outline. "You will observe," he said with satisfaction, "that the big toe is short and appears to be separately jointed."

For a long time we stared at the prints in disbelief: as might men who have come across the fresh spoor of a dinosaur on the Sussex Downs.

"If we follow them," I said at last, "they may lead to the top of the cliffs."

It was, the others decided, a possibility worth looking into. So we struck camp, loaded the sledge and set off in the best safari tradition to follow the trail.

The footprints stretched away in front of us: intriguing, enigmatic, luring us on like the song of Sirens heard faintly over a mist-encompassed sea. For some time they kept parallel to the cliffs, at a distance of roughly a hundred yards; then, quite suddenly, they cut in toward the shadow of an overhang. We came to a halt peering up at the fearsome-looking cornices of ice, which looked as though if a bird so much as dropped on them they would come avalanching down. Westerman pursed his lips, "Don't fancy the look of them."

"It could," McBride said, "be a trap."

Discretion, we agreed, was the better part of valour. We decided to give the cornices a wide berth, and try to pick the footprints up again on the far side of the overhang. This, much to our satisfaction, we managed to do, Corbella re-sighting the trail as it emerged from the shadow of the cliffs three or four hundred yards farther round the Viedma. The prints were more blurred now by wind and freshly fallen snow, but they were still unmistakably the spoor of a heavy, long-striding biped. We followed them round the bottom of the cliffs, eagerly: the excitement of exploration supplemented now by the excitement of the chase. Every half hour we stopped for a short rest; and it was during one of these halts that Christina motioned us to be quiet. "Listen!"

Faintly above the bluster of wind we could just make out,

in the far distance, another sound: a deeper, steadier roar, which didn't fluctuate but boomed on and on. It was a sound I had heard before when I was climbing in the Cairngorm after weeks of rain. "I think," I said, "it's a river."

We came to it an hour later, a fast-flowing torrent boring its way through the ice. Most ice-fed streams are crystal clear; but this one had a curious muddy appearance, and a curious not very pleasant smell which none of us was able at the time to identify. The footprints led straight into the water, at a place where it was a good six feet deep; and as far as we could see they didn't reappear on the far bank. We came to a disappointed halt. There was, however, nothing we could do about it. Losing one's trail in water was, as McBride pointed out, one of the oldest and most effective tricks in the world.

We spent the rest of the day by the river, Corbella and Christina taking a great number of samples, photographs and fixes, while Westerman, McBride and I explored its banks. We found a place to ford it, where the water was comparatively shallow; but of the footprints we found no sign, although we followed the river downstream for more than a mile and upstream as far as the cliffs, where it disappeared into a Stygian cavity, en route apparently for the bowels of the Viedma. The creature, whatever it was, seemed to have vanished off the face of the earth.

We pitched our tents that evening in the open, where no one could creep up on us unobserved; and we all, I think, took our turn at sentry duty a deal more seriously than usual. We had, however, no more nocturnal visitors.

What we did have was a surprise of a different kind. I have already mentioned, I think, that from the moment we left El Condor Corbella had been keeping a detailed plot of our route and environs. This he now produced in its finished glory: a dozen sheets of survey paper, each covered with a network of correlated bearings. "You will observe," he announced with satisfaction, "that tonight we are camped on Chilean soil."

We studied his map of the Moreno, with the peaks meticulously triangulated and the watershed delineated in detail and with accuracy. "So the Viedma," McBride said, "is in Chile?"

"It is indeed. As you see, the line of the highest peaks runs at least half a mile to the east of it. As for the watershed, it too lies to the east. For the river we have just crossed is clearly on course for the Pacific."

The wind howled over the ice cap. Through the entrance to the tent we could make out the mass of the plateau, etched starkly against the stars. "I'm sure you're welcome to it," I said.

Christina and Corbella exchanged glances. And smiled.

"We're here," Westerman said sharply, "to explore the Viedma, not to prejudice who it belongs to. So I suggest we put our minds to how we're going to climb it."

We tried. But we hit on no panacea that evening. Indeed the only thing we could think of was to continue sledging round the plateau in the hope of finding a spot where the cliffs were less precipitous.

We were out of luck. It took us three days to circle the Viedma, exploring as we went every possible nook and cranny. But not once did we see the slightest crack in the bastion's defenses. The cliffs, all the way round, remained between two and three hundred feet in height; in some places they were festooned in arrases of ice, in others the bare striated rock rose sheer into the mist; everywhere they were too vertical to climb. Only in two places, Westerman and Corbella agreed, might a team of expert mountaineers with pitons have got to the top: nowhere was there the slightest hope for amateurs such as Christina, McBride and I—much less for our supplies.

On the fourth day we completed our circuit of the plateau, and found ourselves back in the area of moulins, mist and thermal springs. We were a disconsolate party, for our survey had been painstaking enough for us to feel sure that no possible route had escaped us. What were we to do? We had used nearly half our supplies, and in less than a fortnight shortage of food would be forcing us off the Hielo Continental. Yet the prospect of returning home with so many mysteries unsolved was not to be thought of. My last recollection that night was of McBride squatting like some monstrous bullfrog in front of the Primus, apparently deep in dejection and quite oblivious to the good-night that I wished him.

It was, however, a very different McBride who greeted us next morning: a McBride with bristling beard and the glint of false modesty in his eye. "Eureka! The problem, gentlemen, is solved!"

"You've thought of a way up?"

"I venture to think so."

"How?"

"To an analytical brain the problem admits to only one solution. Bearing in mind the forays of the *Paranthropus*, there has to be *some* way on and off the Viedma. So if we can't go up the cliffs, then clearly we have to go *under* them."

For a moment we stared at him blankly. Then I got it. "You mean the underground river?"

"Exactly."

I remembered the sinister cavity at the foot of the cliffs out of which the water had come boiling fast as a millrace, and shivered. But the idea was obviously one that had to be explored; and by midday we were back at the spot where the footsteps had disappeared.

The cavity where the river cascaded out of the Viedma was shaped like a tunnel: about twelve feet high and twenty feet wide, with water discharging through the bottom two-thirds of it. There seemed at first to be no way in, for the current was flowing too fast to be waded against. Then Corbella spotted what looked like a narrow ledge running along the nearside wall. On closer inspection the ledge turned out to be reasonably level but less than two feet wide; it was slimy with algae, wet with spray and only a few inches above the creaming water.

"You can count me out," I said. "I've done my share of swimming!"

But we all knew in our hearts that the river had to be explored. And the ledge was the only way in.

We cached our surplus equipment in as safe a spot as we could, beneath the cliffs; then we reorganized our packs. Obviously we had to travel light. So we took with us only our climbing gear, a single tent, four days' food, a Primus, a Tilley lamp, a camera and one of the Parker-Hales. Every item that was left behind we would have liked to take. But underground exploring with heavy packs simply wasn't on.

As we made our way back to the cavity, Westerman took the lead. "I'm the smallest," he said. "I'll go first."

Christina looked at him reproachfully. "You're not very gallant about my vital statistics."

We stared at her.

"Thirty-six–twenty-three–thirty-six," I said.

She favoured me with a disarming smile. "I didn't know you were so observant. . . . But seriously, let me go first. I'm the smallest. When I'm in, I'll belay the rope, and the rest of you'll have something to hang onto."

She was right, but I could sympathize with Westerman in his dilemma; he wasn't the sort, when there was danger, to lead his army from the rear. It was Corbella who helped him make up his mind. "Let's be realistic," he said. "You're the last person we could afford to have hurt. Let her go."

So we took Christina's pack, and secured her with two ropes (two, in case one of them got severed). Then we hoisted her onto the ledge. She tested the rock, then took off her boots and socks, having decided, I suppose, that she'd get a better purchase with bare feet. It must have been because the two of us were much the same age that it was to me she turned at the last second for comfort. "Wish me luck, Pete."

She looked small, frightened and far from sure of herself— as well she might, for if she fell into the river there was no guarantee that the ropes would save her. On sudden impulse I kissed her. "Take care of yourself," I said.

A surprised and rather frightened smile, and she was crawling onto the ledge.

To start with she inched forward on hands and knees; then, after a long pause, she went flat on her face. I thought for a moment that she had lost her nerve. Then I realized that the ledge, as it went round a slight curve, narrowed: narrowed so much in fact that she had somehow to get a grip with her fingers and toes while the rest of her body swung out over the millrace. It was the most hair-raising thing I have ever seen. Beside me I heard the breath suck in through McBride's teeth, and Corbella muttering exhortations to the Virgin Mary. Then she was past the curve and out of sight.

We went on paying out the rope, and after about fifteen yards had been uncoiled, we heard her shout—a shout, thank God, not of fear but of satisfaction. Her voice came out of the cavity muffled, distorted and indecipherable above the roar of water; but we got the message.

"Can I go next?" I said.

Westerman nodded. "And take the Tilley."

Even with the rope to hang onto, the crawl was a nightmare: slime, darkness and the frenzied roar of water foaming past only a few inches below me. I tried not to look down as I inched forward with my face to the wall, one hand on the rope, the other clawing for fingerholds in the rock. And it was even worse once I was round the bend, for here, cut off from the glare of the ice field, the darkness was Stygian. "Where are you?" I shouted nervously.

"Here." In the confined space her voice had an unearthly resonance, as though caught out of tune in an amplifier. "Another five or six yards. And there's a cave."

I was almost alongside her before I realized where she was, crouched in a sort of alcove at the edge of the river. She was cold, wet and trembling, and to my consternation in floods of tears.

"You hurt, Chris?"

"No. Just frightened."

In the dark we cannoned into each other, and my arms went round her. It came as an almost pleasant surprise to realize she wasn't as tough as she liked to make out. I held her close to me, somewhat fatuously stroking her hair, until after a while the muffled shouts of the others brought us back to the present. "I'll light the Tilley," I said. "Make it nice and cozy."

But the scene that flared up in the circle of light was more macabre than comforting: the walls of rock, beaded with moisture; the river disappearing into the darkness; and on the far side of the alcove, sloping slightly upwards, a curious sort of tunnel which might at first glance have been either an old bed of the river or a passage made by man. There was a good deal of loose rock about, and the whole formation struck me as none too stable. "We'd better," I said, "keep our voices down."

She nodded. And we tugged on the rope to signal the next man in.

Corbella was the third to arrive. "I'd never have made it," he panted, "without the rope."

I showed him the unstable rock, and from the moment he saw it we spoke in whispers. I also showed him the tunnel, and we took the Tilley lamp and made another and closer inspection. In years gone by it had, we decided, been the bed of a river, for its floor was strewn with smooth well-rounded boulders, and its walls sculptured with the swirl-marks of water; there was no indication of whether or not it led to the surface of the Viedma. Christina, meanwhile, had been rigging up a double line and pulley so that we could hook on and haul in the packs. In the course of the next half hour our five loads were pulled through successfully; and such is man's dependence on his bric-a-brac that as soon as we were surrounded by our equipment and food, we felt happier.

McBride was next on the roster for entry. We heard him puffing and grunting as he wormed his way down the ledge, then a pause and a muttered curse as he contemplated the bend. He had our sympathy. His enormous strength, here, was no compensation for his breadth in the beam. We exchanged glances. And sure enough a second later there came a frightened shout and the most almighty splash. I slithered anxiously along the ledge. "You all right?"

He surfaced almost beside me, like a bedraggled walrus; if he hadn't had the presence of mind to hang onto the rope, he might well have been swept out through the cavity and drowned. As it was, the current was so strong and the water so deep that he was hard pressed, even with my help and the help of the rope, to haul himself along hand over hand to the alcove. At last, however, with much heaving and panting, we managed to drag him ashore. For several seconds he lay inert in a widening pool of water, like a great stranded whale. Then very slowly he levered himself to his feet. "I am much obliged to you," he panted. "My premature demise would have been a grievous blow indeed to the world of science."

I pointed to the unstable strata in the roof. "You'll get a grievous blow yourself if you don't keep your voice down!"

He was, I could see, about to give me the rough edge of his tongue—for never was man more intolerant of criticism—when there occurred an incident terrifying both in itself and in its implication.

After Corbella and I had made our reconnaissance of the old riverbed, we had left the Tilley lamp at the far side of the cave; there it had remained ever since, lighting up both alcove and tunnel. We had just given a tug on the rope, as a signal to Westerman to start crawling in, when we heard a distant rumbling: faint at first, but building up within seconds to a deafening crescendo. It sounded as though a runaway train was bearing down on us through the bowels of the earth. It was Corbella who saved our lives, "Quick! Backs to the wall." He half-flung Christina against the side of the cave. And a second later a gigantic boulder came hurtling down the dried-up bed of the river. It flattened the Tilley lamp, bounced like a cannon ball across the cave and smashed with terrifying violence into the rock face. The whole formation quivered like jelly; dust rained down from the roof, and little avalanches of rock broke away from the face of the alcove and cascaded into the water. I thought for a terrifying moment the walls were about to cave in. Then the debris rolling down in the wake of the boulder came to rest. The dust settled. Everything was deathly quiet. And Westerman came crawling into the cave. He at once took charge. "Christina, Fergus, Peter, Eduardo. Anyone hurt?"

It seemed that everyone, almost miraculously, had escaped unscathed. I felt for the emergency torch which I carried sewn into the lining of my anorak. It was amazing how clumsy one was in the dark; it took me at least a minute to extract it, but at last a thin beam of light lit up our frightened faces and the aftermath of the landslide.

It was Westerman who came out with the question that was at the back of all our minds. "Was that deliberate?"

We showed him the bed of the old river, sloping away into darkness beyond the beam of our torch. There was of course no way of knowing if the boulder had come down it of its own volition or if it had been thrown; but the prospect of crawling on hands and knees up the tunnel while someone at the top took pot shots at us with boulders was not inviting. "I suggest," McBride whispered, "we seek an alternative route."

I must admit it struck me as highly improbable that there would be another way out of the cave. But a closer inspection revealed that the ledge continued to run parallel to the river, and that on the far side of the alcove it seemed to get broader rather than narrower. We therefore collected our kit and our composure, and set off into the maw of the Viedma, like latter-day Jules Verne heroes en route for the center of the earth.

Our eyes by this time had become a little adjusted to the dark, and we realized that the underground passage was not in fact in utter blackness. There was a faint phosphorescence from the water; in one place a tiny colony of glowworms hung clustered from the roof; and in another a pale anemic glimmer of sunlight filtered down through a crevice in the rock. We examined the latter hopefully, but nothing larger than a house spider could have wormed its way through. After two or three hundred yards the roof of the passage grew higher, and the ledge broadened out to form the floor of a fair-sized cave. There were more glow-worms here: tiny pinheads of light, which vanished as we approached, then lit up again behind us as the noise of our footfalls diminished. There were stalagmites and stalactites too: slender columns rising from the floor and hanging from the ceiling, several of them streaked with veins of a curious coppery-green. Christina and Corbella seemed to be fascinated by the veins. They peered at them in the light of my torch, tapped them, scratched them, broke bits off them and tasted them, and finally shoved a couple of sample fragments into their packs. Westerman quite lost patience. "Come on, you two. And put out that torch!"

We hurried after him, Christina and Corbella whispering *sotto voce* like a couple of conspirators, "Pale green in rounded bosses."

"I'm afraid it's malachite."

"It tasted acrid enough."

"What on earth," I said, "is malachite?"

They looked vaguely uncomfortable. "It's a long story," Corbella said noncommittally, and before I had the chance to question him further there came an excited shout from McBride. "Light ahead!"

We pressed forward eagerly. But the light didn't turn out to be what we expected.

My first impression was of a dull red glimmer, pulsating rhythmically out of the dark like the glow from a Roman candle. Could it, I wondered, be the light of the setting sun streaming down through a moulin? It seemed a logical possibility; but as we neared the light, it gradually dawned on us that its source was below the ground and not above it. McBride came to an abrupt halt, and as we cannoned into him I felt a waft of heat, as though the door of a blast furnace had been flung suddenly open.

"Look out!" Corbella gasped. "It's the vent of a volcano!"

We backed away. And as our eyes became slowly accustomed to the strange red light, we could make out a scene as bizarre as it was terrifying. The cave through which we had been walking terminated in a series of passageways which radiated out of it like fingers from a hand. We had walked down the center of these, and had been brought up short by the vent: a fissure which appeared to drop sheer into the bowels of the Viedma: a minifumarole, white-hot in its center, and pigmented through scarlet, crimson and vermilion to a pale rose-gold at its periphery. It was a scene all the more frightening for the complete and utter silence. For as we watched the waves of heat and light pulsate across the face of the rocks, we were conscious of the fact that only a little way under the ground on which we stood, titanic forces were straining at the leash: forces the more dangerous for being held so mutely in check. Instinctively we drew closer together. Yet for all its power to terrify, the fumarole had the power to fascinate as well. We couldn't take our eyes off it, but peered at it in fearful anticipation, half-expecting any second to see streams of lava, the very stuff of creation, well redly out from the center of the earth. Corbella, as a geologist, was more conscious than the rest of us of danger. I saw him eyeing the faulted strata of the rock. "The sooner we're out of here," he muttered, "the better."

We backpedalled, shading our eyes against the red pulsating glow. My last impression of the fumarole, as we rounded a bend in the passage, was of a sudden welling up of flame and light and a shower of white-hot sparks: a *feu de joie* at our retreat.

Back in the cave we held a council of war, huddled together beneath a cluster of glow-worms which, when they heard us talking, most inconsiderately put out their lights.

"What a ghastly place," I muttered. "Do you suppose these passages are old volcanic vents?"

McBride shook his head. "In my opinion they are the work of man: *Paranthropus* man."

We looked at Corbella. "I reckon," he said slowly, "they're

volcanic in origin. But I must admit in places they seem to have been improved. Look there"—he flashed his torch at the entrance to one of the passageways—"that rock's been cut by hand."

Christina shivered. "Strikes me," she said, "we're skating on thin ice."

I had the same sensation. The atmosphere of the underground passageways was redolent of mystery and danger. So, I told myself, must Grecian captives have felt when they first set foot in the labyrinth of the Minotaur. "I vote," I said, "we get the hell out of this."

Westerman looked at his watch. The luminous hands were coming up to five o'clock, indicating that we had been inside the Viedma a mere three hours. It seemed much longer. "We don't want to give up too easily," he said. "Let's have another look round."

McBride nodded. "I don't fancy that ledge again—unless I have to."

So we set off once more into the bowels of the earth, having agreed on certain elementary precautions: no talking, minimal use of the torch and Corbella making a diagram as we went along to ensure that we didn't get lost. We also agreed to turn back, exceedingly smartly, at the first sign of volcanic activity. The first passage we investigated soon petered out, but the second went on and on.

It was shaped like a tunnel, about eight feet wide and six feet high, although in places the ceiling lowered abruptly, so that we were forced to crawl forward on hands and knees. The rocks that lined it, Corbella said, were Mesozoic: principally basalt and granite; although here and there were strata of a very different formation: softer and flecked with veins of a yellowy-green. These once again seemed to interest Corbella and Christina, and I got the impression that if they hadn't been afraid to use the torch, they would have liked to examine them more closely; as it was they merely took samples. We pushed on, the passage becoming gradually more narrow and the glow-worms gradually more scarce.

Soon we were edging forward into complete darkness. We formed a chain, holding hands like children in the night, half-expecting that any moment the passage would peter out. But it didn't. It wound on and on. Once, as we were crawling under a projecting ledge, we thought we could hear away in the distance the roar of water—another underground river, perhaps, boring its way through the rock. Once, as we stamped our feet, the floor rang hollow. "Careful," Corbella whispered, "there's a cave underneath."

"The whole plateau," McBride muttered, "is doubtless honeycombed with caves. Like the scarps of the Dordogne."

We crawled on, fear giving gradual way to boredom, then boredom to exhaustion. We were about to call it a day when Westerman, who was in the lead, held up his hand. "Listen!"

At first we could hear nothing. But after a while our ears picked up a tiny murmur of sound—as if a thousand distant taps were dripping intermittently onto a stone floor. We pushed forward, and, rounding a bend in the passage, realized that the darkness ahead was fading from indigo to mother-of-pearl. Yet another bend, and we stood staring in amazement at the magnificent vista that opened up ahead.

The passage ended in a cave. Cave, however, is an altogether inadequate word to describe the magnificent formation we now stood looking into. Imagine a vast church, windowless but dimly lit from above by unseen shafts; imagine its pillars to be stalagmites and stalactites, many of them beautifully fluted; imagine its floor to be a mosaic of greys and greens and subtle blues; and imagine the whole structure to be three or four times the size of the largest cathedral. No wonder we stood for several minutes in silence: a silence broken only by the continual drip-drip-drip as moisture from the roof splashed down on the stalagmites beneath. As our eyes grew gradually accustomed to the light, we noticed that in the farthest corner was a stairway of rock, bathed in light, spiralling upward like the steps to a pulpit. "It looks," Westerman whispered, "like a way out."

And this it proved to be: our gateway to the Viedma.

The sun was setting as we climbed wearily up the ice-veneered staircase of rock, and onto the plateau.

I can't begin to tell you how thankful we were to exchange the claustrophobic labyrinths of the volcano for the open vistas of the ice field. The wind and snow which swept down on us the moment we appeared above ground level we greeted if not as friends at least as acquaintances whose moods and foibles we understood; as for the hard white light, though it was strong enough at first to hurt our eyes, the fact that we could see more than a couple of feet ahead was like ambrosia to the gods. We were filled with the sort of elation that is next of kin to overconfidence.

The sun, as I say, was setting; and it was clearly too late that evening to explore farther. We did, however, climb to the top of a small mound in an effort to find out what sort of terrain it was whose secrets were so sedulously guarded. The view was reassuringly normal; almost in fact an anticlimax. The summit of the Viedma appeared to consist of a featureless, more or less circular plain some half-dozen miles in diameter. There was a gentle rise from the point where we were standing up to a flattish cone in the center, so the far side of the plateau was hidden from view. Apart from this central cone, the only features were a number of outcrops of rock: little excrescences of black, standing out sharply against the snow. We decided to make for the nearest, with a view to pitching our tent in its lee.

The outcrop we headed for was less than half a mile distant, and there seemed no reason at first why we shouldn't reach it well before dark. However, some hundred yards short of it, we noticed that the snow was becoming increasingly soft and unstable. We came to a halt.

"Don't fancy this," McBride muttered.

We all felt the same way; the last thing we wanted was to venture into another area of moulins and thermal springs. We therefore decided to camp in the open, some 150 yards from the rocks.

It was bitterly cold that evening as we set up the tent.

Little wisps of cloud were scudding west, being absorbed into a hard green sky, and as the light faded the ice pack took on a frozen pallor. We were tired, and after an improvised meal decided to doss down early. For a while the long sub-Antarctic twilight kept us awake; and I tossed and turned in my sleeping bag thinking nostalgically of the soft colours and gentle lights of the hills round St. Andrews; but after a while the green fields of sunset were swamped by the rising tide of night, and I slept.

I slept badly. It was, to start with, my turn for the midnight watch—always an unpopular one, for it broke up the night—and I had, it seemed to me, no sooner dozed off than Corbella was shaking me by the shoulder.

"All quiet?" I asked him.

He nodded. "Thought I heard a sort of clicking noise once. But I guess I imagined it."

His face, I noticed, was drawn and pale; and I looked at him curiously. "But you didn't see anything?"

"Not a thing. The rifle's loaded, by the way."

Again I looked at him curiously. For we had agreed to load the Parker-Hale only in emergency.

Corbella didn't waste any time dossing down, and soon he was snoring peacefully while I was pacing up and down outside the Pyramid like a cat on hot bricks; for I hadn't been on watch ten minutes before I was obsessed by the old fear that we were being watched.

It was a lovely night. The cloud and mist had lifted, and although there was no moon the Southern Cross was close to its zenith, and the peaks of the Moreno were etched against a sky so brilliant with stars that the ice fairly sparkled with phosphorescence. On such a night, I told myself, there was no fear of our being surprised, for the ice cap was devoid of cover and bathed in light. All the same, I was nervous. I kept the rifle loaded and patrolled assiduously round and round the tent.

Much to my relief, however, there were no alarms or excursions; and a little before two o'clock I heated some drinking chocolate for Christina, whose turn it was to relieve me. When I had woken her we stood for some minutes outside the tent, sipping our drinks. It was bitterly cold, with the wind whipping up loose particles of snow and spinning them in flurries over the ice.

"Why," she asked, "is the rifle loaded?"

"Corbella thought he heard something. A sort of clicking, he said."

"But *you* didn't hear it?"

I shook my head.

A few minutes later I was on the threshold of sleep, half-conscious of the comforting pad of Christina's snow shoes as she circled the tent: round and round, round and round, round and fading *pianissimo* to silence.

I don't know what it was that woke me; but I woke suddenly, all of a piece. I was lying on my back. And the first thing I saw when I opened my eyes was the hands: the great, red, hairy, strangler's hands delineated like some nightmare fantasy against the wall of the tent. They were moving toward my throat.

I screamed.

I tried to roll aside. But the hands came down on my neck, quick as a cormorant, tight as a vise. The night was filled with a foetid animal stench and a frenzied click-click-click-ing. I was vaguely aware that beside me the others, too, were threshing about like harpooned fish. Then the hands tightened their grip, unbearably. I tried to claw them away; I tried to bite them; but I might as well have blunted my teeth on handcuffs of steel. Redness, like a tide of blood, welled up in front of my eyes. I know what's happening to me, I remember thinking: my head is being screwed off. Then I blacked out.

10

In the Hands of *Paranthropus* Man

A veil of red was rising and falling in front of my eyes. Waves of pain were surging across the back of my head. I felt myself being lifted clean off the ground, as if in the grip of a gargantuan vise. Then dropped, suddenly. I lay still, no more than half-conscious. At first I was thankful only that the pressure on my neck had relaxed; then, as the pain subsided and my head cleared, I opened my eyes. But what I saw was too fantastic to believe. I wouldn't, I told myself, look; it was easier to lie blind and unthinking in the dark.

After a while, however, the evidence of my nose (the foetid animal stench) and the evidence of my ears (the curious click-click-clicking) convinced me that I wasn't in the grip of a nightmare, so I opened my eyes again.

It was dawn. The light was grey but strong enough for every detail to be sharply defined: the canvas of the tent ripped to shreds, Westerman and Corbella flat on their backs either dead or unconscious, and McBride on his feet, stark naked, in confrontation with the most incredible creature I have ever clapped eyes on. I say "incredible creature," yet the first thing that struck me about him, the thing that almost made me burst out in a cackle of half-hysterical laughter, was his extraordinary resemblance to McBride! The creature was, it is true, a great deal bigger and hairier than the professor; but he had the same thick-set body, the same barrel chest, the same short, somewhat bandy legs, the same tangle of rust-red hair, the same pale, near-translucent skin and the same intolerant "what-do-*you*-want-damn-you" expression; only the shape of his head was different, the low backward-sloping skull of the ape-man being in sharp contrast to the broad cranium of the man-of-science. Their faces were inches apart, and they were glaring at one another with the ferocity of tom cats, each trying to make the other slink discomforted away. It would have been a sight to laugh at if my instinct hadn't told me that our lives depended on whose eyes were first to drop.

I lay still, hardly daring to breathe, trying to work out what had happened. Somehow, in spite of our sentry, the ape-men had managed to rush us. I looked for Christina, and realized she was missing—very likely stretched out in the snow, I told myself, with her head screwed off. Anger and grief welled up in me, the ice cap started to undulate like the waves of the sea, and I thought I was going to black out. Then I forced myself to take stock of our predicament— about as nasty a one, I fancy, as ever men were faced with.

There were a couple of dozen ape-men: big, ugly-looking customers, not one of them under six foot and most of them nearer seven. They encircled the tent; and if looks could kill, we would have been already past human aid. I have never seen eyes so full of hate. They had clearly burst into the tent with the amiable intention of screwing our heads off. What, I asked myself, had made them stop? I could think of only one possible reason: the fact that McBride might have been their next-of-kin. I stared at the two figures —the professor and the Stone Age ape—locked in a battle of wills. There was no doubt who was the stronger; any one of the apes could have flattened McBride with a single blow; but *Homo sapiens* has climbed the ladder of evolution not by brawn but by brain, and every iota of McBride's formidable intellect was concentrated now on asserting his will over his opponent. And after what seemed an eternity—

but must, I suppose, have been something less than a minute—the creature began to shift uneasily. The hatred in his eyes gave way first to uncertainty, then to fear. He backed away, snarling, little flecks of saliva slobbering white out of the corners of his mouth.

McBride then made the mistake that all but cost us our lives. He glanced round, just for a second, to see what had happened to the rest of us.

The moment he took his eyes off the ape, the wretched creature leapt forward and dealt him a great backhanded blow that knocked him clean off his feet. The others set up a frenzied click-click-clicking, and I thought for a moment they were going to finish us off there and then. It seemed, however, they had other ideas. For we were hauled to our feet; our hands were lashed behind our backs—the fellow securing me could tie knots like a boatswain—and we were frog-marched out of the tent. Westerman, I was glad to see, had been lying doggo and was apparently unhurt. Corbella, however, looked in a bad way; his left shoulder hung forward, blood was streaming down his arm, and he was clearly in a good deal of pain. Of Christina there was no sign. Nobody, thank the Lord, stretched out in the snow, no blood, no footprints, no rifle; incredibly she seemed to have vanished off the face of the earth. As for McBride, he certainly didn't lack nerve. When one of the ape-men tried to grab hold of him with the obvious intention of trussing him up, he fixed the creature with a stare of such outraged ferocity that it hesitated, gave a perplexed grunt and sidled away.

The result was another outburst of "conversation." And since the ape-men's language was half-click, half-mime it wasn't difficult for us to follow their train of thought. They didn't know what to make of McBride.

It was their hair that made them so ridiculously alike. Now that I had the chance to study both professor and *Paranthropus* (for such I assumed the creatures must be) more closely, it was obvious there were a thousand-and-one differences, many of them basic. But the rust-red, thickly matted hair that covered their bodies was identical; a professional dyer couldn't have matched the colour more perfectly.

We were not, however, given time to speculate on this lucky coincidence. One of the ape-men gave me a none-too-gentle shove, and gestured toward the center of the Viedma. "For Christ's sake," McBride hissed, "get going!"

And so we moved off in single file, one of the ape-men leading, the others forming up on either side of us like guards surrounding prisoners of war. I doubt, however, if prisoners of war ever presented such a sorry spectacle as we did. For we were half-naked, dazed with shock and frightened out of our wits. Westerman, Corbella and I had, it is true, slept partially dressed and were not too badly off; McBride, however, after his involuntary swim in the underground river, had stripped off his wet clothes for the night; the only things he had been able to snatch up as we were bundled out of the tent were his boots and underpants; and striding across the ice cap clad in nothing but these he was, to say the least, an incongruous sight. Westerman caught my eye and winked.

I can't begin to tell you how much that wink did for my morale. It was a reaffirmation of sanity: an assertion that we weren't after all caught up in some nightmare beyond our control, and that the classic virtues of courage, humour and resource still had a meaning.

We were herded toward the center of the Viedma, sometimes sinking up to our knees in the soft, wet snow. Westerman maneuvered himself alongside me. "Did you see Christina?" he whispered.

I shook my head.

"Nor I." He worked his way across to McBride, and I saw the professor shake his head. What on earth, I wondered, could have happened to her? It seemed impossible she had escaped. Yet if the apes had caught her, why wasn't she with us? What in God's name, I asked myself, had they done with her? And thoughts too terrible to be contemplated in cold blood passed through my mind.

We had covered a bare hundred yards when Corbella pitched forward onto his face and lay still.

We stopped. The ape-men didn't like this. They set up an impatient clicking, forcing us on with kicks and blows, and there wasn't much that Westerman or I could do. McBride, however, whose hands had not been tied, bent down and hoisted the Chilean over his shoulder in a fireman's lift. Then the bizarre cavalcade moved on, more slowly now, Westerman and I dragging our feet as much as we dared to give McBride the chance to keep going. Most men would have given up inside a hundred yards, but McBride carried his unconscious companion for the best part of half a mile. I don't know how he did it! It was the most fantastic feat of strength; for the snow was heavy and cloying, and Corbella weighed a full 170 pounds. Within seconds McBride was gasping for breath; within minutes his face was wet with sweat; and long before we had struggled through to our destination his skin was grey, his eyes were rolling and the muscles of his arms and legs were standing out like knotted cords.

Then, mercifully, we were at the end of the road.

For some time we had been plodding up an almost imperceptible rise. Now, at the top of it, the snow slopes fell steeply away in front of us, and we stood looking down into the heart of the Viedma: the crater of the volcano itself.

So many strange things had happened in the last twenty-four hours that I would hardly have batted an eyelid if we had found ourselves gazing at a lost city (some Shangri-la of the Andes), or a fertile valley or a shantytown of the apes. But the scene we stood looking down at was not nearly so fanciful: indeed it seemed at first glance almost normal. Almost but not quite. For gradually, as our eyes took in the details, we spotted a number of features that were to say the least unusual. To start with, although the temperature was well below zero, the lake in the center of the crater was ice-free; so it must, I told myself, be fed by springs flowing hot from the heart of the volcano. As for the volcano itself, there was no doubt as to its activity, for a continuous banner of smoke was pulsating out of a vent on the rim of the crater. And it was this smoke, I now realized, mingling with the near-perpetual cloud, which formed an unbroken canopy over the Viedma: a canopy which had for centuries kept guard over its secrets. On three sides the slopes of the crater were a continuous concave sweep; but on the fourth side, just below where we were standing, they were broken up into a series of cliffs and terraces. And lining the terraces, like cardboard silhouettes against a backdrop of snow were whole families of red-haired apes: there must have been forty to fifty of them, peering up at us half in fear, half in expectation.

I say apes, but I realized almost at once that the word was a misnomer. For spread out at intervals along the terraces were a series of fires: little oases of warmth.

Here, it seemed to me, was evidence of the skill that had raised man above the level of the beasts. Bird can call to bird, a lioness may lay down her life for her cubs, termites may live in highly organized communal towns. But they can't make fire. Man alone has the intelligence to master the elements.

And so, I told myself, our captors must be men: men certainly who were still on the very bottom rung of the evolutionary ladder, but nonetheless blood of our blood, kith of our kin, cousins one hundred thousand times removed. Surely we could establish some sort of rapport with them?

I felt a great blow on my shoulder. A sharp-nailed toe dug painfully into my groin. Our "cousins," it seemed, were anxious to move on.

I thought McBride was never going to make it. The second we came to a halt at the edge of the crater, he had collapsed in the snow, sucking in great gulps of air like a man about to drown; his face had a greyness I didn't like the look of, and he was clearly, in boxing parlance, out on his feet. But now, after only a few moments' rest, and before his breathing was back to normal, our captors were urging us on. When Westerman tried to remonstrate, he was given a clout which tumbled him head-over-heels down the crater in a little avalanche of snow. This the ape-man seemed to think was funny. They danced up and down, click-click-clicking and miming Westerman's fall. My hopes of a rapport receded.

I did what I could to help McBride hoist the still-unconscious Corbella over his shoulder. Then we were stumbling forward again: forward and downward, into the crater of the Viedma.

As we approached the terraces, more and more of the *Paranthropus* materialized, apparently out of thin air, to watch our arrival. I couldn't make out at first where they were coming from. Then I noticed the mouths of caves: the dark little openings, some only a few feet high, that honeycombed the lower strata of the terraces. And McBride's words as we stood by his desk in The Harbour Wall came back to me: "I expect to find the creatures existing in caves, close to the volcanic fumarole." It was uncanny how his every prediction was coming true.

But again we weren't given time to speculate. None too gently, our captors shoved us along the terraces, to the accompaniment of a mounting crescendo of clicking-cum-hissing from the apes. It was the most unnerving sound I have ever heard: primitive, bestial, malignant. Such a cacophony of hate, I told myself, must have been the last thing on earth heard by gladiators about to die. I felt little beads of sweat prick up across the nape of my neck.

McBride was at the end of his tether—I doubt if he could have staggered more than a few yards farther—when we came to a halt at the mouth of a cave: a cave that was narrow at its entrance, but opened up inside to a height and depth that our eyes couldn't plumb. We were pushed in. An enormous stone was rolled across the entrance. And we were on our own.

McBride collapsed like a felled oak, spilling Corbella awkwardly onto the floor. We laid the pair of them out as comfortably as we could, and loosened the Chilean's clothing—all of which, with our hands tied, was a great deal easier said than done.

"We've got to get free," I whispered.

Westerman nodded. "There's a knife in my pocket. If it's not fallen out."

I tried to get it. I remember that I once saw Laurel and Hardy tying themselves in knots with a similar routine, and I dare say our antics would have looked to an audience every bit as comic. I got both my hands stuck in Westerman's pocket; wrenching them free I made a rip in his trousers; several times, like a pair of clowning dancers, we almost overbalanced; and at the end of it all the wretched knife first fell to the floor and then refused to open. But at last Westerman was sawing awkwardly away at the thongs that bound me. They seemed to be made of some sort of hide, and were not too difficult to cut. After two or three minutes, they parted. A moment of agony as the blood came coursing back through my wrists; then I was freeing Westerman.

We had been too preoccupied up to this point to pay much attention to our surroundings. But as I sawed away at Westerman's bonds, I became increasingly aware of a curious smell which I had noticed *en passant* the moment we entered the cave: not the overpowering stench of the *Paranthropus*, but a farmyard smell that was vaguely familiar and had not unpleasant connotations. I was trying to identify it when we both heard the movement at the same time. A surreptitious scuffling: coming slowly toward us, out of the darkness at the back of the cave.

We froze.

I am ashamed to admit that I was absolutely terrified. My

imagination by this time had got altogether out of hand, and I wouldn't have been in the least surprised if a saber-toothed tiger had come leaping at us out of the dark. Westerman, however, was made of sterner stuff. The moment he was released, he unearthed a pocket-torch out of his anorak, and set off purposefully toward the back of the cave.

"Careful!" I muttered, falling in behind him with more discretion than valour.

The torch didn't give much light. I had a vague impression, as he flashed it from side to side, of walls of rock rising sheer and black into the darkness above our heads; then the ground in front of us seemed suddenly transformed to an undulating sea; eyes glowed like oriflammes in the dark; and Westerman jumped back with a frightened curse. I was about to take to my heels when I heard—and never was sound more welcome—a succession of plaintive baas. What anticlimax! We had stumbled into a flock of sheep.

There must, I suppose, have been twenty or thirty of them: gaunt, frightened-looking creatures, huddled up against the side of the cave. Their eyes, in the light of our torch, looked opaque and staring, and they kept bumping into one another.

"I reckon," Westerman muttered, "they're half-blind."

Such was our relief at finding our bedfellows were harmless that we didn't worry our heads, for the time being, as to how and why they came to be imprisoned with us, but pushed past them and reconnoitered the back of the cave.

As I expected, there was no way out, though in one place a glimmer of light filtered down through a vent high above us in the roof, and in another place a trickle of water dripped intermittently down the face of the rock. The water was bitter to the taste, but we collected a little and carried it back to the mouth of the cave, to where the others were stretched out still unmoving, the one unconscious, the other prostrate with exhaustion.

McBride lay flat on his back; his eyes were closed, but his breathing, much to my relief, had returned to normal, and he had lost his frightening pallor. We covered him with as much spare clothing as we could muster, and left him to recover his strength.

Corbella was more of a problem. Both Westerman and I had a smattering of first aid, and we agreed that his collarbone was broken. "We'd better," Westerman said, "make him a sling."

"And the sooner the better," I added. "Before he comes round."

So we freed Corbella's hands, pulled off his anorak and pullover as gently as we could and passed an improvised bandage from elbow to shoulder. It must, I suppose, have been the shock of our somewhat ham-fisted ministrations that made him come round, wincing.

"You're O.K.," I said. "Lie still." I moistened his lips with water.

He was suffering from shock. It was some time before he seemed to realize that I wasn't one of the ape-men about to twist his head off; but eventually the fear ebbed out of his eyes, and after a while he was able to sit up and take part in our conversation. "Did you see Christina?" I asked him. "Back in the tent?"

He shook his head. And the mystery of her disappearance and our fear of what could have happened to her deepened. But our only chance of helping her—if by some miracle she was still alive—lay in helping ourselves. And we decided our first step should be to make an inventory of our effects. This didn't take long, but it did produce one or two articles that might be useful—two knives, two torches, two boxes of matches, two pencils, a number of spare bootlaces, a compass, a roll of bandage and, last but by no means least, three emergency food packs. The latter contained cubes of dehydrated meat and tablets of glucose, Horlicks and vitamins. We suddenly realized we were hungry, and though the food could hardly be described as appetizing, we all felt decidedly more human once we had had something to eat.

Our next step was to look at the great stone blocking the

entrance to the cave. It must have weighed a couple of tons, and our combined strength couldn't shift it an inch. Not that it would have done us much good if we had shifted it, for outside were a pair of *Paranthropus*. The moment they saw us heaving away, they set up an angry clicking. Immediately some dozen more of the loathsome creatures, armed with clubs, came rushing up. When they saw that we couldn't move the stone, they pranced up and down in derision.

"Bloody monkeys!" Corbella muttered.

I looked at their clubs—not picked-up fragments of timber, but workmanlike weapons made with skill; I looked at their fires on the terraces, well-tended and under control; I listened to their conversational clicking; and I knew that no monkeys had ever climbed this far up the ladder of evolution.

Our next step was to make a more detailed inspection of the cave. At the back of our minds was the hope that a skilled rock climber such as Westerman might be able to work his way onto the roof, and thence to the shaft through which we had noticed the glimmer of light. We were disappointed. With the help of our torches we examined the cave meticulously, section by section. The walls were sheer, with hardly a crack or crevice; the floor was solid; and the roof, except in the one place, an impenetrable slab. The general effect was that of a prison cell, impervious to assault from within or without. The only spot where there appeared to be the slightest flaw was where the shaft of light, softly diffused, came slanting in at an angle, some thirty feet above our heads. But the thirty feet, as far as I could see, might as well have been thirty miles. There was no way up. We shone our torches backward and forward over the roof, more in hope than expectation.

"I think," Westerman muttered, "there *is* a hole."

We all knew it was impossible, but we knew too that we had to try. Three times Westerman used every iota of his skill and expertise in an effort to work his way up the smooth, slab-sided rock. But he never even got halfway, and the third time he fell awkwardly, bruising his shoulder and leg. Though he was reluctant to admit defeat, the rest of us insisted he give up. One would have needed the prehensile feet of a fly to get within spitting distance of the roof.

We sat in a disconsolate circle, wondering what on earth to do next. We were exhausted, both physically and mentally; and it was tempting to forget our predicament in the opiate of sleep. Westerman, however, insisted—and quite rightly—that we stay on the *qui vive*, ready to snatch any opportunity, no matter how fleeting, of escape. So we sat, and waited, and talked.

We talked first of Christina. None of us had seen the slightest sign of her, either during the hiatus in the tent or while we were being frog-marched away. "I don't see," McBride's voice was sepulchral, "how she could possibly have survived."

Corbella rocked to and fro. I knew what he must be thinking: it was he who had insisted she come with us.

"What I can't understand," Westerman's voice was puzzled, "is the timing. Peter, your spell as sentry was from midnight to two?"

I nodded.

"So Christina's was two to four. But the apes didn't rush us till dawn, well after six."

We thought it over, but I can't say we arrived at any very satisfactory conclusion; there were too many imponderables. I didn't contribute much to the conversation. I was, I suppose, numb with grief. Also it seemed to me that nothing I did or said could in any way help Christina. This didn't stop my thinking of her. Far from it. And it was the same, I am sure, with the others. Many, many times in between the hair-raising events of that terrible day, our thoughts turned to her. But thought without action is a barren pastime; and in the end our attention was taken by a more mundane but also more immediate mystery: our fellow prisoners, the sheep.

There was only one place they could have come from:

the abandoned *estancia* at the head of Lago Viedma. Obviously, however, they hadn't been kept in the cave, where there was nothing to eat, ever since they had been stolen; so we asked ourselves what were they doing here now? An exceedingly nasty suspicion crossed my mind—shades of the one-eyed Cyclops and his dwindling flock—but I dismissed the idea as moonshine: it was too horrific to think of. And after a while our conversation turned to the *Paranthropus* themselves.

It says much for McBride's powers of recuperation that he now proceeded to embark on a monologue for the better part of an hour. Picture him seated on a slab of basalt, clad only in boots, underpants and a motley of cast-off clothes, addressing the three of us as though delivering a lecture in the Younger Halls. "We are privileged indeed," he boomed, "to be observing at first hand the last survivors of a bygone age—the Pleistocene Age to be precise. A million years ago *Paranthropus*, almost identical to our captors, were widely distributed throughout the world. They were vegetarians—witness their descendants' powerful jaws and heavy skull musculature—and existing as they did on green shoots, leaves and fruit, they had little need of weapons. The same could not be said of their cousins *Australopithecus. Australopithecus* were eaters of meat: great hunters, and scavengers of game—for which pursuits they needed sharpened flints and spears. We have evidence that for several millennia the two species of pre-men coexisted. But in the lean years it was *Australopithecus* who turned out to have not only the sharper flints, but the sharper wits; and the eaters of flesh must sometimes have looked thoughtfully at the *Paranthropus'* young." His voice dropped to a sonorous whisper. "Came the day when Cain killed Abel. . . . It was the start of five hundred thousand years of war. Step by step the unfortunate *Paranthropus* were driven out of their green pastures: driven to seek refuge in the lonely places of the earth, in desert hideouts, mountain fastnesses. Their numbers dwindled. About half a million years ago, the pundits said, they became extinct. But we know otherwise." He got to his feet and peered through the crack between the boulder and the entrance to the cave. "If only," he murmured half to himself, "our cameras hadn't been left in the tent. Never in history have scientists been blessed with so rich a field for research."

"I'd prefer to do *my* research," I said, "from a safe distance."

He treated the remark as beneath contempt, and proceeded to lecture us on the unique combination of circumstances which in the Viedma had enabled a last remnant of the ape-men to survive. And it came to me in a moment of admiration tinged with envy that McBride had the true scientist's complete and utter disregard for his own safety.

At the end of an exposition as lengthy as it was erudite, Corbella scratched his head. "What *I* can't understand," he said, "is why they didn't finish us off right away? In the tent?"

"I reckon they would have," I said, "if Professor McParanthropus hadn't looked like their next-of-kin!"

McBride transfixed me with the sort of glare that had quelled the apes. "Upon my word, young man, you take the most remarkable liberties."

"Well, it's a fact."

"I must ask you, sir, to choose your words more nicely. What saved our lives in the tent was the fact that the *Paranthropus* recognized, and were not unnaturally cowed by, my superior intellect. I was able to impose my will on them. When in a misguided attempt to help the rest of you my concentration lapsed, the spell was broken. Brute force won a temporary triumph. I do not doubt, however, that in the long run intelligence will reassert itself."

"I hope," Westerman said quietly, "you're right. Because here comes King Kong himself!"

The stone was rolled to one side, and about a dozen of our captors came marching into the cave.

I say "came marching," because that is exactly what their entry was: a ceremonial procession; two lines of guards, armed with clubs, flanking a central figure who was clearly the ape-men's leader or chief. He was a big, ugly-looking customer: a foot taller than any of us and a good fifty pounds heavier. His physique was magnificent, but his expression had an arrogance and cruelty that didn't augur well for our future. He clicked impatiently and beckoned McBride forward. When the much-vaunted intelligence was a bit slow on the uptake, he gestured angrily, and a pair of guards sprang forward and dragged the professor into the center of the cave.

The ape-man planted himself in front of McBride. He stared at him, first with curiosity, then with mounting disdain. He walked round him, stiff-legged, like a dog assessing the potential of a rival. Then, almost derisively, he dealt the professor a savage clout in the stomach: a clout that doubled him up, retching, on the floor of the cave. The rest of the creatures set up an excited click-click-clicking, and formed themselves into a circle; and I realized in a moment of horror what was going to happen. McBride and the leader of the apes were expected to fight.

It was a fight which could, I knew, have only one ending. Instinctively, I sprang to McBride's aid. It was a foolish gesture. Quite casually and without any sort of effort, one of the apes grabbed me by the scruff of the neck, kicked my feet from under me, picked me up and slung me half across the cave. I landed—luckily—on top of one of the sheep, which let out a frightened bleat and blundered into its companions. For a moment the cave seemed full of hooves, dust and fleece; then as the hubbub subsided I picked myself up, half-blind with dizziness and rage.

If there hadn't been cooler heads about than mine, it would for all of us have been the end of the road. For perhaps ten seconds rocks, sheep and apes gyrated like a kaleidoscope in front of my eyes; then they snapped back into focus; and this is what I saw. In the center of the circle McBride and the leader of the ape-men were crouched like Japanese wrestlers about six feet apart, glaring at one another with sustained ferocity. As I watched, half-fascinated, half-appalled, I realized that McBride was talking. "Throw me the torches. Quick."

Westerman, thank the Lord, was more on the ball than I was. He lobbed the torches over. And McBride, taking his eyes off his opponent for no more than a second, caught them. The ape-man didn't know what was going on. What he didn't understand, he feared. He let out a rumbling bellow of rage, and the muscles tensed in his legs.

"Look out!" I heard myself yell. "He's going to spring."

And in that second McBride switched on the torches. Both at once. Straight into the creature's eyes.

In the semidarkness of the cave the beams were certainly powerful; but they had, it seemed to me, an effect out of all proportion to their strength. The ape-man sprang back with a cry of pain. He flung up an arm, trying to shield his eyes from light which he obviously found blinding in its intensity.* McBride played it exactly right. With the torches at arm's length, he advanced relentlessly on the ape; too fast and he would have goaded the creature into a panic-stricken charge; too slow, and he would have given it the chance to recover its wits. But he made no mistake. He drove it back, snarling and bewildered, toward the mouth of the cave. The circle of onlookers, sensing their leader's fear, gave way also in a retreat that wasn't far from panic; and I wondered in a moment of quite unwarranted elation if we might not be able to walk clean out of the cave and escape. But in fact we had only one trump card: surprise; and once we had played it we had nothing but our wits to fall back on. Inevitably there came a time when the leader, weaving and ducking, managed to escape the questing beams of the torch. He screened himself behind a coterie of his guards. McBride didn't dare to follow. And we were in trouble.

At the mouth of the cave the ape-men stood their ground,

* Since troglodytes spend most of their lives in semidarkness, their eyes are peculiarly sensitive to strong light.

and I had a terrifying presentiment of what was likely to happen if we couldn't keep them on the run; they would recover their nerve, they would launch a counter-attack, and that would very definitely be that. My fears would, I am sure, have been realized if it hadn't been for Westerman.

The apes were, as I say, beginning to recover their composure, exhorted by their leader who, however, like the Duke of Plazatoro was now directing his army from the rear. Their clicking and miming were all too easy to interpret. They were reminding themselves that they had us outnumbered and outgunned; they had nothing, they were telling each other, to fear. One of them took a sudden swipe at McBride's torch, and came within a hairsbreadth of ripping away both torch and hand.

It was at this moment that Westerman ran forward, straight at the most belligerent of the apes. He was holding something—I couldn't see what—in his hands. As the creature, with a dreadful snarl, moved to meet him, Westerman flung a handful of blazing matches straight into its face. I had a momentary glimpse of green eyes, a warty leprous skin, huge teeth aslobber with saliva; then with a scream of pain, the ape turned tail. Another volley of matches. Another scream. And again the *Paranthropus* were on the run.

They backed away, snarling, their eyes aflame with hate and fear. Their retreat, however, was not so much a rout this time as a withdrawal. And the moment the last of them was clear of the cave, they seized and rolled back the stone—all but crushing Westerman who had rashly attempted to set foot outside. When we tried to peer through the cracks between stone and entrance, we were driven away by a well-directed volley of rocks. It was our turn to back away now, huddling together in a sheltered alcove beside our companions in misfortune, the sheep. It was several minutes before we had got back our breath, and several minutes more before we realized, with almost hysterical relief, that the *Paranthropus* were not about to launch another attack.

Thanks to McBride's wit and Westerman's courage, we had, in military parlance, won the battle. But it seemed impossible that we should win the war.

"God help us," I muttered, "if they come back."

"I'm afraid," Westerman said quietly, "it's not 'if' but 'when.'"

Silence. And the fear that was in us welling up like blood from a cut, until even McBride shifted uneasily. "At least," he said, "we're alive. Sufficient unto the day . . ."

The afternoon that followed was for all of us the most terrifying in our lives. At first, we were obsessed by an almost feverish compulsion to *do* something. We reexamined the cave; we studied the *Paranthropus*; we dreamed up the most fantastic schemes of escape. It was only gradually, as the hours dragged by, that reality began to sink home. We were prisoners; there was no way out; like those whose last appeal has been turned down, we could only wait.

Wind howled over the terraces. Flurries of snow blew in through the mouth of the cave. Light gave way to twilight. And in the gathering darkness the *Paranthropus* began to emerge from their caves. By the time the sun had disappeared under the rim of the Viedma there must have been over a hundred of them milling about on the terrace. We watched apprehensively. "Looks like they're building up the fires," Westerman observed.

McBride hadn't lost his thirst for knowledge. "It would be interesting to know," he boomed, "what material they are burning."

"It's not wood," Westerman told him. "It looks like a sort of charcoal. They're bringing it out of the caves."

"Sounds as if they're getting ready," I said, "for a barbecue."

The moment I'd spoken, I could have bitten my tongue off. Never had humour sounded so sick.

"I very much hope," Westerman said drily, "you are mistaken."

When the fires had built up to their satisfaction, a group

of the *Paranthropus* came striding purposefully toward the mouth of the cave. They rolled back the stone.

We had agreed that our only hope was to try and act as if we were unconcerned; then, if they looked as though they were going to manhandle us, to make a break for the mouth of the cave in the very forlorn hope that anyone who managed to reach the open might be able to outrun them. But we wouldn't have won any Oscars. Animals, it is said, can smell fear; and certainly the *Paranthropus* the moment they set foot in the cave sensed that we were petrified. They were watchful, it is true, as though uncertain what trick we might be up to next; but their mien was that of captors, their arrogance that of the strong. There were half a dozen of them, and they stood in a cluster at the mouth of the cave, swinging their great clubs, clicking away and pointing at us derisively. "The bloody things," I muttered, "are laughing at us."

Suddenly two of them sprang forward. I thought our last moment had come. But it was not, thank God, us they were after; it was the sheep. They separated one of the flock from its companions, and half-herded, half-dragged the unfortunate animal to the mouth of the cave. The moment they appeared with their victim, the concourse of apes on the terraces below set up an excited clicking, and a group of them ran forward and began to erect a sort of tripod over the largest of the fires.

The *Paranthropus* who appeared to be in charge of extricating the sheep beckoned us to come forward. When, not surprisingly, we hesitated, he sprang at us snarling, club upraised. We were in no position to argue.

I don't know what the others' thoughts were as we stood huddled together at the mouth of the cave, looking down at the bizarre scene on the terraces below. But I don't mind admitting that I was filled with a numb, disbelieving terror. This can't be happening, I told myself, in our day and age, and to me. Yet the flicker of flames was making me shield my eyes, the clicking of the apes was building up to a crescendo in my ears and every fiber in my being cried out that this was real. I think we all knew in our hearts what was going to happen next.

The luckless sheep was bludgeoned down the terraces in the direction of the fire, helped on by kicks and blows from our "cousins" the *Paranthropus*. A few yards short of the flames it came to a halt, exhausted, bewildered, terrified. The second it stopped moving, one of the *Paranthropus* leapt forward and struck it a great blow with his club, cracking its skull. The wretched creature must have died instantly; it fell as if pole-axed, and the ape-men spitted it with a hardwood lance and slung it over the fire.

This cheerful little scene had been acted out so far against a background of clicking from the apes. The clicking had been unnerving enough, but it was superseded now by another sound: a sound that brought out sweat on the palms of my hands, the hissing that had first greeted our arrival in the crater. Up to now the *Paranthropus* had been preoccupied with the sheep, but as soon as this excitement was over they transferred their attention to us. More and more of them turned to stare at us, posturing angrily, jumping up and down, miming (all too explicitly) the fate that they had in store for us. The fate of the sheep.

McBride caught his breath. Corbella reached for his crucifix. Even the imperturbable Westerman turned pale.

The cacophony of hissing swelled to a climax, then faded gradually to silence as the leader of the ape-men clambered onto an outcrop of rock on the terrace immediately below us.

It wasn't hard to get the gist of what he was saying. Their old enemies, he told his people, had dared to set foot in their stronghold, but they had been captured, they were powerless, and now they were going to die. Green eyes, cold and malevolent, stared at us out of the dark. Here and there an ape-man's face, etched in firelight, was thrown into fragmentary relief. Every expression was the same. No Klansman ever looked with such primordial hate at a Negro, nor

Arab at Jew; for the petty antagonisms of colour or creed are nothing compared to the bitterness of a blood feud that has lasted half a million years. The ape-man pointed first to us, then to the entrance from which we had been dragged. We would, he was telling his people, be flung into the cave; here we would remain like the sheep until such time as our captors chose to pluck us one by one, to drag us down the terraces, to club us to death, and to hang our bodies over the beds of red-hot charcoal.

No monarch ever promulgated a more popular decree. The apes went wild with delight: leaping, posturing, hissing, hugging each other like a soccer team who have scored in the last second of extra time. They pointed to us in derision: miming our fall down the terraces, cowering under the thud of imaginary blows, twitching their limbs to the lick of imaginary flames. Then one of them picked up and flung a stone.

It was an ill-directed throw, but it sparked off a veritable hail of missiles, several of which whistled by uncomfortably close. McBride stepped to the edge of the terrace, hands upraised. With his tangled beard and wild eyes, he reminded me of some Old Testament prophet about to invoke Jehovah's wrath on the children of disobedience.

"Stop!"

He was a commanding figure, and his voice, vibrant with authority, echoed and reechoed round the bowl of the Viedma. But he was chaff in a storm. Indeed the sight of him seemed to incense the apes to a new pitch of fury. A wave of hissing welled up from the terraces. The hail of rocks became a veritable blizzard. I was struck on shoulder and thigh; beside me Westerman was doubled up clutching his stomach, and a great boulder flashed by within inches of McBride's face—if he hadn't jerked back his head he would certainly have been killed. We fled.

Our retreat was greeted with jeers and hisses from the crowd and with kicks and blows from the guards. We were booted unceremoniously into the cave; the stone was rolled back; and in darkness and silence that were never more welcome we collapsed on the floor, bruised, dazed and sick with fear, but—for the time being—alive.

For several minutes we lay quite still, breathing heavily, like animals licking their wounds. Then gradually, as the effects of shock wore off, we began to appraise the situation. None of us was badly hurt; but this, it seemed to me, was the one ray of comfort in an outlook that was otherwise completely without hope. We huddled together in an abject cluster at the back of the cave. They say that necessity is the mother of invention and that danger sharpens wit; but we could think of nothing, absolutely nothing, that seemed to offer us the slightest hope of survival.

Corbella had a haven to run to. "Only God," he said quietly, "can save us. We must trust in Him."

"God helps those," Westerman said sharply, "who help themselves. There must be *something* we can do. Think."

We thought. We looked at the great stone blocking the entrance. We looked at the sheep. We looked at the shaft of light—moonlight now—seeping in from high above our heads. We made yet another survey of the cave. But at the end of it all it seemed more certain than ever that we were going to die, and in a way that didn't bear thinking of.

You might have thought that sleep for men in a position such as ours would have been out of the question. But exhaustion proved itself that night more potent even than fear, and one by one, as the moon rose over the Viedma, we dozed off.

My last conscious thought was of Christina. If she had been surprised by the apes, say, soon after 3 A.M., why, I asked myself, hadn't they rushed us until after 6 A.M.? What in God's name had they been doing in those three hours? My thoughts were too horrifying to be endured, and my mind went blank. But I couldn't stop myself dreaming. And in my dreams a monstrous russet-haired King Kong was leaping from rock to rock, a girl in his arms. I felt sure it was Christina, till I saw that her hair was not dark but a corn-coloured gold and her eyes not brown but green as the sea. "Alison!" I whispered. It was, I think, the grinding together of my teeth that woke me.

The *Paranthropus* left us alone that night, except for one terrifying incident. It must, I think, have been a little after 1 A.M. that the stone was rolled back and a group of them appeared at the entrance. They were carrying torches—flaming branches of *nothofagus*—which bathed the cave in a weird, red, flickering glow. They jumped up and down, pointing at us in derision, revelling in our helplessness; then they tossed something into our corner of the cave. I couldn't to start with make out what it was, though I heard McBride swear softly under his breath. Then, as one of the branches flared up, I saw in a little pool of light what the *Paranthropus* had thrown in: the bones of our erstwhile companion in misfortune, the sheep.

It was quite a time after this before any of us slept.

The more I thought about our position the more hopeless it seemed. For we were beyond all human aid: cut off from hope as surely as astronauts who have spun out of orbit. Between the boulder and the mouth of the cave I could see a little fragment of sky. It was clear of cloud for once, and dotted with stars. Death, I told myself, came to all men in the end. But our end was now. And the stars looked cold, uncaring and very far away.

11

Escape

I thought that I must be dreaming: dreaming I lay trussed up on a beach, and that a toy ship was standing offshore and firing broadside at me. The shells were landing close-by, kicking up little fountains of sand. I was telling myself it was all very strange, when something hit me flush in the face. I sat up with a frightened grunt.

It was dark. The pocket-handkerchief of sky was a featureless grey, and what little light there was came from a fire on the terrace outside. The flames flickered and flared, throwing patterns of red light onto the walls. I was about to turn over and try to get back to sleep when another fountain of sand spurted up alongside me. I looked down and saw a fragment of rock.

Someone was tossing stones into the cave.

I got to my feet and tiptoed to the entrance. There was no one in sight; no one, that is, except for a pair of the *Paranthropus* on guard beside the fire. I looked at the shaft in the roof. In the small hours of the morning not much light was filtering through, but it looked as though a hand—a disembodied hand—was waving to and fro.

"Chris?" I whispered incredulously.

The hand disappeared. There was an agonizing pause, during which I wondered if I had imagined the whole thing.

Then a screwed-up ball of paper landed noiselessly in the sand at my feet. I unwrapped it, held it to the light and in a flood of amazement and relief recognized her handwriting.

"QUIET! APES VERY CLOSE. WILL LOWER ROPE."

My tramping about the cave had woken Westerman, and together we peered at the shaft. For a long time nothing happened. Then we saw the rope: the lifeline which, at the eleventh hour, looked as though it might be going to save our lives. It came coiling down. It landed with a little thud on the floor. I gave it a tug. And Christina stopped paying it out.

We woke the others. They thought at first we must be delirious or dreaming; they couldn't believe Christina had managed to survive. Then they saw the rope. "I told you," Corbella whispered, "to trust in God."

"It's not God on the other end of that rope," Westerman hissed at him. "It's Christina. So don't expect more miracles!"

Another screw of paper came fluttering down. "QUIET! APES RESTIVE. ROPE SECURE."

We went into a huddle at the back of the cave. It was Westerman who took charge. "McBride, watch the entrance. Corbella, see nothing's left behind. Peter, up you go. Quickly, while I steady the rope."

It was no time to argue as to who went first. I gave our lifeline an experimental tug. It *seemed* secure. So I began to haul myself up, hand over fist. I soon found, however, that the ascent was more difficult than I had expected—what with shock and lack of sleep and lack of food none of us was at peak fitness; also the rope was thin and I could get little purchase on it with my feet. By the time I was halfway up my arms were aching, and long before I got to the top I was wet with sweat and puffing for breath like a grampus.

The opening in the roof looked a comfortable size to squeeze through. As I neared it I saw Christina peering down, and no vision from heaven was ever more welcome! She put a finger to her lips, and I did what I could to restrain my puffing and panting. At last I was level with her, swinging clear of the rope and scrambling onto a ledge of rock. We half-stumbled, half-fell into each other's arms. "Chris"—I could feel the beat of her heart as I held her close to me—"you all right?"

She nodded.

"What happened?"

"Later. The apes are too near."

"But you're O.K.?"

She nodded again. And it was as though a great weight which had been dragging me underwater was suddenly released. Hope and the will to live came flooding back, and I began to take stock of our surroundings. We were not, to my disappointment, in the open but in another cave: a bigger and better cave, however, and one which ended not in a blank wall but a well-worn passageway. "Where are the apes?" I whispered.

She pointed to the mouth of the cave.

We couldn't from where we were crouching see the entrance, for the cave was dog-legged. I tiptoed to the bend, peered round it and nearly let out a yell of fright. Not a dozen feet from where I was crouching a family of *Paranthropus* were sprawled out on the rocks. There were five of them, and even as I watched, one of the children scratched itself and rolled over, half-awake, half-asleep. Considerably shaken, I backed away. We were, it seemed, far from out of the woods.

McBride was halfway up by the time I got back, and making heavy weather of the ascent. I saw Christina lean over anxiously, her hand to her mouth. But at last he was squeezing through the shaft, puffing and panting and making as much noise, it seemed to me, as a traction engine. He took Christina into his arms. His eyes, rather to my surprise, were full of tears. "Thank God, my dear, you're alive."

"Quiet!" I hissed. "There's a crowd of bloody great apes round the corner."

He nodded, his face pale and strained. After he had recovered his breath, he motioned me closer. "Corbella," he whispered. "We'll have to haul him up."

The Chilean, I remembered, had his arm in a sling; and I now realized why Westerman had insisted that McBride and I were first to make the ascent: it would take our combined strength to haul in 170 pounds of deadweight mountaineer.

We explained the situation to Christina. She looked anxious. "You're bound to make a noise."

"A bit."

She patted the Parker-Hale. "Then I'll keep an eye on the apes."

I can't say that I cared for the prospect of her facing a pack of charging *Paranthropus*, but she obviously lacked the strength to be as effective as McBride or I on the rope. "Don't fire," I whispered, "unless you have to."

We waited until she was in position, then payed out the last few feet of rope so that Corbella could tie himself on. Peering down through the shaft, we could see him and Westerman moving about, now silhouetted in the glow of the fire, now fading into the surrounding gloom. They seemed to be taking a very long time over securing the rope. Eventually, however, we felt a tug, the signal to start hauling in.

He seemed more like 170 tons than 170 pounds; and once again it was McBride's strength that saved the day. He hauled Corbella up, hand over fist, like a fisherman his lobster pots. Only the knotted muscles in his arms and legs and the beads of sweat on his forehead gave a hint of how much the effort cost him. And after a couple of minutes' heaving and straining, the Chilean was swinging up through the shaft.

He came awkwardly, spinning round and round like a payed-out fish. I was terrified he was going to cannon into the side of the shaft and dislodge a fall of loose rock, of which there was a good deal lying about; so the moment he was level with us, I seized him round the waist and swung him unceremoniously onto the ledge. It can't have been much fun for him with a broken collarbone, but he had the guts not to cry out. "Quiet, Eduardo," I whispered. "The apes are just outside."

He nodded. I untied the rope, and he stepped carefully clear of the shaft.

Carefully, but not carefully enough. For at the last moment his foot caught in a coil of the rope and, shaking it free, he dislodged a small rock, an innocuous-looking fragment of basalt no larger than a tennis ball. The rock rolled toward the shaft. I thought it was going to lose momentum before it got there, but at the last moment it gathered pace; it collected one or two fragments of debris in its wake and disappeared over the edge.

I would never have thought so small a fall would have made so fiendish a din. The shaft, I suppose, must have acted as an amplifier, for a clattering boom echoed throughout the cave. The noise sounded loud enough to wake the dead, let alone the *Paranthropus*.

"Quick," I hissed. "Down with the rope."

As McBride payed it out, I peered anxiously through the shaft.

I couldn't see Westerman at first, but after a moment I spotted his silhouette, outlined in firelight on one of the walls. There was something about the way he was crouched that I didn't care for. I craned forward, peering farther into the cave, and saw to my horror, stalking in through the entrance, one of the *Paranthropus* who had been acting as guard, club upraised.

"The rope!" I screamed. "Grab the rope!"

Westerman jerked up his head. A pause while he weighed the odds. Then his silhouette seemed to launch itself into space; there was a violent tug on the rope, and McBride was hauling him in.

As I leaned over the cavity the whole terrifying scene swung into focus: Westerman swarming hand over fist up the rope, and below him the *Paranthropus,* snarling with rage, about to take a swipe at him with its club. I shut my eyes. But the sickening crunch that seemed inevitable didn't come. For Westerman managed to jack-knife aside so the club whistled by within inches of his stomach. And when I looked again, he was several feet higher and the *Paranthropus* was about to take a second swipe at him, this time at his legs. Again he escaped by inches—McBride at the last moment giving a desperate heave on the rope, so that he shot suddenly upward. Then the two of us were hauling him out of reach, and the *Paranthropus* was bellowing and slobbering with rage, and from the terraces there started up an excited clicking, muted at first but quickly swelling to an angry crescendo: the alarm.

The rifle cracked. In the confined space the noise was deafening, and another avalanche of rock cascaded down through the shaft. "Quick!" Christina's voice reflecting the panic that was welling up in me. "They've seen us."

We made a dash for the mouth of the cave. But at the bend Christina stopped us. "It's no use," she gasped. "They're outside. Dozens of them."

There wasn't a *Paranthropus* in sight—they evidently knew about rifles—but their excited clicking and the nauseating stench of them came to us, clear and unmistakable, on the night wind. We were trapped.

"That passage." Westerman pointed to the back of the cave. "Where does it go?"

"There's a whole maze of passages—they go on for miles." Christina fired again as a hand appeared briefly round the entrance.

"It's not a dead end?"

She shook her head.

I guessed what Westerman was thinking: that we'd stand more chance in the open than hemmed-in in a cul-de-sac. For a moment the five of us stood irresolute. Then he pointed to the passage. "Quietly. Don't let 'em know we've gone."

We backed away from the entrance. We tiptoed past the shaft. We walked quietly through the cave. Not until we were round a bend in the passageway did we break into a stumbling run. I worked my way next to Christina. "What happened to you?" I whispered. "In the tent?"

"No talking." Westerman's voice was sharp.

We jogged on in silence. The light waned. Soon we were feeling our way forward in absolute darkness.

After about a hundred yards we came to a V-shaped intersection. We looked at Christina. "That way," she whispered. "I think. It goes round in a loop, and comes out at the end of the terraces." We plodded on: Westerman leading, Christina still carrying the rifle next, then myself, then Corbella, and McBride bringing up the rear.

The passage was like the one we had followed from the underground river. Originally the bed of a stream, it seemed to have been enlarged by the *Paranthropus*, and was now seven or eight feet high and about the same width. The air, we noticed, was fresh, which made us think the passage had more than one exit; it was also warm, which we took as an indication that we couldn't be far from the fumarole. After a while we came to another intersection, a veritable crossroads, and one that Christina didn't recognize.

We stood in an uncertain circle, peering this way and that. Christina had to admit she was lost. But Corbella, luckily for us, had been taking bearings with the compass. He pointed to the right-hand passage. "I reckon," he whispered, "that's the way out."

Now the right-hand passage looked very much like the others: a dimly seen tunnel, lit here and there by glowworms, and streaked with occasional veins of whitish rock. I can't say what it was that I didn't fancy about it, but the thought of entering it filled me with a sudden unreasoning terror. "No," I whispered. "Not down there."

The others looked at me in astonishment. I was trying to explain how I felt when Westerman raised his hand. "Listen."

In the stillness under the earth every sound was magnified. I could hear the breathing of my companions; I could hear the thud of my heart; I could hear, from far away, the trickle of water. And after a while I could hear something else: the distant tread of feet. Coming nearer.

Westerman pressed his ear to the floor. Christina unslung the Parker-Hale. I looked for somewhere to run to.

We were at the intersection of five passages. It would be fatal, it seemed to me, to retrace our steps; the *Paranthropus* seemed to be advancing down the right-hand passage, which left us three to choose from. There was no time for reconnaissance: we could only take our pick and trust to luck. After a moment's hesitation Westerman pointed to the central passage, and we tiptoed into it silently, in single file. There seemed no reason why it shouldn't, like the others, go on for miles. But rounding the very first bend, we were brought up short by a solid wall of rock.

There was no way out. We were trapped in a cul-de-sac.

My first instinct was to rush blindly into one of the other passages. Then I realized, from the pad of feet, that the *Paranthropus* were too near. There was only one thing we could do. We flattened ourselves against the walls of the cave, hardly daring to breathe, hoping against hope that the apes wouldn't bother to look into what they probably knew was a dead end. We could hear their muted clicking now as they came jogging along, doubtless with the amiable intention of taking us in the rear. At the intersection they paused. It was the most agonizing moment of our lives. For we knew very well that if one of them looked into the cul-de-sac, we wouldn't stand a chance. The rifle might account for two or three. But our end would be inevitable, bloody and, we could only hope, brief.

There was a good deal of what I can only describe as whispered clicking, during which the pounding of my heart seemed so loud that I felt sure the *Paranthropus* would hear it. Then, to our indescribable relief, they moved on: one party, to judge by the sound of their feet, following the passage we had just emerged from, the other the passage to our left.

Limp with fear, we unpeeled ourselves from the walls of the cave. I reached for Christina's hand. It was cold as ice. I gave her fingers a reassuring squeeze, but there was no return pressure. She was in a state of shock. She was neither crying, trembling nor hysterical; she had simply withdrawn into a world of her own where nothing could frighten or hurt her anymore. "It's all right," I whispered, "they've gone." But she didn't understand. And I wondered again what could have happened to her in the twenty-four hours since we had been captured.

"Stay with her," Westerman said quietly. "I'll see if the coast's clear."

While McBride covered him with the rifle, he inched cautiously out of the cave and into the open space where the passages met. He took a good look around. Then he walked a little way down each of the passages in turn, with a view, I suppose, to triggering off any ambush that might have been set. I watched him with a sort of agonized fascination, half-expecting any moment to see him snatched up by a pair of great hairy hands. But all that happened was that the glow-worms put out their lights at his approach; and it wasn't long before he was back, smiling his imperturbable smile. "All clear."

We decided to follow the passage the apes had come down—presumably if we kept to it long enough it would lead to the open. To start with Christina wouldn't let go of my hand; she followed me like an automaton, clumsily, tripping and stumbling over protuberances in the sand; and it was only very gradually that her coordination improved, and a suspicion of warmth returned to her fingers. I smiled at her. "All right now?"

She drew a shuddering breath and clutched my hand so tight that I winced. We stumbled on, through a labyrinth of apparently never-ending corridors of rock, until after about a quarter of an hour, rounding a bend, we saw in the distance a semicircle of white: like a sixpence cut in half. It was some moments before we realized that what we were looking at was the morning sky.

The underground passages were claustrophobic, and the prospect of getting out of them gave a much-needed boost to our morale. We had enough sense, however, not to charge blindly into the open. "Without doubt," McBride boomed in a sonorous attempt at a whisper, "the *Paranthropus* are imbued with a degree of cunning. We cannot exclude the possibility of a trap."

We agreed that one of us should make a reconnaissance while the others hung back and provided covering fire in the best military tradition. "I'll go," I said without enthusiasm.

After a good deal of whispered discussion, we decided to draw lots for the time-honoured shortened match. Since I had volunteered, I shouldn't, I suppose, have felt aggrieved when I picked the broken matchstick. I shouldn't have, but I did. Christina too obviously felt that fate had dealt us a shabby trick, for she wouldn't let go of my hand. She battened onto me like the proverbial clinging vine, and I was beginning to think I'd have to drag her along too when Corbella said something sharply in Spanish. She blinked, and dropped my hand like a hot potato.

"Teach me Spanish sometime," I said. Then I was inching my way along the wall toward the semicircle of light.

The passage for its last twenty or thirty yards ran straight. There was no cover. But I took heart from the fact that I was in shadow, whereas anyone guarding the entrance would be silhouetted against the light. And how strong the light was; after twenty-four hours' incarceration in the underground caves it seemed almost blinding in its intensity; and a few yards short of the entrance I paused to give my eyes the chance to adjust.

It was a pause that saved our lives.

For as I stood looking out through the opening, the light seemed to grow brighter still, and I suddenly realized what was happening. The Viedma, as usual, was wreathed in mist-cum-cloud, but behind the cloud the sun was rising, and its rays were now streaming over the rim of the crater, bathing the amphitheater in a white ethereal light, the sort of light that makes shadows stand out clearly. And what a strange lot of shadows there were: monstrous-looking silhouettes etched darkly against the snow. I stared at them first in bewilderment, then in fear. It couldn't, I told myself, be true. But when one of the shadows moved, there was no mistaking the heavy body, the bandy legs and the backward-sloping skull. Crouched up against the wall of the terrace, on either side of the opening, the *Paranthropus* were lying in wait. Even as I stared at them in impotent despair, the cloud thickened, the light grew pale and their shadows merged into the snow. If it hadn't been for the ephemeral brightness of the sunrise, we would have blundered straight into a trap. I crept back to my companions.

When they heard the news, McBride swore softly and Christina reached for my hand; Westerman, however, was strictly practical. "Did you see how many there were?"

"A good half-dozen on either side."

"Too many to try and break out?"

I nodded.

"Then we'd better get back. Fast. Or we'll be trapped."

He was right. In our hearts we all knew it. Yet the thought of retreating once again into the labyrinth of passages filled us with dismay. "I suppose," McBride muttered, "there's no alternative?"

Well, if there was we couldn't think of it. For a moment we gazed longingly at the semicircle of daylight—tantalizing as a vista of freedom seen through bars—then we were plodding back the way we had come. The passages seemed darker now, the floor bumpier, the ceiling lower. Every couple of hundred yards we stopped and listened, half-expecting to hear the pad of advancing feet, but the only sound to break the silence was a very faint murmur of water, so far away as to be almost indiscernible. Eventually we found ourselves at the familiar intersection: five passages radiating out from a central hub. "At least," I muttered, "we know which *not* to try."

"In my opinion," McBride whispered, "we should investigate the left-hand passage. The one the *Paranthropus* didn't go into."

"Perhaps," I said, "they didn't go into it because they knew it was a dead end."

We eyed the five openings without enthusiasm. After a good deal of whispering we agreed to McBride's suggestion— I think we all felt that anything would be preferable to coming face to face with the apes; so we set off in single file, heading still more deeply into the core of the Viedma.

I quite expected the passage to end any moment in a cul-de-sac. But it didn't; it wound on and on; there were even one or two intersections where smaller corridors branched off it. After a while I became conscious of two things that I didn't care for: the passage seemed to be sloping slightly but continuously downward, and the air seemed to be getting steadily hotter. I told myself I was imagining things; but when we next came to a halt I noticed that Westerman had to wipe the sweat out of his eyes, while McBride collapsed puffing and panting on an outcrop of basalt. "Phew! It's like a damned Turkish bath."

I tried to talk to Christina, but she was at the end of her tether; she wanted only to drop off to sleep; her head kept lolling limp as a rag doll's against my shoulder.

Corbella, meanwhile, was poking about at the wall of the passage. Carefully screening the torch, he examined the rock with a professional eye. "Lava," was his verdict. "And only recently cooled."

We were peering at the rough grey rock when Westerman raised his hand. "Listen!"

In the deathlike silence I expected to hear once again the tread of the *Paranthropus*. But it was a very different sound that came to us faintly out of the gloom: a curious plop-plop-plop, like soup bubbling in a cauldron. "It's coming from there." I pointed to a bend in the passage a little way ahead.

There was no future in going back; we could hardly stay where we were; we had, therefore, no alternative but to investigate.

As we edged cautiously round the bend, the smell of sulphur hit us like an almost physical blow. "Light," Westerman muttered. Corbella flicked on the torch, and there at our feet lay a pool of boiling mud, thick as porridge, erupting in little gaseous bubbles. We stared at it in silence, shading our eyes against the heat.

It was obvious now why the *Paranthropus* hadn't come into the left-hand passage. And a nasty suspicion that had been lurking for some time at the back of my mind was confirmed. We hadn't escaped at all. We had underestimated the cunning of the ape-men. They were outwitting us: maneuvering us into a more and more helpless position, driving us closer and ever closer to the fumarole of the volcano.

The pool of mud simmered gently, wreathed in steam and acrid with the stench of sulphur. There was sulphur everywhere, ingrained in the walls, crystallizing in cascades of gold on the rocks and drifting in particles in the air; it left a bitter taste in our mouths, and reminded us that we were thirsty as well as lost and had no water. There was no way round the pool; it halted our advance as effectively as a wall of rock; we could only hope that the intersections we had passed farther back were not sealed off in the same way. We retreated, and sat down on the floor of the passage to consider what to do next.

"We'll get nowhere," Westerman said, "dashing this way and that like a lot of frightened mice. We must have a plan. Eduardo, you've been plotting our course?"

"Roughly. We've been heading east: straight into the mountain. To get back to the crater we want to head west."

"And another thing we want," McBride muttered, "is water."

"We heard it once," I reminded him.

We tried to remember where we'd been standing when we had heard the underground river, and from which direction the sound of it had come. Christina took no part in the conversation. She seemed to have retreated once again into a world of her own; it was only when I looked at her closely in the light of the torch that I realized she was in the last stages of physical exhaustion, almost literally asleep on her feet. "If we found water," I said, "we could lie up somewhere, until they call the search off."

The idea had no supporters. "The longer we're cooped up in these damned caves," Westerman said, "the weaker we'll get."

The words were barely out of his mouth when a catastrophic roar, like a collapsing house, reverberated from the passage behind us. Dust rained down from the roof, there was a frenzied bubbling from the pool and the ground on which we were standing trembled and shook. The noise went on for perhaps ten seconds, then faded to the rumble of an occasional boulder rolling down in the wake of what had obviously been a cataclysmic fall of rock.

The torch had gone out, and for a moment we stood huddled together, shocked and frightened. Then with one accord we began to run: back the way we had come. In the silence, the pant of our breath and the thud of our feet sounded unnaturally loud—in one place, I remember, our footfalls had a curious echoing ring, as though we were running over the roof of a cave. I think we all had a premonition of what we were going to find: the passage blocked, and the five of us on the wrong side of it, walled up beyond hope of rescue in the darkness under the earth. And sure enough, after about a hundred yards the air became thick with dust, and as we rounded a bend, our worst fears were realized: we were brought up short by the sort of landslide that bulldozers and dynamite would have been hard put to shift. It looked as though thousands of tons of rock had caved in, obliterating all trace of what had once been a passage.

Corbella by this time had got the torch working, and as its beam moved slowly over the debris, our hearts sank. There was no possible way through. We were buried alive.

I don't know how the others felt, but I'd had about as much as I could take; I sat down on the floor, my head in my hands, like a punch-drunk boxer who has been floored so often he has no intention of coming up for more. Beside me McBride was swearing softly in Gaelic, Corbella was toying with his crucifix and even the stoic Westerman was at a loss for words of comfort. Death from thirst and suffocation, sealed up in a living tomb, was a prospect that drained us of manhood as a pricked balloon is drained of air.

12

Out of the Frying Pan

It was Westerman who snapped out of it first. "Eduardo, shine the torch up and down the wall, section by section. I'll climb to the top and see if there's any loose rock. The rest of you strike matches along either side of the wall; see if there's air coming through."

We set to work with feverish energy, soon dampened down in my case when I cracked my head on an overhanging slab of rock. After this I proceeded at a more leisurely pace, working systematically along the walls of the passage until I was down to my last couple of matches. I found not the slightest suspicion of crevice or crack. The rock was solid as a watertight door. The others had no better fortune. And after a while, exhausted and utterly depressed, we gave up and squatted in a forlorn little huddle at the foot of the landslide. Christina dropped off to sleep. I envied her; the sleeping cannot think.

After a while Westerman asked what the time was, and Corbella switched on the torch. "A few minutes after nine."

The sun, I thought, would be full on the Hielo Continental now, transforming the peaks to citadels of rose and gold. In St. Andrews street lamps would be shining like daubs of butter through the mist. But sunrise and street lamps, for all the chance I had of seeing them again, might have been in another world.

"We'd better," Westerman said at last, "have something to eat."

McBride's voice was fatalistic. "I question the necessity."

"While there's life," Westerman said, "there's hope."

Accordingly we ate the last of our cubes of concentrated meat and sucked a couple of Horlicks: a meager enough meal, but one that at least did something to alleviate our thirst. After a while I was struck by an encouraging thought. "Have you chaps noticed the air?"

The others looked at me inquiringly.

"Near the pool," I said, "it was thick with sulphur. After the landslide it was thick with dust. Now"—I sniffed—"it's clear."

"You're right." Westerman's voice had a suppressed excitement. "If we were sealed in, the air would be getting worse, not better."

It was wonderful how even the smallest spark of hope lifted our morale. In a moment we were back on hands and knees, feeling for even the faintest suspicion of a draft. We found nothing; but after a while Corbella had a brain wave. "Remember where the passage rang hollow. Perhaps the rock has shifted, and there's air coming up from below."

We hurried back. Since we weren't sure exactly where the weak spot was, we halted every twelve or fifteen yards and stamped our feet. And eventually, after about the fourth bout of stamping, the floor not only rang hollow but positively shook. "Steady," Corbella muttered, "or we'll have the whole lot down."

We shone the torch this way and that. At first the rock looked depressingly intact, but after a few minutes' poking and prying Westerman discovered a narrow crack at the junction of wall and floor. We crowded round it, like starving men who have unearthed a bone.

"Looks promising!" McBride indulged in a series of elephantine hops. The ground trembled, and from not far under our feet came the rumble of loosened rock.

"Stop that!" Corbella, as a geologist, was more alive to

danger than the rest of us. "If we start a fall, God knows where it'll stop. We might even trigger off the volcano."

Considerably chastened, we drew back while he cast a professional eye over what appeared to be an embryo fault— a split where two types of rocks (schist and basalt in this case) joined in a diagonal traverse that ran from ceiling to floor. He spent a long time examining not only the crack but also the surrounding rock structure. He tapped the floor, broke off and tasted the schist, peered through the cavity and lit a couple of matches to test the oxygen content of the air. "I *think*," he said at last, "there's a cave not far below us. I *think* we could break through. The trouble is we're likely to start off a fall we can't control."

"Could we shore the passage up?" I suggested. "With rock from the landslide?"

"Too big a job."

"Could we shore the opening up?" This was Westerman.

"We could try. But there'd still be a chance the whole lot would collapse on top of us."

"We've no chance at all," I said, "if we don't do something."

We decided to try and break through. At the back of our minds, I am sure, was the thought that if we had to die, a quick death would be preferable to a slow one.

It was Corbella who took charge. "Fergus, would you and Peter go to the slide. Bring back two or three blocks of basalt. As heavy as you can manage, and as square. Eric, you and I'll have a look at the fault." He shone his torch on Christina. She was asleep again, crumpled limply against the wall of the passage. "I suppose she's O.K."

We bent over her. Her eyes were closed, and her face in the light of the torch looked pallid as wax, but her breathing seemed more or less normal. I took her pulse. It was faint but regular: a steady 70. "I reckon she's simply payed out," I said. "God knows what happened to her while we were in the cave."

McBride hadn't many clothes to spare, but he took off the

pullover we had lent him, rolled it into a ball and eased it under her head. She didn't wake but clutched the pullover like a child its doll and curled up with it in her arms. "Don't wake her," Westerman said, "till we have to."

When McBride and I arrived at the landslide he selected the most enormous boulder. I can't say that I fancied our chances of shifting it, but I hadn't allowed for his strength; and after about ten minutes of heaving and straining, we managed to lug it back. When we dropped it—rather more heavily than we meant to—the floor of the passage trembled. We collected four blocks in all, none of them, I am glad to say, quite as heavy as the first, but all weighing over three hundred pounds. Westerman and Corbella, in the meanwhile, had loosened about eighteen inches of rock immediately under the crack: had loosened it, but had not yet knocked it away. Corbella explained his plan. "The moment we knock out the rock, you two Tarzans push in your block of basalt. We'll try and jam a holding wedge on either side, like a doorpost. Then excavate in between."

He showed us just where to push the basalt. He chose a block that looked the right size. He told us—though this in our hearts we already knew—that if we didn't get it in fast enough and the wall collapsed, we would almost certainly be crushed to death. "I'll wake Christina," he said.

"Why not let her sleep?"

He shook his head. "She'd want to know."

It seemed cruel to me, but the others didn't seem inclined to interfere. For several minutes the two of them muttered away in Spanish, and Christina's fingers closed round her crucifix—though it seemed to me that she was too exhausted to take in what was happening. Then McBride and I moved into position, and Westerman and Corbella began, very carefully, to knock out the loosened rock.

It gave way easily, falling with a rumbling thud into the cavity below. The second the gap was wide enough, we began to ease in our block of basalt. And it was as well we did. For from above our heads came a sudden crack, and the whole great mass of the schist began to slide down. I snatched my hand out of the opening a split second before the schist crashed into our wedge. It's bound, I thought, to give way. I looked in terror at the rift above our heads: widening, widening, then quite suddenly widening no more; still, except for the haze of dust drifting down like drizzle out of a windless sky.

"It's holding," Westerman whispered.

Corbella nodded. "Push the loose rock through. Gently."

Half an eye on the unstable schist above us, half an eye on the growing cavity below, we broke the rock away and lowered it into the darkness. To judge by the time gap between our dislodging the rock and its landing, the floor of the cave was no more than ten or twelve feet below us. We worked slowly, breaking away only a fragment at a time, for fear of triggering off another slide. When the hole was wide enough, we inserted a second block of basalt: a double-insurance, in case the first gave way; and from this moment we made faster progress. At the end of an hour we had excavated a hole large enough for even the bulky McBride to squeeze through.

We shone our torch into the cavity, spotlighting the walls of what appeared to be another cave. The air coming out of it was fresh, so there must, I told myself, be an exit.

"Listen!" Westerman cupped a hand to his ear.

At first we could hear nothing. Then it came to us faintly, like the voice of an old friend: the murmur once again of the underground river.

"I'll go first," Westerman whispered.

He could, I think, have leapt down easily enough; but there was a good deal of loose rock on the floor of the cave, and the last thing we wanted was a twisted ankle. So we lowered him by rope, together with the torch and rifle.

The floor turned out to be only about a dozen feet below us; and after Westerman had taken a quick look round, he cleared a landing space and told the rest of us to jump. I was a bit anxious about Christina and Corbella, but both made the drop safely. I was last out, and though we had no means of knowing what lay ahead, I have never been so thankful to get out of a place in my life—I would rather, I think, be toasted alive by prehistoric apes than left to die walled up in a living tomb in the darkness under the earth.

As soon as we were down, Westerman led us to an alcove at the side of the cave. He spoke in a whisper, urgently. "We've underestimated the apes"—beside me I could see McBride nodding in agreement. "Twice we've escaped them by the skin of our teeth. We won't be so lucky again. Now I reckon it was the apes who started the landslide"—more nodding from McBride. "With luck they'll think we are walled up. So our first priority is to *stay hidden.* No noise, no light and no talking unless we have to. O.K.?"

We nodded.

"Now we've quite a few things in our favour. The rifle, the fact the apes think we're dead and the fact they don't seem able to track us—obviously they've a poor sense of smell."

"The musculature of the *Paranthropus'* nose—" McBride began.

But Westerman cut him short. "Save it for your seminars, Fergus. . . . Now I reckon we've had about as much as we can take. So I vote we head for the river. This was your idea, Peter, I know, and I've come round to it. With water and the food that's left in our packs, we'd be able to rest: to lie up for days if we wanted to."

It was, I think, the prospect of being able to lie up that decided us. For seldom could men have needed rest more urgently. Both physically and mentally we were at the end of our tether—indeed I believe that if the *Paranthropus* had, at that moment, come charging into the cave, I for one would have lain down with sheer exhaustion while they clubbed me to death. We therefore agreed to head even more deeply into the Viedma: to make for the underground river, whose murmur came to us faintly out of the dark. McBride pointed down the cave. "It sounds almost dead ahead."

[152]

Westerman nodded. "Ahead and below."

The cave tapered off into a passage; and the passage, to start with, seemed to lead in the right direction. We groped into it in single file.

Events which one would expect to remember clearly have a habit at times of staying blurred. Such was the case with our adventures during the next few hours. I have a vague recollection of trudging through endless passageways, often so much alike that I was convinced we were going round in circles; of the atmosphere becoming unpleasantly hot, with coils of steam writhing white through vents in the floor; of my feet aching, my head aching and my whole body becoming more and more debilitated, as though I were in the grip of some creeping dystrophy; of the sound of the river becoming louder, receding like a will-o'-the-wisp, then growing louder still, until at last late in the evening, peering down through a chimney, we saw it: a mud-coloured, fast-flowing torrent boring its way, some twenty feet below us, through a channel cut deep in the rock.

For the last hour we had been plodding forward in morose silence, but the sight of water unleashed a spate of whispering. "Let's hope it's fit to drink"—this was McBride. "Hang onto Chris. We don't want her falling in"—this was Corbella. I helped her down the chimney and onto the narrow terrace that bordered the river. She was like a sleepwalker, her movements coordinated by instinct rather than brain. I hung onto her while we leaned over and scooped up the water. It was faintly tepid, faintly bitter too, with the taste of sulphur. But drinkable. We drank and drank and splashed our faces and drank again and felt a little more human.

The river flowed fast as a millrace, and we couldn't touch bottom; it was not, however, especially wide—there were several places where, even in our weakened condition, we could jump it—and on the far side was a natural gallery honeycombed with caves. The rest of us, I think, would have made for the nearest hole, stumbled into it and fallen asleep. Westerman, however, insisted that we choose our hiding place with care. "We want a cave," he whispered, "that's warm, dry and near the water, *and* has only one entrance and a good field of fire."

We knew he was right, but this didn't make us curse him less. We stumbled wearily along the bank of the river, inspecting cave after cave, until at last we found one to his satisfaction.

I was too exhausted by this time to take in the details of our surroundings. I have only the vaguest recollection of a cleftlike opening, high walls and a sandy floor. A vague recollection too of Westerman's warning: "Doss down at the back. Away from the entrance." Then I shut my eyes, thankfully, surrendering to the waves of tiredness that engulfed me the moment my head touched the sand. The last thing I remember was Christina nestling close to me. Then the flood tide of exhaustion was too strong to be denied.

We slept for ten hours, soundly, and woke refreshed.

The first thing I noticed when I opened my eyes was the light. There wasn't much filtering in through a crevice several hundred feet above us, but what little there was seemed to be reflected and refracted, so that the upper portion of the cave appeared to be colour-washed in gold.

The second thing I noticed was Christina. She was awake, and watching me. Our hands met. "Feeling better?" I asked her.

She nodded. And for a while we lay quietly, side by side, content for the moment to be together and alive. But man is an inquisitive animal, and it wasn't long before I found myself, not for the first time, asking questions about Christina that I couldn't answer. For her escape from the apemen, it seemed to me, was not an isolated incident but the climax of a whole series of mysterious events. "Chris!"

"Hmmm?" Her voice was wary.

"How did you manage to get away? When they rushed the tent?"

"It would be easier for all of us," she said, "if you'd just accept the fact I'm here."

"Why make a mystery of it? Do you wonder I'm curious?"

"You know what curiosity did to the cat."

I was very much put out. "Look," I said with some asperity, "I like you. I want to get to know you. How do you suppose I feel when every time I ask you a question you shut up like a clam?" A pause. "So, how did you get away?"

She was silent for so long that I thought she had withdrawn once again into her shell, but at last, after a look at Corbella to be sure he was asleep, she said in a small, rather frightened voice, "I wasn't in the tent."

"Where were you then?"

"Hanging upside down in a moulin."

"And looking very attractive, I'm sure. But why?"

Another pause, another glance at Corbella, then it came out with a rush. "I'd gone prospecting. . . . You remember the laccolith—that outcrop of rock not far from the tent. Well, it was sort of glinting in the moonlight, as though it was flecked"—she hesitated—"with copper. I didn't think there'd be any harm in having a look. So I walked across to it. But as I was chipping off a sample, the snow gave way and I fell"—she shivered—"right into this awful moulin."

"You weren't hurt?"

She shook her head. "I was lucky. I fell down and down, whacking away at the wall with my ice ax. And at last it held: about twenty feet from the bottom and God-knows-how-many feet from the top. It took me"—another shiver—"three hours to climb out. And you can guess what I found."

"Footprints and an empty tent?"

"And silence, Peter. Blood on the snow, and the most awful absolute silence. I thought I'd go out of my mind."

I reached for her hand.

In the end, she told me, she had plucked up courage to follow our trail. She had followed it easily enough to the terraces. But it had taken her the rest of the day to locate us; and she had come more than once within an ace of being captured as she had worked her way to the cave above us. It added up, though I still had the feeling she was holding something back.

"You and Corbella," I said, "*expected* to find copper in the Viedma."

She nodded. "But I've told you enough."

"Enough," I said, "to whet my appetite. What I want now is the whole story: the truth, the whole truth and nothing but the truth."

Our eyes met. "You're very demanding, aren't you?"

"I could be."

She was, I could see, torn by conflicting loyalties, but at last she said quietly, "My story is simple to tell. But not so simple perhaps for you, a Britisher, to understand."

"Try me."

She sat up and folded her hands in her lap, like a little girl about to recite. "You must understand first," she said, "that the families who have settled round the great lakes of the border country are Chilean. They may live on a frontier the position of which has been in dispute for a hundred years, but whatever governments may decide about the frontier, the settlers owe their allegiance to Santiago, not to Buenos Aires. All right?"

"I'll take your word for it."

"You must understand second that we Chileans—especially perhaps those who live on the frontier—are very patriotic. I am told that in Europe it is not fashionable now for young people to be patriotic. But we"—she smiled complacently— "are very backward. We love our country. And we do not like to see it exploited by the Imperialists. It irks us that our national assets—nitrates and copper—are in foreign hands, bringing wealth not to us but to Americans, British, Germans. We would like to find other assets, especially other minerals, which we could work ourselves. For the good of our own country. Can you understand this?"

I nodded. "But where do *you* fit in?"

She continued unabashed. "One of the places we hope to find minerals is the Moreno. But the area is unmapped and unexplored. From Chile it is inaccessible. So the conventional type of survey, you see, is impossible. A few years ago, however, our government was asked—and helped—by the United States to make an aerial survey of the range by helicopter. And at the same time as we photographed it for the map-makers, we did a secret gravity survey for minerals. You know what a gravity survey is?"

I shook my head.

"If you fly over an area, it is possible to detect deposits of mineral in it by a technique known as X-ray spectroscopy. You carry equipment in the plane—or in our case in the helicopter—which emits a beam of radiation into the ground. This beam will, if faults and extraneous minerals are present, induce a return beam which the equipment can measure. By changing the isotope of the beam it is possible not only to detect minerals but also to hazard a guess as to what they are." She hesitated, then went on. "The isotope which induces a reply from copper is plutonium—two thirty-eight, and when this was used over the Moreno we got a response."

I began to get the picture. "So the Chilean government thinks there's copper in the Moreno. But before they do anything about it, they want to be sure it's on Chilean soil?"

She nodded. "The Moreno is where the border is in dispute. We don't want the whole range, just the part we're entitled to: *our side of the watershed.* And in particular we want the Viedma."

I remembered the percentages pencilled on the back of the charts in naval headquarters. "Is that," I asked, "because the Viedma's rich in copper?"

"According to survey," she said, "it contains deposits that'll put El Teniente in the shade."

It sounded straightforward enough on the impersonal level, although I had the feeling that she was still holding something back. Also it didn't answer the questions I wanted answered. "But what about you, Chris? Where do *you* come into it all?"

"I suppose," she said slowly, "it began as a sort of romantic dream. I was only sixteen when the helicopters did their survey. One of them got damaged by bad weather and had to land at El Condor. There was a lot of fuss, I remember, from Argentine officials. A guard was put on the helicopter. And Father and the pilot had to hide the X-ray equipment. For a girl of sixteen it was like *Don Quixote* and *The Three Musketeers* all rolled into one. I managed, months later, to wheedle out of Father what the helicopters were searching for. And"—she shrugged—"you can surely guess the rest. There were the Moreno, right on our doorstep: they looked so close sometimes you'd think you could climb them in a couple of days. Do you wonder I dreamed of stumbling across an El Dorado, that I studied metallurgy, that when I heard an expedition was being formed to climb the Viedma I moved heaven and earth to join it?"

"But how *did* you hear of the expedition?"

"Cedomir," she said, "has a brother in the Chilean Navy."

I was thinking this over when she laid a hand on my arm. "There's one other thing, Peter, I want you to understand. My country means more to me than anything—or anybody. I have been to other parts of the world—Boston, Paris, your Oxford for a couple of weeks—but I could never live anywhere except Chile, and southern Chile at that." Her eyes took on what I can only describe as an erotic fervour—it made me quite sad to see such talent misapplied! "It's the last really wild and beautiful corner of the earth that's not been spoiled by man. And we want to keep it that way. Oh, I don't mean we want to lock ourselves up in a nature reserve—a sort of ivory tower—but if there *was* a mineral strike in the Moreno, don't you see how much this would mean to Chile? It would mean we could develop our country ourselves, as we want to, on our own terms."

"And will there be a mineral strike?"

She nodded, "Corbella and I have got samples. Though God knows if we'll live to get them back."

I was filled with a not very logical content. "Your secret's safe with me," I told her. "I won't sell your mine to the Imperialists!"

"I am glad"—she seemed to take the remark quite seriously. "I would much prefer us to be friends."

"Me too," I said. "So come here and be friendly."

She hesitated, gave me a thoughtful look, then rolled over and laid her head on my shoulder. "I must say you don't make a bad pillow."

For a while we lay without moving. In fact I think we both dozed off, and I am not sure that I wasn't half-asleep when our lips met. Then, quite suddenly, I have seldom been so wide awake in my life. Her eyes in the strange half-light were amber, very still and very wide. "What," she whispered, "would Cedomir say?"

"Cedomir," I said, "isn't here." It was hardly the most profound remark I have ever made, but it seemed to satisfy her.

We left the cave in mid-afternoon; and if the others noticed that Christina and I had established a new rapport, they were tactful enough to say nothing.

Before we pulled out, we ate what was virtually the last of our food, drank our fill of water and discussed our next move with the care of those who know that a wrong decision is likely to cost them their lives. We agreed in the end to follow the underground river. As Westerman pointed out, it had to emerge from the plateau somewhere—perhaps in the area of moulins and thermal springs that we had bypassed in our early reconnaissance.

As we were getting ready to move off, I noticed Corbella dislodging a fragment of rock from the wall of the cave and shoving it into his knapsack.

"Is it chalcopyrite?" I asked him.

He looked first at me, then at Christina. "It could be a low yield," he said. "Quite valueless."

We headed downstream.

We were able at first to follow the river easily enough, for the bank along which we were travelling consisted of a flat terrace flanked by caves. We edged forward in near-darkness, keeping a respectful distance from the water which boomed and roared like a millrace; if one of us had slipped and fallen in, there is no telling where he'd have fetched up. For a while we made slow but steady progress. Then the inevitable happened: the terrace petered out, and the river disappeared into a tunnel.

We didn't like using the torch, but we had no option, and Westerman shone it into the cavity. There was neither ledge nor crevice we could cling to, and no bottom we could plumb. "We'll have to go back," Westerman muttered. "Try and find a passage that runs parallel to the river. And follow it by ear."

It was a technique we used God-alone-knows-how-many times in the next eighteen hours.

The river twisted and turned, disappeared into Stygian whirlpools and was joined by tributaries so hot that we couldn't set foot in them. It sometimes took us an hour to cover a couple of hundred yards; and at the end of some particularly hair-raising crawl we would often find ourselves brought up short by an impenetrable barrier. Corbella did what he could to cheer us up. We were, he insisted, with frequent references to his compass, making progress: were pushing our way, albeit with painful slowness, through the core of the Viedma; if only we kept going long enough we were bound to work our way out. It sounded logical, but I for one had visions of our going round and round in circles, like mice on a treadmill, until we were overcome by exhaustion. In the light of day I am, I like to think, no more a coward than the next man; but in the claustrophobic darkness of the Viedma I am ashamed to admit that if it hadn't been for the steadfastness of my companions I would have given way to despair. After three hours we were tired, after six hours we were exhausted, after twelve hours we were past caring or thinking of anything but sleep. Sleep, however, was a luxury Westerman wouldn't allow us. "We must," he whispered, "get out *now*. Before we lose strength." So we dragged ourselves on, sometimes plodding down corridors dark as the catacombs, sometimes crawling on hands and knees through dripping tunnels in the rock, sometimes wading up to our waists in the fast-flowing river. The river was our hope and our despair. We were bound together in a love-hate relationship. When we were with it we cursed it, deploring its depth, appalled at its rapidity, swearing at its sharp-edged rocks and grumbling at its devious twists and turns. When parted from it, we were terrified we would never see it again; we struggled frantically to get back to it, like a man to the arms of a mistress he despises but cannot do without.

In the small hours of the morning we came to a place where the river was joined by a broad, well-defined passage, a veritable motorway compared to the tunnels we had been crawling through. Sheltered behind a convenient outcrop of basalt, we considered this new development.

The passage, lit faintly by random colonies of glow-worms, disappeared into the darkness less than a dozen yards from where we were crouching. "Looks like the main road to somewhere," I whispered.

McBride nodded. "In my opinion it would lead us out of the Viedma. It has always been my view that there must be some means of access which is relatively easy. Otherwise the *Paranthropus* wouldn't make such frequent forays into the world outside."

He had been right so often that we didn't bother to argue. We were about to climb into the passage when Westerman froze, like a pointer scenting game. "Quiet!"

At first we could hear nothing except the cacophony of the river. Then Christina and I picked up the noise at the same moment. We shrank back, holding our breath as the pad of feet came nearer and nearer, until on the wall of the passage two monstrous shadows were thrown into momentary relief: a pair of the *Paranthropus*.

They were in view for only about five seconds, then they merged ghostlike into the gloom. But it was the better part of five minutes before we dared to speak. Then McBride swore softly, "God damn it! I reckoned we'd seen the last of them."

"It seems," Westerman said mildly, "that your exit's going to be guarded."

We eyed the passage in silence. It looked a good deal less attractive now we knew that a hunting party of *Paranthropus* might be lurking round the next corner. "Do you reckon," I whispered, "those two were on their way to take guard?"

"Could be. Why?"

"Perhaps the pair they relieve will be coming back."

It was a complication. Being troglodytes, the apes could see in the dark a great deal better than we could, and the last thing we wanted was a surprise confrontation in the underground passages. We agreed to wait.

And it was as well we did. For after rather less than twenty minutes we picked up a muted clicking and the pad of feet; and a moment later another pair of the loathsome creatures appeared briefly out of the gloom. (We knew it wasn't the same couple because one of them, this time, was a female.) They were moving fast—anxious, I suppose, to get back to family, food and fire or whatever it is that warms the cockles of a *Paranthropus'* heart—and almost before we were alerted, they had come and gone. We looked at each other uneasily.

When they were out of earshot, Westerman handed me the rifle. "I'll go first," he said briefly. "The rest of you follow, about ten yards behind. Peter, cover me. But don't fire unless you have to. O.K.?"

We nodded.

I remember that as we set off down the passage, I glanced at my watch. The hands were coming up to 5 A.M. On the

Hielo Continental it would soon be dawn, and I don't think I have ever longed for anything so much in all my life as to see, just once again, the first faint flush of sunrise on the peaks.

We made about as good time down the passage as a family of timorous snails. It was Westerman who set the pace: inching forward a few feet, listening, waiting for us to close up, then inching forward again. We knew he was doing the right thing and that our lives depended on being neither seen nor heard, but I couldn't help wishing he'd get a move on. It was hot and airless in the passage, or to be precise, what little air there was seemed to have a curious stifling quality, as though tainted by extraneous gases— among them I thought I detected sulphur dioxide. It would, I told myself, be ironic if after all our threshing about in the underground passages, we found ourselves back at the central crater! After a while the river veered off at a tangent, its roar fading first to a murmur, then to an unnerving silence. We had become so accustomed to the river, we were bereft without it. The silence was eerie and oppressive; there was, it seemed to me, something sinister about it; it got on my nerves; and it wasn't long before I found myself fighting an almost uncontrollable impulse (a sort of death wish I suppose) to burst out singing at the top of my voice! I must, I told myself, be going out of my mind. I concentrated on the physical trivia of our advance: twenty-four shuffling steps and thirty seconds' wait, twenty-two shuffling steps and thirty-two seconds' wait. It irked me that our advance had no logical sequence. I cursed Westerman for not establishing a rhythm, then cursed myself for being a neurotic fool.

There came a time when I couldn't understand why we were waiting so long. I must have stood there a full couple of minutes, swaying with exhaustion, insensate as a patch of amoeba in the ocean swell, before I realized that the darkness ahead was giving way to light.

Persephone herself could not have been more thankful to emerge from incarceration; and hope, to which we had for long been strangers, came seeping back. We continued our advance with a new-found purpose while the light ahead gained slowly in intensity, until we could see little spirals of what we took to be mist eddying in through the mouth of the passage. The prospect of breathing air that was fresh, of feeling again the bite of the wind and the warmth of the sun, was like a shot in the arm. I found myself gripping the rifle more tightly: not all the *Paranthropus* in the Viedma, I told myself, were going to stop us now.

As we neared the end of the passage we became conscious of a strange sound, so faint as to be almost imperceptible. It was a sound I couldn't identify: a sort of slow, rhythmic sibilance, like the breathing of some gargantuan monster chained deep under the earth. We exchanged glances.

"Stay here," Westerman whispered.

We watched apprehensively as on hands and knees he crawled forward the last twenty or thirty yards. At the mouth of the passage he paused, silhouetted for a moment against the swirling eddies of white. We saw him draw back as if in fear, then raise a hand to his eyes as he took a more careful look at whatever lay in our path. Eventually he beckoned us to join him.

I don't know what I expected—though if I had been more on the *qui vive*, the heat and the stench of sulphur would have given me a clue—but even if I had been prepared for some sort of volcanic phenomenon, nothing my imagination conjured up would have been as bizarre or terrifying as the scene we stood looking down on.

Imagine the fumarole of a volcano: a vortex plunging whirlpool-like into the very depths of the earth. Imagine its walls a circle of sheer black rock, the upper reaches hung with cornices of ice, the lower disappearing into a cauldron of vapour and steam. Imagine the cauldron of vapour and steam to be simmering gently, like soup coming to the boil, then every couple of minutes welling up in a great fountain of molten lava and gaseous liquid—the "breathing" we had heard from inside the Viedma. And imagine, finally, the mouth of the passage where we were standing opening out about halfway up the fumarole, so that above us was two hundred feet of rock reaching for the sky, and below us two hundred feet of rock plunging sheer into the lava. All this our eyes took in at a glance. It wasn't until we studied the fumarole section by section that we spotted the track: the narrow ledge, cut into the rock, which went spiralling up from the end of our passage to the top of the cliffs; an escape route for those with strong nerves and a head for heights.

13

The Fumarole

There was no sign of the *Paranthropus*. But this didn't mean
a thing. They might very easily, I told myself, be close at
hand, hidden perhaps by vapour or screened by rocks, just
waiting to give the alarm the moment we started to climb.
We stood for a long time in silence, weighing the chances
of an ascent. The track was our only hope: everywhere else
the rocks fell sheer into the fumarole. We retreated down
the passage.

We had, it was clear, walked right through the Viedma,
from central crater to outside cliffs, and had emerged at a
spot where a secondary fumarole had burst through the
side of the parent volcano. Since we hadn't spotted this
fumarole during our first reconnaissance, we assumed that
it lay in the area of moulins and thermal springs, screened
by vapour-cum-mist. If only therefore we could climb the
track, we would almost certainly emerge onto the Hielo
Continental.

"I don't like it," McBride muttered. "If we were caught
halfway up, we'd be between the devil and the deep."

"Could we wait till it's dark?" Corbella suggested. "Slip
out without being seen?"

Westerman shook his head. "That path'll be bad enough
to climb by day."

"I wonder," I said, "where the *Paranthropus* have got to?"

"If there're some at the top and some at the bottom," McBride grunted, "I don't want to be caught in the middle!"

"Once we're on the track," I pointed out, "they could only come at us one at a time." I tapped the Parker-Hale. "We'd have a chance."

We decided to make a break for it: not a blind stampede but a planned sortie. Westerman, Christina, McBride and Corbella roped together, in that order; I checked the rifle, and took up my position in the rear; then we crouched for some twenty minutes at the mouth of the passage, partly to study the route, and partly to make sure that our eyes had become completely acclimatized to the light.

It was dawn. Looking up through the shaft of the fumarole we could see, in between eddies of vapour, a kaleidoscope of blue—it was evidently one of those rare fine days when the Hielo Continental lay sparkling under a gentian sky. Was it, I asked myself, possible that in something under an hour we would be out of the primordial world of the Viedma and back once again in the twentieth century? Two hazards in particular stood in our way: the geyser and the cornices.

About forty feet from where we were crouching, the track dipped sharply toward the fumarole before restarting its ascent: dipped so far toward the fumarole in fact that when the geyser fountained up, little globules at its periphery cascaded onto the track. It was all too obvious that if we didn't time our crossing right, we'd get a shower of white-hot lava on our heads.

And if we survived the Scylla of the geyser, we would still have to circumvent the Charybdis of the cornices. A whole row of the fearsome-looking things—like gargantuan icicles—overhung the upper section of the track. They looked as if a fly so much as brushed them with its wing tips, the whole lot would collapse, sweeping the track and anyone on it into the fumarole.

"Come on," Westerman muttered at last. "And don't look down!"

Moving as quietly as we could and as quickly as we dared, we set off down the path.

It was about three feet wide. And slippery. In a few places deposits of sulphur gave a reasonable foothold, but most of the rock was slimy with lichen and moist with globules of steam. Below us the lava bubbled obscenely. A slip was not to be thought of.

As we neared the dip, we were able to look more closely into the fumarole itself, and I have never seen anything so terrifying in all my life. On the surface its lava was a dull red ochre, but here and there, as it welled up in little blisters and burst, we had glimpses of a fiercer red beneath: a glow like that from a subterranean forge. While every two minutes, almost exactly to the second, a great gout of lava and steam erupted out of the depths: a fountain of gaseous liquid flung several hundred feet into the air, then falling back in a scalding downpour into the fumarole. We froze, numb with terror, each time the geyser welled up, fearful that a more-violent-than-usual eruption would scald us to death.

At the approaches to the dip the lichen petered out, and the rocks became first bare, then soft, then puddled with water: water that was hot to the touch. A little way short of the spot where the track began to descend, we came to a halt. We had been timing the geyser's eruptions; they were regular as heartbeats: every 120 to 122 seconds. We studied the gauntlet we had to run. It was less than three dozen yards across, and the rock, though wet, looked level and reasonably firm. We would have plenty of time to cross between eruptions, *so long as nothing went wrong.*

"Check boots and rope," Westerman advised us. We looked at laces and knots with the care of those who know that a trailing bootlace might mean the sort of death that didn't bear thinking of. "We'll go after the next eruption," he said quietly. "The second the geyser collapses, follow me. And take it easy."

Again the upthrust of lava and steam. Again the blast of hot air slamming into us like a physical blow. Again the cataract of boiling water, pitting into the path at our very feet as we climbed down the dip, over rocks that were still steaming and hot.

Don't, I told myself, touch the basalt. Don't hurry. And don't look down.

The path, though soft, was mercifully stable, and Westerman set a steady walking pace. In single file we moved forward, each step taking us that much closer to safety. In the stillness between eruptions the squelch of our footsteps sounded surprisingly loud, and I remember noticing that we had fallen like a well-drilled patrol into step. Left, right, left, right. The gauntlet was proving easier to run than I had dared to expect. If we keep this up, I remember thinking, we'll be over in one minute, let alone two. Soon Westerman, who was in the lead, had only a couple of yards to go.

It was then that we heard the noise, about the last noise on earth that we wanted to hear: the hissing of the apes.

The first three on the rope (Westerman, Christina and McBride) kept going. But Corbella, who was last, stopped and looked back to see where the hissing came from. The rope tightened. He was jerked off his feet. And before the rest of us realized what was happening, he slid with a muffled scream into the fumarole. One second he was there, the next he had gone.

The pull on the rope jerked McBride backward. For a moment his feet scrabbled frantically as he fought for a footing, and I had visions of the four of them, one after the other, toppling like string-jerked marionettes into the boiling lava. Then he regained his balance. I dropped the rifle; and we both at the same moment fell to our hands and knees and, sick with apprehension, peered into the fumarole.

The rope had held. And Corbella was spinning slowly

round and round, some three or four feet below us, his life quite literally hanging by a thread.

A sudden pain in my hands made me jerk them off the rock, and looking down I realized that my gloves, where I had pressed them against the basalt, had burnt through. And, to judge from the smell, something else was burning too. The rope.

I saw it out the corner of my eye, the tenuous thread on which Corbella's life depended. It was pulled taut across a smouldering outcrop of rock. Even as I watched, appalled, a little spiral of smoke coiled up, and the outer fibers withered away and the threads inside began to curl grey in the heat. I looked at McBride. He looked at me. And we each saw our horror reflected in the other's eyes. If someone had shouted, "Leave the rope and run," I'm not sure that I wouldn't have done it.

But there was no face-saving order: no getting out of what I knew had to be done. "Hang onto my legs," I shouted.

As McBride's hands, reassuringly large and firm, grabbed hold of me, I lowered myself over the edge of the fumarole.

I was desperately close to Corbella now, but even with my arms fully stretched out, I couldn't grab hold of him.

"Eduardo!" I screamed.

He had been dangling limp as a rag doll—numb with terror, I suppose—but my scream galvanized him to life. His head and his uninjured arm jerked up, and I managed to grab his wrist. Then the rope parted.

We swung to and fro over the fumarole, like an act on a crazy trapeze. I could feel the sweat, cold and damp, break out all over my body; and I was filled with a quite illogical fear that the sweat would run down my arm and onto Corbella's wrist, making it too slippery to hold. Then I thought: What the hell does it matter if I *do* drop him? The geyser's going to erupt any second. And that'll be the end of us all. I didn't realize that the whole nightmare scene was being acted out in far fewer seconds than it takes to describe.

I could feel the heat building up in my knees and loins where they were pressed hard on the rock, and I tried to shout at McBride to haul us up; but I was so terrified that my vocal chords must have got knotted, because all that came out was a strangled squawk. McBride, however, needed no encouragement. And his strength, once again, saved our lives. Quite a few men, I suppose, might have been able to pull us up with a lot of puffing and panting, given time. But time was what we were short of. And McBride knew it. He got to his feet, and with one almighty heave hoisted the pair of us up, like a couple of fish on the selfsame hook.

For a moment we lay spread-eagled on top of each other, gasping for breath. Then Westerman's voice, sharp and urgent, spurred us to action. "Quick. Run. You've ten seconds."

One second for the message to sink home. Two for us to stagger to our feet. But Corbella was dazed and doubled up with pain; he was facing the wrong way; and it took me several seconds to spin him round and give him a shove in the right direction. Then we were scrambling for the rim of the depression—and safety—only a couple of yards away. The others were there already. I could see quite clearly the distance Corbella and I had to cover, for the rocks out of range of the geyser were a lighter, quite different texture to those soaked recurringly in spray. I was telling myself that, against all the odds, we were going to make it, when I was conscious of a sudden crescendo of sound, and the geyser— it seemed to swell up from right beside me—erupted in a monstrous pyramid of lava, gas and steam. The blast was strong enough to make me stagger, and hot enough to make me feel, though not a drop had touched me, as though I'd been doused in scalding spray.

The events of the next few seconds seemed to be acted out in slow motion. I remember realizing that my life depended on how long it took for the geyser to reach its apex and collapse: two seconds and I'd never make the last few yards; three or four seconds and I'd have a chance. I remember the heartbreaking steepness of the final ridge of rock. I remember Westerman waiting, feet planted on the very line where the rocks changed colour. I remember his outstretched hand. I remember the grunt of his breath as he grabbed me and hauled me over the edge of the depression. Then we were rolling clear while great cataracts of boiling water scythed into the rocks where only a second before we had been standing.

The falling spray missed us by inches rather than feet. Not a drop touched us. Yet such was the heat from air at the geyser's periphery that I felt as though I were being boiled alive. I rolled over and over in a desperate effort to shield my eyes.

The deluge subsided. A moment of shocked silence. Then running footsteps, and Christina's hands cupped round my face. "Pete! You're all right? Say you're all right."

I sat up. "I'm all right," I said.

With true feminine logic she burst into tears.

I felt myself all over. Somewhat to my surprise, I seemed to be still in one piece. I looked at my hands. The palms were singed rather than burned; they weren't even starting to blister. The same was true of my knees. Indeed when I came to assess my injuries I found I had disappointingly little to show for the fact that I had been within inches of a thoroughly unpleasant death. Westerman and Corbella, too, appeared to be more or less intact. Christina was beside me, sobbing as if she was never going to stop. And McBride?— I looked this way and that. He was nowhere to be seen.

I shut my eyes, counted five and looked again. And he was still nowhere to be seen.

It wasn't until I had struggled to my feet that I spotted him walking purposefully back into the depression. I thought he must have gone out of his mind with shock. I was about to scream at him to come back when I saw him bend down and pick up the Parker-Hale. Or rather try to pick it up; it was evidently still hot, for he dropped it exceedingly smartly and it went clattering across the rocks and came within a hairsbreadth of sliding into the fumarole. McBride looked at his watch; then, without the slightest sign of hurrying, he took off his anorak, wrapped it round the rifle, and, cradling it in his arms, brought it back out of the depression. He cleared the danger area less than five seconds before the geyser erupted.

Westerman's hand rested for a moment on his shoulder. "Well done," he said briefly.

"You shouldn't have taken the risk," I muttered.

"The rifle," McBride said, "is our only hope."

For a moment I couldn't think what he meant. Then I remembered what had led to our near-debacle: the *Paranthropus*.

I looked back. There the loathsome creatures were, about half a dozen of them, jumping up and down at the mouth of the passage—whether with rage or excitement I couldn't tell. Their clicking-cum-hissing came to us clearly across the fumarole: a weird accompaniment to the bubble of lava and the rhythmic exhalations of the geyser. They made no attempt to follow us; and this, it seemed to me, was just as well from their point of view, for we could easily have picked them off one at a time as they advanced down the narrow track—assuming, of course, that the Parker-Hale was in working order. McBride was looking at it critically, wiping it dry and checking its loading. "How about a trial shot?" he suggested.

Corbella, it was clear, didn't approve, but Westerman nodded. "Into the air. We don't want to stir up our friends."

He aimed up the shaft of the fumarole, fired, and the bullet ricocheted off an outcrop of granite a couple of hundred feet above us. In the confined space the echo was deafening: a series of staccato reports, like the crack of elephant whips, flung back from wall to wall.

The *Paranthropus* at the mouth of the passage redoubled their clicking. "That's given them something to talk about," I said with satisfaction.

McBride shook his head. *"They're* not the ones we have to worry about."

He was looking not down past the geyser but up toward the cornices. For a moment I couldn't think what he was getting at. Then I spotted them: the pair of *Paranthropus* staring down at us from beside the great blocks of over-hanging ice at the top of the track. And the professor's warning came back to me: "If there are some at the top and some at the bottom, I don't want to be caught in the middle." Well, it had happened. We were trapped. For the second—or was it the third or the fourth or the fifth—time, we had been outmaneuvered and outwitted by a pack of prehistoric apes.

I can see in retrospect that we shouldn't have been sur-prised. For half a million years this last remnant of a once mighty species had managed to survive. I could picture their ancestors being driven from hideout to hideout, prized out from jungle, oasis, plateau and swamp, until they at last found refuge in this least-accessible corner of the habitable world. Here, geology, climate and their own cunning had combined to preserve the secret of their existence. Preserv-ing this secret was what the *Paranthropus* had been doing for half a million years: no wonder they were good at it! Very likely, I told myself, we were not the first to stumble across their hideout. Very likely we had been preceded by Neanderthal man, Inca raiding party or Jesuit priest. Perhaps one day our bones would be found beside theirs: a puzzle for some thirtieth-century archaeologist. For I could see no chance of our getting out of the fumarole alive. If we went back, we would bump into virtually the whole tribe—for even as I watched, more and more of the bestial creatures came crowding out of the passage, their every gesture one of derisive satisfaction. If we went forward, the *Paranthro-pus* at the top of the path had only to avalanche the cornices, and we would be swept into the fumarole. If we stayed where we were, we would either starve or be scalded to death. No wonder the apes looked pleased with themselves!

A sudden anger took hold of me: not the blind, red rage that had clouded my judgment in the caves, but a hard, cold, calculating hatred. It was as though the age-old antagonism of *Homo sapiens* and *Paranthropus* had become synthesized into a personal feud between myself and the apes of the Viedma. It was unthinkable, I told myself, that five armed, intelligent, twentieth-century men should be made fools of by a bunch of Stone Age monkeys. Somehow, somewhere, there must be a way of escape. I took a critical look at the terrain. My mind, as I rejected plan after plan, was crystal clear. And eventually an idea took shape: not especially ingenious, and by no means certain of success, but something that gave us a chance.

From where we were standing I could see the top of the cornices, the unstable snowslopes that folded back from the lip of the fumarole. Anyone who wanted to avalanche the cornices would, presumably, quite simply dislodge snow from the top of these slopes. Now it occurred to me that if we could lure the *Paranthropus* at the top of the path to get in position to start an avalanche, I *might* be able to pick them off. It wouldn't be an easy shot, but the Parker-Hale had telescopic sights; it was a precision instrument, and one's aim is liable to improve when one's life depends on it. "You four go on," I said. "Pretend you're going to make a dash under the cornices."

Westerman got the idea at once. "If we kill those two, you reckon the way will be clear?"

"We'll soon know. Stop short of the overhang. And don't run for it till I give you a wave."

Corbella started to remonstrate, and Christina showed a touching but unwelcome reluctance to leave me.

"Look lively, you lot!" Westerman's voice was sharp. "If our friends think we're plotting something, they'll charge."

As the four of them disappeared up the track, I must admit that I felt like running after them. A scalding geyser and a pack of bloodthirsty apes are not exactly the company I'd choose.

I moved a few yards farther away from the geyser, to a spot where the track skirted a projecting spur. From here I could see a good three-quarters of the snowslopes; they were bathed in sunlight. The apes had evidently been watching these maneuvers; for as I took up position at the edge of the spur, they redoubled their clicking: warning their colleagues, I hoped, of our advance. And sure enough after a couple of minutes, two shadows, long and black in the low morning sun, appeared over the top of the cornices.

I had already loaded and sighted the Parker-Hale. Don't rush it, I told myself: two good shots are worth a broadside of near misses. A wisp of vapour coiled perversely in front of the cross wires. The shadows lengthened. And the heads of the *Paranthropus* rose black over the ridge.

If I had stopped to think, I might have felt almost sorry for the *Paranthropus*. They hadn't missed a trick. They had defended their last fragment of earth with a cunning which would have routed us right, left and center if we hadn't been possessed of weapons beyond their comprehension. Even now it was touch and go if the most modern rifle in the gunsmith's armory would enable us to escape the trap they had maneuvered us into. But I didn't spare the *Paranthropus* a thought. My whole being, mind and body, was concentrated on aligning the bead of the sights on the heart of the leading ape-man.

The sights steadied. My finger tightened, slowly.

A staccato crack, and the leading *Paranthropus* clutched his shoulder and let out a shriek of rage and pain that echoed and reechoed round the vortex of the fumarole. His companion froze. Rooted to the snow in shocked disbelief, he was a better target than I would have dared to pray for. I fired again. For a second I thought incredulously that I must have missed, because he didn't move. Then, very slowly, his legs folded under him, and I knew by the way he fell that he was dead before he hit the snow.

The first ape, however, was far from dead. He was clutching his shoulder, snarling with rage and staring this way and that in an effort to see where the danger came from. I hoped he'd turn and run. But he didn't. He started scrabbling at the snow. Within seconds he would have started an avalanche.

I fired again. The impact of the bullet knocked him clean off his feet. He rolled over and over. Faster and faster, down and down, down the snowslope, onto the cornice and over the lip of the fumarole. In the air, he seemed to fall with a macabre slowness, spinning round and round as he passed me, like a leaf on a quiet autumn day. He didn't stop screaming from the moment he left the edge of the fumarole to the moment he hit the lava.

I wondered if I was going to be sick. My whole body felt as though it had been turned to water. There, but for the grace of God, I thought, go I.

For perhaps ten seconds there was absolute silence. Then one of the apes let out a scream of rage.

The spell was broken. I waved at the others, who were frozen into a shocked tableau some two hundred yards up the path. "Run for it!" I shouted. And the fumarole, which a moment before had been quiet as a deserted church, became filled with the sound and fury of a hunt to the death.

The *Paranthropus* were determined to get us. I could tell by the way they came flooding out of the passage in a great red tide, like a torrent of blood. I had a sudden vision of our five bodies spinning down and round into the fumarole. I ran as I have never run in my life.

Ahead, the others were directly under the cornices now; and it occurred to me—as if we hadn't enough on our plates already—that the noise of pounding feet and bellowing apes might easily crack the ice and set off an avalanche. Then I realized that the cornices were the least of our anxieties. For behind us the *Paranthropus* were gaining.

It was amazing how such ponderous creatures could climb at such a speed. We had a good start on them, the path was so narrow that they could only come one at a time and they were held up by the geyser; yet they were closing the gap with every stride; and it came to me in a moment of terror that somewhere close to the top of the fumarole, they were going to catch up with us. Fear made me reckless. Shutting my mind to the possibility of a slip, I leapt from rock to rock like a terrified but unwieldy goat.

Next time I looked up, the others were past the cornices and on the final stretch of path that led to the ice field. The *Paranthropus*, however, were less than a hundred yards behind. I could hear the thud of their feet and the pant of their breath; in my imagination I could smell the stench of their bodies and feel the rip of their claws. Only a miracle, I remember thinking, can save us.

The path, in the overhang of the cornices, turned suddenly dark. I looked up at the unstable undersurface of the ice; and it came to me that here was the last straw at which we could clutch.

The cornices extended for roughly a hundred yards. I've never done the distance in better time. The second I was out of the tunnel of shadow, I skidded to a halt, unslung the rifle, dropped to one knee and fired again and again and again. Not at the *Paranthropus*: at the cornices.

The bullets passed clean through them, dislodging no more than a few particles of ice. But this I expected. It wasn't the bullets I was pinning my faith on: it was the echo.

The fumarole was a natural amplifier, and the sound of the shots echoed and reechoed around its walls in an ear-splitting crescendo. By timing the shots carefully, I was able to escalate this crescendo into an almost rhythmic succession of high-pitched cracks.

The noise was cataclysmic. I looked imploringly at the walls of ice. Break, I heard myself mutter after every shot: break, break, break.

The *Paranthropus* were under the cornices now, moving fast: sixty yards, fifty yards, forty yards. I fired at the leader. Missed. Fired again. And he staggered against the wall, rebounded like a drunken runner and toppled without a sound

[178]

into the fumarole. But another took his place. Forty yards, thirty yards, twenty yards. Two more shots, I told myself, were all I'd have time for. I fired. And the leading ape-man clutched his stomach. But he didn't fall. He came on. And on and on. There was no stopping the *Paranthropus* now. They came pouring down on me in a torrent of snarling mouths, brandishing clubs and great teeth aslobber with saliva. I stood up—I was damned if I was going to die kneeling down. The sights of the Parker-Hale steadied between the eyes of the leading ape. I'll get you, I remember thinking, before you get me; I remember thinking too that this was hardly a good Christian sentiment with which to be quitting the world.

I fired. The crack was improbably loud. I couldn't think why it went on for so long and was so deafening that I dropped the rifle and clapped my hands to my ears. I couldn't think why sun, sky and fumarole had vanished, and in their place was a swirling kaleidoscope of white. I couldn't think where the *Paranthropus* had gone to, and why the ground under my feet was trembling like ill-set jelly. I remember thinking that if this was death, it was a great deal noisier than I had expected. Then, in a moment of elation mingled with fear, I realized that the cornices had collapsed, and that only a few yards from where I was standing thousands of tons of snow and ice were cascading into the maw of the volcano.

And not only ice. For as I shrank back, fascinated but appalled at the forces I had unleashed, the colour of the kaleidoscope changed: changed from white to black, as the whole face of the cliff—*Paranthropus* and all—peeled away, and with a catastrophic roar fell headlong into the fumarole.

A great gout of lava shot high into the air, the plateau trembled and the vent emitted a hiss of protest, cut suddenly short as more and more rocks cascaded into the orifice of the fumarole. For half a minute earth and sky seemed full of the crash of thousands of tons of basalt and quartz. Then, quite suddenly there was silence.

The path below me had been swept away.

The *Paranthropus* had vanished.

The volcano was sealed up.

And ahead, the way to the Hielo Continental lay open: our escape route to a world that I had despaired of ever setting eyes on again.

14

"Seismographs have recorded an earth tremor in southern Chile."

I don't know how long I crouched there, bludgeoned to an unthinking stupor by the magnitude of the holocaust and the narrowness of our escape; but eventually I realized my friends were waving and shouting, beckoning me to safety. I stumbled toward them, like a frightened child to its parents' arms.

They came down the path to meet me. And now that I saw them in full daylight for the first time in almost a week, I was appalled at their appearance. Westerman got to me first. But was this the dapper little man who had drunk coffee so elegantly in the hotel on the Scores?—his hair was snow-white, his eyes were bloodshot and the hand that he laid on my shoulder was trembling. And was this the well-groomed rider from the pages of *Vogue*, who had greeted me with such self-assurance on the shore of Lago Viedma?—Christina's hair was in rats' tails, and her skin was ingrained with dirt and the colour of parchment. Nor surely was this the dignified naval officer of whom we had stood in more than a little awe?—with his stubble of beard and makeshift sling, Corbella would not have passed muster on a third-rate tramp. As for our learned professor: a club and a bit more hair and he could have doubled more readily than ever for one of his Stone Age "cousins." We were indeed a sight to frighten the daylight. But we were alive.

For a moment we stood in a silent cluster on the rim of the fumarole, staring at one another in disbelief. Then McBride spoke for us all. "Let's get the hell out of this!"

And if it hadn't been for Westerman, I believe we would have rushed off there and then like the Gadarene swine in a panic-stricken stampede. "We won't," he said quietly, "get far without ropes and crampons."

He was, we realized, right. Yet the prospect of going back to pick up our equipment, of lingering even a few hours longer beside the Viedma, was anathema. "Do you reckon," I said without enthusiasm, "the stuff will still be there?"

"If it isn't," Westerman said, "I don't fancy our chances."

Silence, as our situation began to sink home. We had been so thankful to escape from the Viedma that we had imagined ourselves well on the road to freedom. In fact we had taken only a tentative first step. We were still close to the summit of one of the most difficult ranges in the world, without food or equipment; and looked at impartially, the odds on our making a safe descent could not have been good. Corbella, as a mountaineer, backed Westerman up. "Without crampons," he said, "the glacier would be suicide."

I took another look at the fumarole. It was a scene of utter devastation. A whole segment of the cliff had broken away, spewing enormous quantities of rock into the maw of the volcano. Of the lake of lava, not a trace remained: not a coil of steam or a haze of heat. Several hundred feet of the path had been swept away, together with an unknown number of the *Paranthropus*. There was no trace of survivors. Yet it struck me as unlikely that the whole tribe had been obliterated, for thinking back to the moment before the landslide, I remembered that some of them had been climbing the lower, still undamaged, section of the path while others had been emerging from the passage. These unfortunate creatures must, we assumed, have escaped the holocaust and retreated into the Viedma. I wouldn't, I reflected, be in their shoes for all the gold in El Dorado, for they were quite literally sitting on a pent-up volcano with no way of escape.

Or perhaps there was a way of escape? It suddenly crossed my mind that while we were debating our next move, the surviving apes might be making for the Viedma's last remaining exit, the mouth of the underground river, the very spot we had to return to to pick up our equipment. "We'd better not dilly-dally," I said, "or our friends'll get there first."

We had, as we had anticipated, emerged in the area of thermal springs from which we had fled with such alacrity during our first reconnaissance. Luckily, we had emerged on one of those rare fine days when the wind was a dry south-easter, and the usual miasma of mist-cum-cloud had been dispersed. Luckily too we had surfaced quite close to the river; indeed Westerman thought he could hear it—though since the rest of us could detect nothing more than the roar of the wind we were inclined to put this down to imagination. At least, however, there was no doubt about which direction we ought to head. We turned our backs, thankfully, on the fumarole, and set off to follow the line of the cliffs.

Fear gave us wings: fear that at any moment the volcano might break through in an explosion all the more violent for having been dammed back, and fear that through passages deep in the Viedma the *Paranthropus* might also be heading for the river.

Neither fear was realized.

Looking back, I think I can say that we were due for a respite—for in the past week we had surely seen more wonders, suffered more fears and endured more hardships than is the lot of most men in a lifetime. Be that as it may, after a couple of hours' uneventful slogging, we came to the river; and there, thank the Lord, we found our cache of equipment and food, partially buried by snow but undisturbed. It wasn't until we opened the Raslin bags, and saw the meat and potato powder actually swelling up on the Primus, that we realized how hungry we were. Then we ate and ate. And under the influence of fresh air and hot food, our strength came seeping back, like new blood into the veins of an injured man.

The weather helped our recovery too. It was one of those afternoons when the Hielo Continental was like a Disney stage set: almost too beautiful to be believed. There wasn't a cloud in the sky; around us peak after peak rose out of the plateau like castles dipped in icing sugar, and the air was so clear that we could see west to the Pacific and east to the great Patagonian plain. We didn't, however, waste time admiring the view. While eating, we assembled and loaded the sledge. And the moment we had finished, we strapped on our snowshoes and made for the glacier.

Conditions for sledging could hardly have been better. And this was as well, since none of us was pulling strongly, and Corbella, with his broken collarbone, wasn't pulling at all. The sledge, however, was light (for we had lost or eaten three-quarters of our stores), the surface was firm and much to our satisfaction we made excellent progress. There was no sign of the *Paranthropus*. There was no stir from the volcano. It was almost too good to be true.

Light lasts well in the Patagonian summer, and we were able that evening to cover the three or four miles to the head of the glacier. Here, as the sun dipped under the Viedma, we came to a halt. "Do we rest?" McBride panted. "Or push on?"

We were payed out. Yet the idea of pitching camp on the Hielo Continental had no supporters. For we were possessed by an almost pathological compulsion to put as much ground as possible as quickly as possible between ourselves and the Viedma; we therefore decided to rest a mere half hour, then push on through the night.

It was toward the end of this half hour, while we were sorting out crampons and ropes, that there occurred an incident which strengthened our resolve to keep moving.

An earth tremor.

A tremor so faint as to be almost imperceptible—indeed if it hadn't been for the noise that accompanied it, we might have put the whole thing down to imagination. For some five or six seconds the ground seemed to tremble, as a building close to an underground railway will sometimes tremble as a train passes by. The noise, however, was nothing like a train. It was a noise I find hard to describe: a dull reverberating roar, like a wave breaking deep in the heart of the earth.

We sprang to our feet, staring apprehensively at the Viedma. There was neither upthrust of ash nor glow of lava; but Corbella moistened his lips. "I don't like it," he muttered.

I have been told that those who live—as so many Chileans live—in the shadow of a volcano sometimes possess an extra-sensory awareness, a precognition of danger. "You think," I said, "we're in for an eruption?"

"Could be."

McBride picked up his rucksack. "Let's be going."

We eyed the glacier without enthusiasm, its seracs and crevasses taking on a new menace. It was all too obvious what was likely to happen if an eruption took place while we were poised on the unstable battlements of ice. The glacier, however, was our only route: nowhere else was there the slightest possibility of descent. "Come on," Westerman said at last, "beggars can't be choosers."

So we put on our crampons, roped up and headed into the glacial depression.

Our last view of the Viedma was of it silhouetted against the evening sky. There was, I noticed, no coil of smoke from the crater; and the stillness struck me as ominous.

We all of us learned the fallacy, that night, of the adage "out of sight out of mind." For long after the volcano disappeared from view, the threat of its eruption hung over us: a Damoclean sword, casting the shadow of fear over our descent.

It had taken us five days to climb the glacier, but we had been hampered then by bad weather, and had lacked urgency. The weather was kind now: a light wind, no more than occasional flurries of snow, and the ice in first-class condition. As for urgency, we were under no delusions: if we didn't hurry, it was only a question of which got us first, the volcano or the *Paranthropus*. Westerman set a cracking pace and never let up; and we didn't complain—indeed when he paused to suggest a rest, we urged him on. The result was progress beyond our most sanguine expectations. Traverse, belay, pitch and glissade followed each other in rapid succession, while Pisces and Pegasus drifted by overhead through the veil of the Magellanic Cloud. We plodded on, driving ourselves to the limit of our endurance, till the stars lost their brilliance and the sky in the east turned from grey to mother-of-pearl. And at last, as the light gained in intensity, we were able to pick out—mercifully near—the dark forests of *nothofagus* and, at their feet, the sweep of the Lago Viedma. In ten hours we had broken the back of the descent.

We didn't come to a halt until we could see, only a little way ahead, a belt of moraine—not the narrow tongue by which we had ascended, but a broader excrescence farther down the glacier. By emerging via this we hoped to avoid the worst of the *nothofagus*, and reach our base camp after only a short traverse through the woods. And how we longed for the comfort and safety of the base camp: its spring of water, its carpet of moss, its cache of food, its radio and, above all, its Zodiac—our means of escape from the nightmare world of the Viedma. It seemed almost too much to believe that by midday we might be safely embarked: beyond the reach of the "big red devils" of the Moreno.

We had driven ourselves hard during the night, and the question now arose should we push on for the final half-mile or take a breather? It was the look of the ice ahead that decided us; for between the spot where we were standing and the moraine was a difficult icefall, to descend which we would need all our strength. Before tackling it we would, we decided, have breakfast and an hour's rest. So we lit the

Primus, and unpacked a generous helping of powdered milk, chocolate, biscuit and fudge.

We were about to settle down to our meal when the sun came swelling up like a great red peony over the rim of the lake. There are few more beautiful combinations scenically than snow-capped mountains and blue water in the light of a rising sun. Yet the scene on this particular morning had a frailty and transience that I didn't care for: like the beauty one sometimes sees in the face of a very ill child, a promise more haunting for the knowledge it will never be fulfilled. And the stillness was uncanny. I have never known anything like it. No, not even in the passages deep beneath the Viedma; it was as though the whole earth was holding its breath. Another thing I didn't care for was the warmth. This was a phenomenon I have never been able to explain: that although the sun was only recently risen, the atmosphere was close, almost stifling, and the temperature a full ten degrees above normal. If we had been in the tropics I would have thought we might well be in for a typhoon. As it was, we found ourselves peering apprehensively at the Viedma. "The sooner we're across the lake," I heard Corbella mutter, "the better."

We sipped our chocolate, our brains urging us to push on, our bodies crying out for rest.

After a while McBride put into words the thought that had crossed my mind more than once in the course of our adventures. "When we get back, do you reckon anyone'll believe us?"

"I must say," Westerman grunted, "I'd be happier if we'd got our friends on film."

"I've got pictures of them!" Christina announced matter-of-factly, her mouth full of biscuit. She always, she explained, carried a miniature Kodak Instamatic in the pocket of her anorak; and the evening before she rescued us she had managed to take some long-range photographs of the apes—"though God knows," she added, "how they'll come out. It was getting dark, and the camera may have been damaged."

"We are very much in your debt, young lady"—McBride was about to embark on a eulogistic oration when Christina's hand flew to her mouth, her eyes rolled white with terror and she let out an ear-splitting scream.

We spun round and saw what she was staring at. The little black dots, pouring like angry ants down the middle reaches of the glacier. Some of the *Paranthropus* had all too obviously survived. And they had picked up our trail.

Fools that we were to have tarried! In the half hour we had been boiling our milk, we could have been off the glacier and into the forest, hidden from sight. But the *Paranthropus* had spotted us now. I thought of their terrifying agility as they swarmed up the fumarole; and fear, like poison in the blood, seeped into every pore of my body. We would be lucky, I realized, to get the Zodiac launched before they were on top of us. For a moment we stood irresolute, the same thought, I suspect, passing through all our minds—should we make a dash for the camp or fight it out? Westerman looked at McBride. "Reckon we could hold them off? With the Parker-Hales?"

He shook his head. "There're too many. They'd surround us. And wait for night."

"Look lively then. Rope up."

We were in panic. We forgot the Primus and mugs. We forgot Corbella's injured shoulder. Blind as a family of migrating lemming, we half-fell, half-glissaded over the edge of the ice wall. It needed a near disaster—McBride disappearing into a crevasse—to bring us to our senses.

"Steady!" Westerman panted as we hauled him out. "Another one of us injured, and we won't have a chance."

The shock sobered us up. Our fear didn't in any way diminish, but we managed from that moment to bring it under control, with the result that we made better progress, traversing diagonally across the icefall toward the moraine. Our biggest worry was not being able to see our pursuers (for the ice wall rose sheer above us for sixty or seventy feet), and I must admit that I for one conjured up the most terrifying possibilities: apes leaping the crevasses like kangaroos, racing over ice where we had laboriously cut steps and forcing their way quickly through the tangle of *nothofagus* to cut us off; I wouldn't have been surprised, any moment, to hear their hated hissing-cum-clicking, and to see them peering down at us from the top of the ice wall. We didn't, however, spot them a second time until we emerged onto the moraine. Then a group were silhouetted briefly against the skyline as they crossed a ridge of seracs. They were terrifyingly near. In the twenty minutes it had taken us to descend the ice wall, they had halved the distance between us. They were less than a third of a mile now from where we were standing. Closing fast. And it came to me in a moment of what I can only describe as exhausted resignation that we just weren't going to make it: that we would never have time to get the Zodiac launched, that somewhere beside the shore of Lago Viedma the *Paranthropus* were going to catch up with us. For a moment my mind went blank. Then, like a cornered animal, I began to cast round for somewhere to hide.

It was lucky that Westerman weighed up our chances with more discernment. "We've *got* to get the Zodiac. Peter, Fergus, Christina: make a dash for the camp. Grab the boat. Nothing else. Drag it to that spit of gravel"—he pointed. "Get it inflated. Eduardo, you and I'll give them covering fire. Try and draw the brutes off."

A quick look at the terrain, a quick weighing up of the best route to camp and spit, then we were pelting full tilt into the woods: not, thank goodness, the stunted *nothofagus* of the "emerald band," but a forest of tall upstanding trees, with the ground between them free of undergrowth. Fear once again gave us wings. Neither McBride nor Christina, however, would have qualified for the Olympics, and it wasn't long before I found myself having to hang back to let them keep up.

"Go on!" McBride panted. "We'll follow."

So I forged ahead. For maybe a couple of minutes I could hear them crashing along in my wake; then the thud of their feet and the pant of their breath faded to an unnerving silence. I was alone.

Running by myself through the giant *nothofagus,* it was easy to let imagination run riot. What, I asked myself, if the apes had outmaneuvered us again: if they were lying in wait, perhaps in those overhanging branches, perhaps in the camp itself? I began to regret I had outstripped my companions. Instinctively my pace slowed.

The Parker-Hale cracked sharply, once, twice, three times.

Westerman and Corbella, I told myself, were in trouble: it could be that every second was going to count. I shut my mind to the possibility of ambush, and put in a sprint that would have done credit to Ron Clarke. And at last, looming white through the trees, I spotted the overhanging cliff. I splashed through the spring, tore aside the thorn-scrub, and there, thank the Lord, were our stores—radio, food packs and Zodiac—stacked up exactly as we had left them.

The Zodiac, perversely, was at the bottom, and securely lashed down. I tugged at the ropes, cursing Westerman and his double-lashings and the damp which had tightened the knots. I had lost my knife, and I couldn't for a moment think what to cut the ropes with. Then I remembered that our shotguns and bowies had been wrapped in a tarpaulin and stacked away with the food. My fingers, as I tore at the waterproof canvas, were clumsy; I could feel the sweat running cold and salty into my mouth; it seemed an age before I unearthed the knives, an eternity before I had slashed through the ropes.

A scuffling noise from behind the scrub, and I whirled about, bowie poised for the throw.

It was Christina. She was fighting for breath. Her face was grey with fear. "Quick! They're close behind."

We grabbed a corner of the Zodiac, and started to drag it

out through the scrub. It was heavy. We were shifting it piti-
ably slowly, inch by inch, when we spotted McBride. He
came out of the beech woods at a steady walk, breathing
deeply, like a man enjoying a whiff of country air. I remember thinking he was mad not to be running. But his
foresight gave us a hope of survival. For he arrived at the
camp comparatively fresh; he pointed to the Zodiac. "On
my back."

The boat, I realized, would indeed be easier to carry than
to drag, providing his phenomenal strength didn't give out.
It weighed 160 pounds. It was as much as Christina and I
could do to lift it across his shoulders. He staggered, and the
breath came whistling out through his teeth. Then, very
slowly, he started to walk the couple of hundred yards to
the shore.

I grabbed the shotguns and tossed one to Christina. They
would, I was afraid, have no more effect on the *Paranthropus* than peashooters on an elephant, but drowning men
clutch at straws. I ran ahead of McBride, doing what I could
to clear his path of undergrowth and loose stones, while
Christina brought up the rear. From away to our right came
a volley of shots from the Parker-Hales.

Of the two hundred-odd yards we had to cover, the first
hundred was through beech woods, the second across a
shoreline of grass and outcrops of rock. We emerged from
the trees at the same moment as a pair of the *Paranthropus*.

They were less than fifty yards from where we were
standing. For a second the four of us stood rooted to the
spot—in my case by terror. "Chris," I said quietly, "come
here."

I have never admired her more. I was nearer the *Paranthropus* than she was, but she came to my side without
hesitation, cocking the shotgun. I felt sick with fear. I was
surprised that my voice sounded so normal. "Take the one
on the left. Fire at ten yards. At its eyes."

I was vaguely aware, while I was speaking, of Westerman

and Corbella some hundred yards down the shore. Then the *Paranthropus* were charging. Like a pair of bull moose. Straight and fast.

I shall remember every detail of that terrifying scene till the day I die: the blue of the lake, the huge copper disc of the sun, the stillness, the cascade of Christina's hair across the butt of her gun, the flecks of foam on the ape-men's mouths, the glint of their claws and the massive thrust of shoulder and thigh as they came at us like great battering rams of muscle and bone. The crack of the Parker-Hale might have come from another world, but the right-hand ape-man lurched and half-stumbled as the bullet struck him. Another crack. A cough thick with blood, and he rolled over and over, clawing his chest in rage and pain. My sights switched to his companion. He was less than a dozen yards from us, a single stride from his spring, too close for Wester-man or Corbella to fire.

Our shotguns spat into his face, at point-blank range. Then he was on us. Christina flung herself to the ground. I took a swipe at his head, but a flailing arm got in the way, splintering the gun to matchwood, ripping the anorak off my shoulder and spinning me to the ground. If the *Paranthropus* had turned and seen us, he could have killed us with a couple of blows.

He turned. But he couldn't see us. For his face was a mask of blood.

He put his hands to his eyes, keeled over on the grass and rocked to and fro, whimpering like a child. For all his besti-ality my heart went out to him, and if I had had the Parker-Hale I would have put him out of his agony. As it was, I was wondering what on earth I could do, when I realized my shoulder was strangely numb. Looking down, I saw blood welling up through the shreds of my anorak; and such is the selfishness of man that my sympathies were very speedily transferred from the *Paranthropus* to myself! The in-jury, I remember thinking, can't be serious or it would hurt; and immediately a dull ache spread out from my shoulder across my chest and down my arm. There seemed to be a great deal of blood, and I began to feel sick. I was vaguely aware of Christina scrambling to her feet, of McBride plodding doggedly on with the Zodiac and of Westerman and Corbella running anxiously toward us. Then the shoreline began to undulate in long, slow, rhythmic waves, like a following sea. I shut my eyes. "Pull yourself together," I heard a voice mutter. "Don't faint." And much to my satisfaction the undulating eased off, my head cleared and I sat up.

It was all very odd. Everything seemed to have stopped, as if frozen into a tableau. The sun was huge and improbably haloed, the trees were still as cardboard stage props, my companions were motionless in a variety of unlikely postures—McBride reaching for the Zodiac (which he had evidently dropped), and Christina halfway toward me, brushing the hair out of her eyes. Only the waters of the lake seemed to be moving; and they, impossibly, were receding: were being sucked back as though in the grip of a great underwater magnet. For a moment there was absolute silence. Then everything happened at once.

In a great red flood the surviving *Paranthropus* broke cover. They had been gathering in the woods. Now they were closing in for the kill. And I saw at a glance there were far too many of them for us to have the slightest chance. Hemmed in with our backs to the lake, we could neither fight nor run. We could only die.

Westerman's Parker-Hale cracked once, and a single apeman crumpled into the shadow of the trees. But the rest came on. It was like throwing pebbles at a wave. Leading the charge was a group of ten or twelve males, and they came at us in line abreast, moving fast over the short grass between trees and shore. Fifty yards, forty yards, thirty yards. There were no cornices to save us now, no crevices to climb into. Christina buried her face in the hollow of my shoulder. What, I asked myself, should a man be thinking of in his last seconds of life?

There was a roar that all but burst my ear drums, a flash that seared my eyes, and out from the peaks of the Moreno leapt a great cloud of sulphurous vapour: black fingers reaching for the sky. The earth trembled. A moment of shocked silence. Then, with another thunderous roar, a second cloud burst out of the riven peaks: this time a cloud of fire. For a moment it hung poised above the Viedma, an incandescent mushroom of red; then it burst, and twin streams of lava came writhing down the slopes of the Moreno, like glaciers of blood.

The *Paranthropus* went mad with fear. And no wonder. To us the eruption was terrifying enough, an unleashing of the primordial forces that had shaped the earth. But to them it was the death knell of a species; for they must have sensed that with homes and citadel destroyed, even those who lived through the holocaust would have no chance of survival. Some flung themselves to the ground, some ran in circles uttering piteous cries, some fled for the lake and some for the woods.

The line of males who were charging us skidded to a halt. A couple turned and fled. A couple more fell doubled up in terror to the ground. I could read the minds of the others all too clearly. I had felt the same way myself, on the path up the fumarole: If I'm going to die, then you're coming with me. It was a feeling I had regretted then; I regretted it even more now! I saw the ape-men look at one another, then at the flaming mass of what had once been their home, then at us. One didn't need to be clairvoyant to read their thoughts. A big fellow near the center began to stalk forward, stiff-legged, and the others followed. I have never seen such hatred in the eyes of man or beast, and the hair began to prick up across the nape of my neck. When the leading *Paranthropus* was twenty yards from where we were crouching, he tossed aside his club. They're going to tear us apart, I remember thinking, with their hands.

I must have gone out of my mind. I have absolutely no recollection of what I did next. But the others tell me I struggled to my feet, pushed Christina behind me and started snarling at the apes as though I were one of them!

Then, quite suddenly, I found that I couldn't stand up. For the shoreline once again was undulating like a wide-spaced swell. I could see the successive waves rolling slowly toward me. And as they passed through the woods, I could see to my amazement the *nothofagus* toppling over, one after another, like a battalion of soldiers grounding arms. From under our feet came a thunderous roar, like a giant wave surging toward us through the bowels of the earth. It was almost beneath us when, with a terrible crack, the ground split open, only a few yards from where we were crouching, and a great chasm, reeking of sulphur, opened up between woods and shore. Its far lip was crumbling away. And even as I watched, in horror, the advancing *Paranthropus* were sucked into it. Then the roaring noise was past us. And as suddenly as it had opened up, the chasm closed.

There was of course no sound of screaming, no sickening crunch of bones. Except in my mind. But sick with horror and faint from loss of blood, I passed out.

I never heard the wail of terror as the last of the *Paranthropus* fled through the devastated woods. I never saw the advancing columns of lava plunge, in a great cloud of steam, into the lake. I never choked and spluttered as a rain of fine hot ash drifted down out of a sepulchral sky. I was unaware of all my companions went through as they carried me to the firmest and most open spot they could find, bandaged my shoulder and waited for the holocaust to subside. All this I learned later.

The actual eruption, I was told, lasted no more than five or six minutes, but earth tremors went on for a couple of hours, and for the next week a column of black smoke poured out of the riven shell of the Viedma: a reminder that the forces which shaped the world were not dead but lightly sleeping.

I am a bit vague about the events of the next forty-eight hours. I recall everything as through a glass darkly: a kaleidoscope of disjointed happenings seen through a haze of morphia, fever and pain. For the claws of the *Paranthropus* had gouged deep into my shoulder, and their poison must have worked into my blood. I alternated between fever, delirium and bouts of violent shivering.

I remember Corbella calling, calling, calling, late into the night. He was calling Laubaro. Now there's a funny name, I remember thinking, for a girl. It was some time before I realized he was talking into the Manpack radio, and that *Laubaro* was not a girl but a frigate of the Chilean Navy.

I remember Westerman and McBride sitting side by side like a pair of old women, darning socks. What a funny time, I remember thinking, for a "make-do-and-mend." Then I realized it wasn't socks they were stitching, it was canvas; for the Zodiac, they told me afterward, had been damaged, and leaked like a sieve.

I remember too that every time I opened my eyes, a pretty dark-haired girl was kneeling beside me. "Hi, Alison," I heard myself saying. "Why have you dyed your hair?"

It seemed a harmless enough question. I couldn't think why it made her burst into tears.

Then came a time when I couldn't remember anything. I slept and slept, halfway round the clock. And when I woke the fever had gone, and though I was still weak my mind was clear and I was able to take in what was happening.

I can remember very clearly, for example, our excitement when the helicopter was sighted. Our delight when it landed. Our feeling of heaven-sent relief when the pilot told us he would be able to fly us out.

It was a Kaman Huskie of the U.S.A.A.F., on loan to the International Red Cross, that rescued us; and we couldn't get into it fast enough. It was as though we were afraid that even now, at the last moment, the hands of the *Paranthropus* or the lava of the Viedma might reach out to claim us. Within the hour our few remaining pieces of equipment had been hoist aboard. The only person inclined to linger was McBride. I saw him in earnest conversation with Westerman, pointing to the overhanging cliff where—how very long ago it seemed—we had established our base camp. He wanted, I guessed, to go back for something. Westerman first shook his head, then looked at his watch and shrugged; he wasn't, I could tell, at all happy about whatever it was McBride was suggesting; but eventually the professor went hurrying off in the direction of the cliff. He was away for almost fifteen minutes, and when he came back he was carrying something that looked like a football.

Now I was strapped to a stretcher at the time, being hoist aboard, and I can't say that I saw exactly what happened. I have, however, a clear recollection of my companions' expressions as they peered at the mysterious object McBride had brought back. Corbella swore softly. Westerman turned away, his face puckered in nausea. As for Christina, she did what I can only wonder she hadn't done a dozen times before: she fainted.

A few minutes after we had taken off, I asked McBride what it was that he had brought back. He smiled. "Evidence," was all he would tell me. Then the peaks of the Moreno were slipping past the rear window as the Huskie set course for Río Gallegos. We watched the peaks grow smaller and smaller, till at last they were no more than a fleck of white on a far horizon. I can't speak for the others, but I didn't feel safe until they were out of sight. Nor did I really believe our expedition was over until the pilot passed back a copy of *La Prensa.* I read:

EARTH TREMOR IN THE ANDES

Seismographs have recorded an earth tremor in southern Chile. The tremor, of moderate intensity, is thought to have originated in the Mariano Moreno, a mountainous, uninhabited area close to the border. Helicopters are being used to assess the damage.

It was only then that I realized our adventures were part of history.

Epilogue

The Royal Geographical Society, London

To say we were well looked after in Río Gallegos would be an understatement; the authorities went out of their way to be helpful. Part of their helpfulness may have been due to the fact that we were the first people to emerge from the stricken area, and they were anxious to know what damage the eruption had caused; but a good deal of it, I am sure, was pure hospitality, of the sort that is often proffered to travellers in the lonely places of the world. Nothing we asked for was too much trouble. It seemed a poor return for our hosts' kindness that we should hoodwink them as to what we had found in the Viedma. We had, however, agreed to say nothing about our adventures (partly through fear of being disbelieved) until we had talked to our sponsors in London and produced evidence to substantiate all we claimed. Christina and Corbella too were anxious to return to Chile before issuing a statement. We therefore ignored the spate of phone calls and telegrams which greeted our return to civilization, and set about winding the expedition up.

Within forty-eight hours Christina and Corbella had been picked up by the *Laubaro;* and Westerman, McBride and I had been flown to Buenos Aires.

Parting was a wrench for us all, especially Christina and

me; and one scene in particular I recall with the sort of poignancy that I have a feeling the years will never completely dim. We were sitting prosaically enough in the customs shed waiting for our equipment to be cleared, and Westerman was comparing the Andes to some of the other ranges he had climbed in. "Which," I asked him, "do you like best?" His loyalty, it seemed, was divided between the Himalaya and the Andes; and I remember saying that though these lonely parts of the world were doubtless fun to visit, I would never want to live in them.

"Where do you want to live?" Christina's voice was deceptively casual.

"Why, in England of course," I told her.

"And I," she said, "in Chile."

We looked at each other. "Perhaps," I said, "you might be persuaded to change your mind."

She muttered something in Spanish that sounded extremely impolite, and walked quickly out of the customs shed.

Well, I realized I had put my foot in it, but I consoled myself with the thought that she would soon be coming to England, and we could continue our friendship there under more normal circumstances—for the five of us had arranged a reunion in London in ten days' time at the annual meeting of the Royal Geographical Society: this, it seemed to Westerman, being an opportune occasion at which to spring our secret.

I shall skim briefly over the events of the next few days, if only for the very good reason that I spent most of them flat on my back in a coma. For soon after leaving Río Gallegos my fever returned. Indeed it returned with such malevolence that there are only two things I can remember clearly about the flight back: McBride's preoccupation with his "evidence" (which he insisted was kept in a sealed case, specially packed with ice) and my steadily mounting temperature (which had reached 104 by the time we landed). Much to my disgust, I was rushed to St. Thomas's Hospital, where

I recall a flurry of consultants, all of them asking what sort of animal had mauled me, a battery of bright white lights and a welcome spin to oblivion.

When I came round, I found my shoulder in plaster, and McBride's green-eyed daughter at the side of my bed. "Hi, Tarzan," she said. "We wondered when you'd wake up." She had, I learned later, been waiting at the hospital ever since they decided to operate.

Looking back, I am quite sure that of all our expedition I had the most enjoyable time in the week that followed. For I was screened from the impatience and skepticism which the others had to face because of their refusal to issue a statement prior to the R.G.S. meeting—there is nothing the press hates more than being kept deliberately in the dark. For my part, however, I was retained under observation in St. Thomas's, and was allowed no visitors except relatives or members of the expedition. I was glad of the rest. When one has rubbed shoulders with adversity and death, all the little things that one normally takes for granted assume a special delectability: the feel of clean sheets, the warmth of the sun through an open window, a nurse's smile. I lay there hour after hour, doing little and thinking less, happy quite simply to be alive. And after observation came convalescence. I was told to disappear for a quiet weekend: to go somewhere by myself where I would get plenty of fresh air and rest and wouldn't be pestered by reporters in search of a scoop. I went to the Helford River—which no one in his right mind visits in winter. It was certainly quiet. In the morning, walking the cliffs in alternate flurries of rain and sun, I saw no living creature but seabirds and the occasional rabbit; in the evening I drank beer and played darts by myself in the bar of a pub where in four or five months' time holiday-makers would be jammed tight as the proverbial sardines.

I got back to London on February 14, the day before the R.G.S. meeting; and in the evening Alison telephoned to suggest the two of us have supper. The expedition photographs, she said, had been developed, and she thought I might like to see them.

Three or four months ago I think I'd have refused; but I now found myself, rather to my surprise, asking if there was anywhere special she'd like to go.

"I hoped you'd come here," she said. "If you'll risk my cooking?"

"Here" turned out to be a microscopic bed-sitter, shared with two other girls—both on this occasion diplomatically absent.

Alison seemed to have blossomed out in the three or four months since she had seen us off from London Airport. She had, she told me, been tempted to London by a modelling-cum-secretarial course promoted by some avant-garde employment agency, and her new-found freedom certainly suited her. We had quite an evening, starting with photographs.

Of our two cameras, the movie camera had gone up in flames on the summit of the Viedma, and the Hasselblad (which we had left at the mouth of the underground river) contained no pictures of the ape-men. Our only evidence of the latter, in other words, were the half-dozen shots which Christina had taken with her Instamatic, and these as we had feared were of poor quality, for the camera had been damaged and had let in light. I remembered the incredulity with which McBride's original prints had been greeted. "I'm very much afraid," I said, "people will think these are faked."

We regarded our evidence, or rather the lack of it, with some consternation; but it was no good worrying our heads over what we hadn't got, and after a while I began to take an interest in the very pleasant aroma wafting out of the kitchen. "I hope," I remarked, "you're a *cordon bleu!*"

"*Mais naturellement. Et tout de suite.*" She disappeared into the kitchen and emerged almost at once with a steaming tureen, from which she removed the lid with a flourish. "*Minestrone à la Supermarket.* Has it not an appetizing aroma?" Drinking from the tureen, she suggested, would double togetherness and halve washing up. I didn't demur.

"And what famous dish have you prepared to follow?" I asked, when the soup had been demolished.

"Madame Fray Bentos's Steak and Kidney Pie," she announced, "direct from the tin, tomatoes direct from the fridge and the very best Nu-loaf bread—isn't it lucky you didn't come just for the food!" We ate the main course in the same communal style as we had drunk the soup.

"Now let me guess," I said, when we had done justice to the pie, "what we have for our grand finale."

She looked at me expectantly.

"Could it be Monsieur Nescafé's Instant Coffee?"

She clapped her hands. "You are so discerning, Pierre. But Nescafé's Gold Blend, of course."

The rest of the evening was as therapeutic as the meal.

I was still thinking about it, somewhat guiltily, when I went next afternoon to the Royal Geographical Society to welcome Christina. But as it happened, she and Corbella didn't turn up until a few minutes before the meeting, for their plane had been delayed by fog.

The Royal Geographical Society, perhaps I ought to explain, is far more than a club for explorers. It is the headquarters of an organization from whose august portals expeditions such as the first ascent of Everest and the first crossing of the Arctic are conceived, blueprinted and nurtured to fruition. Its roll of Gold Medallists reads like the *Who's Who* of Exploration—Livingstone, Amundsen, Scott, Peary, Nansen; next year, I suspect, Westerman. On the evening of February 15 the general business of the Society had been quickly transacted in camera, to allow time for the main event of the evening: *A Report by Mr. Eric Westerman and Professor Fergus McBride on a Recent Expedition to the Andes in Search of the Vulcan Viedma.* To say this report was eagerly awaited would be the understatement of the year. For ever since its inception in the Younger Halls, our expedition had aroused skepticism and controversy; while our silence over the past ten days had added fuel to the critics' flames, and had had the natural effect of focusing public attention on the R.G.S. meeting. The Society's lecture hall seated a mere five hundred, and was obviously too small to house the vast concourse of would-be attenders. Admission was therefore limited to Fellows and the press. Even so, on the fateful evening the hall was jammed tight, with many a distinguished explorer perched on the stairs, and many an angry pressman brandishing his card in the corridors outside.

A full account of the amazing proceedings that followed will be found in the appropriate volume of *The Geographical Journal*. I won't bore you with details; the highlight, however, was, to say the least, spectacular.

The meeting got off to a brisk start with the president, Rear Admiral Jardine, introducing us with commendable brevity. Westerman, who was giving the first half of the lecture, was an experienced speaker, and his account of our climb to the plateau of the Viedma was listened to in respectful silence. When, however, he came to describe the footprints that we had found circling our tent—"the spoor of what was clearly a heavy, long-striding biped"—it became obvious that a section of the audience was not in the mood to be easily convinced. There was much shuffling of feet, exchanging of glances and coughing. The dissenters, however, held their fire until Westerman had conducted us through the underground passages and onto the summit of the Viedma; at this stage he handed over to McBride—"for the second part of our report is his field rather than mine: anthropology rather than mountaineering." It was then the trouble started.

I have to admit that McBride was provocative in the extreme. He addressed his distinguished audience as though they were children; and although he never deviated from the truth, he made no effort to put the truth across in a manner that would make it credible—listening to his bald recitation of the facts one would have imagined it quite an everyday occurrence to bump into a tribe of prehistoric apes! The result was first unrest, then dissent, and finally derision.

I expected McBride to get angry, but he chose instead to treat his denigrators as beneath contempt; he simply stood on the rostrum smiling benignly at the growing chorus of protest, his hand upraised as though bestowing a blessing. His complacency was like a red rag to a bull, and cries of "Prove it," "Tell it to the Marines!" and "Charlatan!" began to swell up from every part of the hall.

A gavel rapped sharply, and as the hubbub subsided, Jardine rose to his feet. "I must ask you to give Professor McBride a fair hearing. If you feel that some of his observations are open to question, the proper time for your questions is at the end of the address, not in the middle."

The rest of McBride's report was listened to in silence, albeit the silence of incredulity rather than enthrallment. And I have to admit that I wasn't wholly out of sympathy with the skeptics: for listened to in cold blood, our adventures did indeed sound too farfetched to be believed.

The moment his narrative was finished, McBride began to show photographs. And these at least did something to substantiate our claims. There could be no denying, for example, that we had actually found and triangulated the Viedma; and Corbella's wealth of statistics and magnificent photographs were greeted with approval. When, however, it came to our photos of the ape-men, these had all been taken with Christina's damaged camera; and I must admit that several of them were so blurred as to be almost unintelligible to the layman. When the last of the prints had been thrown onto the screen—and greeted with ominous silence—Jardine let slip the hounds. "The meeting," he said, "is now open for questions."

I don't think it an exaggeration to say that in an instant a quarter of the hall were on their feet, baying for McBride's blood.

For several minutes accusation and rebuttal, jibe and repartee flew thick and fast. McBride, it seemed to me, was needlessly abrasive, treating his questioners as though they were either mentally defective or motivated by spite. Tempers were beginning to run high, when the dissenters found a spokesman whom McBride seemed happy to cross swords with: a Professor Lander, who I gathered was his opposite number at a rival university. I quote their exchanges verbatim.

Lander: "This expedition, as I see it, had two objectives: one cartographical, one anthropological. On the first score, I accept Mr. Westerman's findings without reservation. I congratulate him, indeed I am sure we all congratulate him, on a job well done." (Applause.) "On the second score, I do not accept Mr. McBride's findings. He has spun us a quite preposterous story without a shred of evidence to support it." (Cries of "Shame," "Hear hear," and "Well spoken, sir.") "I consider it the duty of this meeting to see that the myth of these so-called *Paranthropus* is exploded by a team of competent and impartial scientists."

McBride: "Are you calling me a liar?"

"I prefer in public to say you are guilty of terminological inexactitude." (Laughter.)

"My reputation, sir, is esteemed by men of science throughout the world. Your reputation has failed to penetrate the mists of a minor Scottish University! You must feel you are on very sure ground to challenge me?"

"I feel—and I believe this meeting feels—I am on surer ground than you are!" (Much applause.)

"Well, well! Setting aside the photographs then, although they have been examined and pronounced genuine by experts, we come to our other evidence. I refer to the vast amount of data we have been able to collect on the characteristics and habits of the *Paranthropus*." (Cries of "Rubbish!" "Rhubarb!" and a number of more explicit epithets.) "Data, for example, on the creatures' bone structure. I could show you charcoal drawings of a head made by myself on the spot—"

"This meeting," Lander interrupted, "is in no mood to be convinced by drawings."

"You want the actual thing?"

"Yes."

"And this would satisfy you?"

Lander (smiling): "But of course."

It was McBride's hour of triumph: the vindication of his years in the scientific wilderness, the moment of recognition which in his heart he had always longed for. Two men brought in a packing crate which they stood in front of the projector. The hall became suddenly quiet, and I found myself holding my breath. McBride was in his element. Svengali-like, he made much play with the preliminaries: adjusting the projector so that its beam threw a silhouette onto exactly the center of the screen, and removing ice from the bottom of the crate so that its lid could be lifted cleanly; then, like a conjurer about to produce a veritable string of rabbits, he took the long wooden pole used by lecturers to pinpoint objects on the screen and rapped it twice on the floor. The men who had brought in the crate whipped off its front and top, and a gasp of fear and amazement swept the hall.

For there, black and bloody, its lips writhed back in the agony of death, was the head of a *Paranthropus.*

A shuddering sigh, part horror, part incredulity, ran through the audience. Someone screamed, and a girl immediately in front of the platform slumped unconscious to the floor. McBride paid not the slightest attention to the hubbub. Matter-of-factly he began to point out the characteristics by which the head could be identified—"the heavy skull musculature, the gorilla jaw, the huge molars and premolars, and the bony ridge along the top of the skull, the anchoring ground for the muscles that work the creature's oversize teeth." And as he spoke I could sense incredulity ebbing, and a gradual flood of conviction sweeping over both Fellows and press. Person after person seemed to be rising to his feet, applauding, gesticulating, pressing forward to get a closer view of the head. The murmurs of doubt were silenced; and those who a moment before had been thirsting for McBride's blood were now united in shouting his praise.

[206]

Nor did the tide of enthusiasm wane. Indeed as more and more people thronged round the head, and word was passed back that it was genuine, the applause mounted. Eventually the tumult reached such proportions that we were thankful to escape via a door at the back of the platform into the quiet passageways that led to the Society's archives and libraries. Here we had a brief respite in which to get back our breath before the press flushed us out.

"So," in the sober words of *The Geographical Journal*, "ended what was perhaps the most remarkable meeting ever held in the Society's premises."

It was a day for surprises. I was in for two more before the evening was over.

About the first, since I am no masochist I don't intend to say more than I have to. Looking back, I can only wonder that I hadn't spotted the warning signs: they were all there, but I suppose it's a well-known fact that love is blind. . . . I didn't get a chance to be alone with Christina until after the meeting. It was a moment I had been longing for for weeks, and I dare say that I kissed her with more enthusiasm than discretion. She drew back. I thought at first that maybe she was embarrassed at such a display of affection in public, then I became aware of someone hovering in the background.

"Peter," she said breathlessly. "Let me introduce you to Cedomir."

I found myself shaking hands with a pleasant, innocuous-looking young man with glasses and slightly buck teeth.

"Cedomir and I," she went on quickly, as though she was out of breath, "were married last Saturday."

"Oh, yes," I heard myself say as the bottom dropped out of my world. "Congratulations!"

There followed an awkward silence as we surveyed one another with embarrassment; I couldn't think of anything to say that wouldn't sound melodramatic, maudlin or trite.

To start with, Christina's eyes refused to meet mine; but

as the silence built up to an awkwardness that neither of us could stand, she forced herself to look at me very straight. "Sorry, Pete," she said quietly. "It just wouldn't have worked."

"I suppose not," I said.

"I did warn you," she tried not very successfully to smile, "my first love was Chile."

There didn't seem anything to say. I felt like an actor in some corny music-hall drama. "I think," I said rather desperately, "I'd better be going."

"Please, Pete," her eyes were full of tears. "Don't be bitter."

I must admit that bitter was exactly how I felt, but I was damned if I was going to let her see it. "Of course not," I said. "If you'd have sent me an invitation I'd have come and danced at your wedding!"

"I'll not forget you," she said softly. "But we were ships that pass in the night. Different courses. Different ports."

Another silence. "I think," I said for the second time, "I'll be going."

And I went—in the time-honoured manner of broken-hearted heroes—into the night, not knowing whether to burst into laughter or tears. I had gone several hundred yards before I realized I hadn't even said good-bye.

Frankly, I was too mixed up to think clearly: I simply walked the foggy streets, anger and grief bubbling inside me like a witches' brew. I tried to convince myself I had had a lucky escape: I thought of ringing Alison; then, after I had walked a fair number of miles, I began to wonder if after all Christina hadn't quite simply been right—different creeds, different backgrounds, different continents to think of as home; they say love is all, but would I *really* have wanted to spend the rest of my life waving the flag in darkest Patagonia? Maybe indeed "it just wouldn't have worked." I looked at my watch and remembered with dismay that Corbella had invited Westerman, McBride and myself to his hotel for a nightcap. That was a couple of hours ago, and with one thing and another the invitation had gone clean out of my head.

I don't think I would have bothered—I would have rung up and made my apologies and gone home, feeling thoroughly miserable—if at that moment a taxi hadn't come crawling down the street, its "For Hire" sign glowing gold through the fog. "Park Lane Hotel," I said.

Half an hour later the four of us were sipping whiskey and soda in a corner of the lounge while Corbella unfolded the final surprise in all our surprising adventures.

"You will be glad to hear," he announced as we settled into our chairs, "that Argentina has agreed to our proposed line for the boundary."

"Giving you the Viedma?"

He nodded.

"Copper or no copper," I said with a shudder. "You're welcome to it!"

"Do you think," McBride asked him, "the eruption will upset your plans? For mining?"

"I don't see why." Corbella beckoned a waiter. "Would you," he asked, "bring the box—number three hundred ninety I think it is—that you're keeping in the safe for me." He smiled at our mystification. "I have," he announced, " a small present for each of you."

We sipped our whiskey in a pleasant glow of anticipation. When the box arrived (it was about the size of a box of tennis balls) Corbella didn't open it at once; he went off instead on an unexpected tack. "Didn't it strike you as odd? Our prospecting in the Viedma for copper?"

McBride and I shook our heads; Westerman said nothing.

"Eric?"

"Your extramural activities," our leader said mildly, "were no business of mine. But since you ask: yes, I did think it odd."

"Why?"

"Even if the field is a rich one, as rich, say, as El Teniente, I don't see how you're going to work it, not economically."

"Just so."

A puzzled silence. Then Corbella leaned forward, the tips of his fingers pressed lightly together. "Would your view be something like this: 'The Hielo Continental is about the bleakest, remotest spot on earth; from the Chilean side of the Andes it is virtually inaccessible; the cost of developing a field there would be astronomic, not on the cards for metal worth only a shilling an ounce.'"

"I'd say that was about right."

"But what if the metal was worth ten pounds an ounce?"

We looked at him in astonishment. And I remembered the little yellow veins that Christina had been so interested in in the underground passages. They had almost rung a bell at the time, but I had been too preoccupied to puzzle out where I had seen the same sort of thing before. Now the penny dropped. The veins were like those I had seen in pictures of the underground reefs in the Transvaal: soft, auriferous ribbons hacked out by Negroes deep under the surface of the earth. "You mean it *wasn't* copper you were prospecting for?" I said. "It was gold?"

He nodded. "You just can't be sure with a gravity survey. We knew there was *some* metal in the Viedma. We thought, from the structure of the veins, that it *might* be gold. But there was only one way to find out: to get hold of a sample. Well, lodegold it turned out to be: a field to put El Dorado in the shade." As Westerman began to say something, Corbella raised his hand. "Please, Eric! I know what you are thinking: that we used you; that we led you, how do you say it, up the garden path. It is true. But think how much was at stake. At the start of the expedition, remember, I hardly knew you, hardly knew any of you, and men all through history have done terrible things to one another for gold. Anyhow, my friends, the end has justified the means. My country is rich now. And so"—he opened the box—"are you."

There were four official-looking documents in the box, and four gold crosses: big rough-hewn crucifixes wrought, Corbella told us, out of the samples he and Christina had brought back. He handed us one apiece. They were inscribed with our names and the message "From Chile, with gratitude." They were heavy, and I was wondering how much I could sell mine for when I suddenly cottoned on to what Corbella was saying . . . "So we set up a board to develop the field. And you," he handed round the documents, "are honorary non-voting members with a salary of ten thousand pounds a year for ten years."

A moment of disbelieving silence, then Westerman drained his glass. "This very generous gesture of the Chilean government," he said, "calls for another round!"

And on this happy note I end my account of our expedition—although for those who like their odds and ends tidied up, I add a postscript.

The others, I understand, sat up into the small hours, reliving our adventures and discussing plans for another expedition. As for me, as befits a man with a five-figure salary, I hired a Mercedes 280SL, drove to Alison's bed-sitter and sat on the horn. The time was a little after 3 A.M.

After a good deal of whispering and delay, she appeared at the window. "Go away, Tarzan," she said. "You're drunk."

"I'm not drunk," I said. "I'm rich. Look!"

She peered at the Mercedes. "Did you pinch it? Or," she giggled, "did your girl friend give it to you?"

"I don't take presents," I told her, "from girls who are married."

When this had sunk home, she asked what I wanted.

"Just a drive and a talk," I said. "With you."

She obviously thought I was mad; but in the end she came down, well muffled up in sweaters and jeans and carrying a thermos of cocoa.

We drove south through the night while I told her all the things about the expedition that I hadn't told her before, and how I'd become suddenly rich, and how Westerman was planning another trip to the Viedma and wanted me to go too. Then we were climbing the gentle approaches to the

Downs. Alison's eyes in the glow of the dashlights were emerald. "May I ask, sir, where you're abducting me to?"

"You'll know soon enough," I told her.

We touched 100 on the Chichester by-pass, with the flood-lit cathedral to our right and the mud flats diaphanous with predawn mist to our left. Then we were in Emsworth. The village was asleep except for a downstairs light in a news-agent's where the morning papers had just come in. I bought half a dozen. "Missing Links," the headlines blazed, "Alive in the 20th Century," "Explorers Captured by Stone Age Apes." Like it or not, we were headline news in every coun-try in the world. I drove to the harbour and out along the narrow, rutted track between houses and sea. "*I* know where we're going," Alison said. "Which was Uncle David's house?"

We pulled up outside it. A small, very ordinary house: pebble dash, and green-framed windows too small to let in a great deal of sun; an untidy garden, the roses not yet pruned and the grass too long. "So this," she said, "is where it all started."

I nodded.

"I bet Uncle David's happy now."

I nodded again. And for the second time in my life I swear I could feel the old man's presence. It was as though he was there in the car with us, come back from God-alone-knows-where to say thank you. The feeling was over almost as soon as it had begun, but at the end of those few seconds I knew I'd never go back to the Viedma. That episode in my life was over: a mystery solved, a quest fulfilled.

As to the future: the Mercedes' seats were real leather, a pretty girl's head was on my shoulder and in the east the first faint flush of dawn was breaking over a quiet sea.